THE MILER

A novel

Hap Cawood

For information, contact the publisher:
CIMARRON BOOKS, P.O. Box 808, Yellow Springs, Ohio 45387
. Fax (937) 767-1499

Quote from *The Holy Science*, by Swami Sri Yukteswar, copyright © 1990 Self-
Realization Fellowship; Los Angeles. [www.Yogananda-srf.org].
Reprinted by permission.

Cover design by Jesse Ranly
Map by MB Hopkins

Printed in the United States of America on acid-free paper
by Lightning Source, Inc., LaVergne, Tennessee

Library of Congress Control Number: 2003094290
ISBN 0-9659075-1-1

CIMARRON
BOOKS
- Publisher -

To Kenney Schryver
Naples High. Class of '57.

With special acknowledgement to my brother
Ray F. Cawood
who ran the mile alone for Harlan High
in 1959 and 1960

Chapters

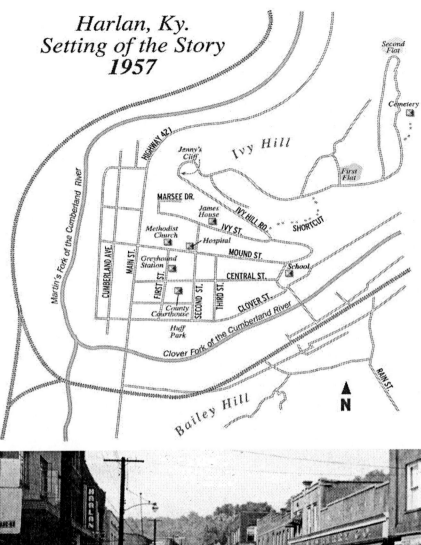

Harlan, Ky.
Setting of the Story
1957

MAIN STREET

THE MILER

Prelude

HIS BILLOWING WHITE SLEEVE BARELY TOUCHES A BULGE OF SAND-stone as he strides around the base of the cliff, quick and certain. He's a Cherokee, but not clothed in native dress. The time feels like the late 1800s.

He swerves away from the cliff and through a patch of woods on a path he knows. He doesn't have to think of which way to go; he puts his mind elsewhere.

As he leans around the trees, the sound stirs as a feeling before it can be heard. This is not the sound of wind against leaves, nor the rush of the river he is following close by. The sound hums from inside him.

He breaks into the open, down the gentle slope toward the water, on a path packed smooth around the stones. The sound enlarges and closes in, as if from all sides, like a deep bass gong holding its resonant tone. Then, inside the sound, a rhythm forms, sparingly at first, beneath the cadence of his gait.

As his body glides, the majesty of the chord rises in him, taking his senses beyond the clatter of the valley, consuming the weight of his body and the strain of his legs.

Then the scene fades, and with the fading of the tone, the sweet expansion folds.

Awakening from this, feeling the difference between the worlds now pressed against each other – the world of the bedroom fresh with the morning sun flickering through the oak tree, and the world of a Cherokee on the path of a century before – a child of seven in the mountains of Kentucky, in the year of 1947, is left to wonder: Which place is the dream?

1

A little prophecy

SO, HOW DID JOSEPH KNOW WHAT THE PHARAOH'S DREAM MEANT, that's what I wanted to know as the sunlight warmed through the windows of the Harlan Methodist Church, making the red of Mrs. Tompkins' rouge redder as she tried to open the minds of us twelve-year-olds, fidgeting in the spring of 1952 as she told us about Old Testament prophets who knew history before it happened.

At least we could ask questions out loud in Sunday school, which was looser than church where, halfway through the service, the preacher called on Mr. Garrett to say the prayer. Mr. and Mrs. Garrett sat in the right section, five rows from the front. My mother, father, sister Sarah and I sat four rows from the front on the left. Most people pretty much sat in the same place on Sundays unless some newcomer sat in *their* place and upset the order.

Mr. Garrett came loaded with things to be thankful for, starting with the particulars of the weather and the beauty of plant life. When I got my first wristwatch, I timed him. Generally Mr. Garrett prayed in the two-minute range unless he read something bad in the newspaper, in which case he could go three; a flood in Harlan took him to four. Whenever Mr. Garrett went past the three-minute mark, even the preacher opened his eyes. I wondered if Mrs. Garrett let her husband say grace at meals.

As to my question about how Joseph knew the pharaoh's dream meant Egypt had a famine coming, Mrs. Tompkins said God must have showed him.

"How?"

"The Bible doesn't say. Through the mind, I think."

"How?"

"You have to listen."

I told her that when I asked something I didn't hear anything. I asked if she thought a prophet could see the future when he was a kid. Mrs. Tompkins said she didn't know at what age prophets could see the future or how much they could see. She said Jeremiah could see the terrible things that were going to happen to the people of Judah and Jerusalem because of the bad things they were doing. That wasn't a good time to be living in Judah.

That stuck in my mind, partly because I asked the question and partly because my parents named me Jeremiah. Or I should say Mom named me Jeremiah – for a next-door neighbor friend in Vicksburg, Mississippi. Dad just went along. At times I wished Dad had been the one who had named me. He was a civil engineer. Engineers are practical. Left alone, he would have named me something modern like Bill or Frank. Dad's name was Steve; that tells you something. Mom's maiden name was Elizabeth McLain, a nice regular name. A woman of warm dignity, she would not answer to anything less, not to Liz or to Beth, just Elizabeth.

Jeremiah seemed as good a name as any for a prophet. As for me, Jeremiah James, I couldn't see even what my final years of high school would bring. If the real Jeremiah had been there and I had been able to ask him what those years would be like, he would have told me I would run the mile but that I couldn't guess where that mile would take me. He would have told me that growing up would have rough parts but that a woman and a girl would show me magic.

I would have wanted to believe him, and would have looked for that girl especially. Three months later, in the brightness of the summer, I even would have thought she had appeared.

2

First sweat

THE SUMMER OF 1952 CAME NONE TOO SOON AFTER SEVEN YEARS of descent from the first grade peak of two loves, one of them being Laura Green, who lived on Marsee Drive about a hundred yards from my home if I walked through the woods. In her utility room we played "Doctor," but despite my wish to be cared for in the gentlest way, all she gave me was shots in the arm with a pencil. The other love was my first-grade teacher, Miss Burke, who patted me on the back of the head when I got an A+, under which influence I became a very good student.

In fourth grade I was informed that Miss Burke had married and had become Mrs. Concini. By then I liked classmate Sandra Sue Saylor and a blonde girl whose photograph I cut out from the pajama section of the Sears & Roebuck catalog.

In the fifth grade Lynn Ann Beyer played tag with me once on the playground, inspiring me to become her boyfriend, except I didn't tell her, and she didn't let on that she knew. After a year of trying to impress Lynn with the way my hair looked greased into a pompadour with Wildroot Cream Oil, I gave up.

Sixth grade life of the heart was just as barren, so I concentrated on getting through fractions.

By seventh grade my body was getting puffier. I could not see my knuckles, only dimpled bumps where the bones should be. All the boys who had girlfriends had knuckles.

Just when life seemed predictable, the sun rose on me – from an unlikely place – next door, at the residence of Mr. and Mrs. Handley. A quiet couple who liked to sit on their screened-in side porch in the warm season, the Handleys could see our playthings tumbling down our side slope into their yard, yet they never complained. They never ordered us off their property the way Mr. Cutler did when he was drunk and didn't want the neighborhood boys playing "Whoever Gets The Ball Gets Tackled" on his lawn. Mr. Cutler's yard had the advantage of being flat, being on the part of Ivy Street that levels out at the bottom of Ivy Hill. One summer afternoon, when four of us climbed his apple tree to pick some fruit, Mr. Cutler strode onto his porch and shot a rifle in the air. We dropped out of the branches as a group and didn't play in his yard after that. Mr. Handley, being an accountant, would never do that sort of thing. Mr. Cutler was a judge.

The Handleys were so quiet that I never expected anything exciting to come from their place. But in that summer after my seventh grade, Mrs. Handley phoned mother and asked if I wanted to meet their nieces from Dayton, Ohio. I was hoping mother couldn't see my hands sweat. After combing my hair with a wave rising off my forehead and putting on my new Wrangler jeans with the cuffs folded up three inches, I headed next door.

When Mrs. Handley introduced her nieces, my hands were so wet I put them in my pockets, which were a bit tight because I had that weight on me. It struck me as peculiar that my hands could be sweating and my mouth could be dry at the same time. It also struck me that her nieces were beautiful, and smiling! Priscilla was my age; Patricia two years older. I asked if they wanted to go downtown to Creech Drug for a soda. When they said yes, I felt excellent, partly because they would go with me and partly because I could talk in that condition.

That was how the sun rose on me. It stood bright for a month. We gathered with the other boys and girls in our neighborhood to tell ghost stories at night on the street and play records in my room. Together alone, our talk was ordinary, but because Priscilla liked me, I felt as if my hand were on the track of my Lionel electric train with the transformer turned low: the juice wanged through until I had to let go in order to breathe right. In a walk in the woods behind my house I offered Priscilla my hand to help her up the path to a foxhole the neighborhood boys dug after watching John Wayne fight to the death in *Iwo Jima*. When Priscilla and I reached what was left of the clay-filled indention, she didn't let go.

On other days I took Priscilla to the attic playroom. Not minding the summer heat that gathered beneath the ceiling so low we could jump and hit our heads on it, we played card games, then sat on the cot to hold hands and kiss. Talk about sweat.

In our last rendezvous in the attic, Priscilla whispered that she would like to come back the next year, to which I replied, "I hope you will," words that kept me awake until two in the morning.

When the four weeks ended, it was wrenching to watch Priscilla and Patricia wedging their luggage into the trunk of their parents' husky blue Hudson. I wished I could say something memorable, but what few words I could think of fell over themselves too much to form a line and get out.

I waved back to Priscilla as her car eased to the bottom of Ivy Street and disappeared around the corner. From then on, my memory had to run on its own battery. A dreamy ache dried up the sweat. By some miracle I had had the affection of someone so pretty that she could have been in the movies.

We hadn't talked about writing to each other. We thought we would meet again the following summer. But Priscilla didn't come back the next year. Nor did she return the next year, nor the one after that, nor the one after that. She wouldn't return until the summer after my junior year. Until then, I would keep the sunshine of her somewhere in reserve, glowing now and then in the dark, the way a dashboard light eases on when the battery is low. I wondered if, when I saw her again, she would remember the sunny days on Ivy Street. I wondered if my hands would sweat the same.

3

Gunsmoke

"IT'S JUST A LOT OF SHOOTING AND KILLING," DAD ANNOUNCED from his armchair that sat so low with such a slanted back that he had to heave forward several times to get up. Dad wasn't preachy or nagging, but every few months he got fed up with gunfights blazing out of our black and white Motorola TV. It didn't help that my favorite show was *Gunsmoke*.

Sarah was dedicated to *The Mickey Mouse Club* and *The Hit Parade*, though in the summer of 1955 *The Ballad of Davy Crockett* wore her down after listening to it for more than three months on *The Hit Parade* as the top song, at which point she switched to *American Bandstand* with Dick Clark. Dad's favorite TV show was *Industry on Parade*, a Sunday afternoon program about how various factories made their products.

I figured that Dad's complaint about shooting and killing on television was a problem of not relating to my generation. He was fifty-five when I was born and fifty-nine when Sarah was born, plus he was eighteen years older than Mom, kind of defying the odds. He lost his first wife, Helen, to a coal truck sliding around a curve at Highsplint where she was driving alone; he wouldn't talk about that. Dad reared my half-brother and half-sister – Harold, a Realtor in Uncle Clyde's real-estate business downtown; and Marci, a violinist and professor of music at Union College in Barbourville, fifty miles west of Harlan. I was proud that he constructed buildings in Harlan that he built coal tipples and mine facilities and the house we lived in, made a comfortable life for us and helped others without talking about it. I was pleased that people in Harlan liked and respected him.

While kids would call me JJ or Jaybird, older people around Harlan would identify me as "Little Steve's boy." Dad was Little Steve because he was five-feet-eight inches tall, compared to his uncle who stood six-three and was known as "Big Steve."

When Dad told me who someone was, he said something like, "That's Jacob Tate, your second cousin once removed." I didn't pay enough attention to memorize how people might be related to me beyond the first cousin level. I just knew that Dad had his bloodlines all connected and layered like the lines of the topographic maps that oozed out of the blueprint machine in his office above the Cumberland Hardware store.

Dad told me to work hard and be fair and, when I slammed the trunk lid on my fingers, he told me to "grit your teeth, just grit your teeth." I could tell he had learned teeth-gritting so well he didn't even show it. His older brother and sister died in early childhood, and his father, Dannon James, died at twenty-eight.

In my sophomore year, my history teacher, Mrs. Riggs, assigned us to write a paper on the life of a grandparent so we could appreciate our family heritage. Dad listed for me his ancestors, explaining how the Jameses first came to Eastern Kentucky when an earlier Stephen James – the family used the same name a lot – was granted 640 acres at the nearby Kentucky-Virginia border as payment for his service in the Revolutionary War.

To help me find out more about granddad, Dad referred me to Petro Blackburn, who lived with his wife in an apartment on Mound Street, a two-minute walk from my house. I called Mr. Blackburn, told him I was the son of Little Steve, and told him what I wanted. He said to come on down. His apartment smelled musty like old folks. Some older people don't open their windows much and don't smell what's around them any more. I could tell that the Blackburns had been boiling string beans and ham hock.

8

Pixie-like, Olivette Blackburn seated herself beside her lanky, mountain-fed husband on a quilt-covered sofa while I sank into the easy chair with a lace doily on the top. The purpose of the doily was to catch the oil from people's hair so it wouldn't grease up the upholstery. By that time, though, I had been off Wildroot Cream Oil for two years. I was clean.

"How old was Dad when you first knew him?" I asked.

"As a little 'un, walking downtown, holdin' his ma's hand."

That distracted me. Dad was sixty-nine when I asked this question. *How old are these people?* I wondered. They still walked around without holding on to anything.

"Little Steve has helped a lot of people," Mr. Blackburn offered. "There's not been as fine a family in Harlan County as the Jameses. Your grandpa was a little rough." All I knew about my grandfather, Dannon James, was that when he sat for a haircut in a barbershop across from the Harlan County Courthouse, his brother-in-law, Calloway Tate, shot him to death point-blank.

"You knew my grandfather?"

"Knowed *of* him more than knowed him," Mr. Blackburn explained. "Everyone knowed Dannon James. When he came into town, people brought their children inside. He liked to shoot the bell at the courthouse."

"Is that why Calloway killed him?"

"He got killed because he provoked Calloway. Those times were heated up anyway, with the feuds. There was some tension over Northern and Southern sympathies, and then there were conflicts due to personalities and meanness and greed. The Jameses was on the Turners' side of the Turner-Howard feud because some of the Jameses had married Turners. I would say your granddaddy did his part giving the town its 'Bloody Harlan' name."

"Did he kill anyone?"

"Lawsy, yes," Mrs. Blackburn interjected.

9

Mr. Blackburn ticked off the names of six people my grandfather killed. I scribbled to keep up. "I don't know the others," he said. "Those were the ones I recall."

"What did he do for a living?" I asked.

"Worked around, but gunslinger's what he was known for, though he did that for himself, not for a living. He got tough early. Had to," Mr. Blackburn explained. "When Dannon was fourteen, Big Jim Tyler rode horseback from Black Snake over to the Jameses place to shoot up the family. Little Dannon jumped him, pulled him from his horse and beat him off. When Dannon growed up and picked off three men coming after him at Bob's Creek, the judge ordered him to the Oklahoma Territory until tempers cooled off here. Now, Calloway, when he kilt your grandpa, the judge sent him and his family to Oregon. If someone stirred up family or feuding trouble and it was hard to tell who started what, this is how they handled it – send them away rather than rile people up with a trial. That how your cousins ended up out there, so as to keep tensions down. It's a wonder they's any Jameses left. I would say at least a dozen Jameses got wiped out. But they breed."

"What side were your folks on?"

"Blackburns stayed out of it, but I was careful where I went. I knowed who was kin to who. You relied on family and loyal friends if you wanted to git by."

"Looks like grandpa didn't get by too well by relying on family, seeing that his brother-in-law killed him."

"Calloway and Dannon was both hot-tempered," Mr. Black-burn allowed. "They left your grandma in a hard way."

That wasn't the family heritage report I expected to write, but Mrs. Riggs, who was new in town, gave the paper an A and didn't write comments in the margins the way she usually did.

Mother told me how Grandmother Martha Tate James – Ma for short – cared for Dad as she could, occasionally sending him to the homes of various relatives. Ma was said to have been beautiful, but the only pictures we had of her were when she was older – a round-faced woman wearing a dark dress, not smiling her thin lips for the camera. Mother said Ma was suspicious of men who courted her after Grandpa was killed. Ma turned away suitors by telling them, "I can ride better than you, I can shoot better than you, and I don't need your money." Word of that got around.

Two years after Grandpa Dannon was gunned down, Robert Andrew Mason, who stood confident and handsome in the scratchy old photograph in Dad's memento file, came courting. He told Ma, "I can ride better than you, I can shoot better than you, and I don't need your money." So Ma married Bob Mason. They gave birth to my Uncle Clyde, who as a young man went to the World War I front in France, where he got gassed, which wasn't the way people fought in Harlan County. He came back quiet but still tough. Uncle Brian, sixteen when the war broke out, lied about his age to join the Army to be with Uncle Clyde. Uncle Brian came back too broken to live more than another five years.

One day while rummaging through a drawer of Dad's papers, Mother pulled out a narrow, weathered letter penciled by my grandfather, from the Oklahoma Territory, April 4, 1888, a year before he returned to Harlan and two years before he was killed. With the spelling of a man who had only a few years of schooling, Grandpa Dannon wrote to Ma how he missed his child.

After reading that, I thought maybe Dad did understand the difference between his generation and mine, and maybe I didn't. By the time I was fifteen, if Dad complained about the colorless TV violence pressing him down in his easy chair, I understood enough to turn the channel.

4

Football break

BY MY FRESHMAN YEAR THE IVY STREET FRIENDS I PLAYED WITH wanted more roughness and glory than they were getting in street games, so they went out for football and beckoned me to do the same. But I held off. I wasn't yet as big as this crew: strong-jawed Sammy Tyron Brown, known as Chief, the guy who led our Boy Scout troop on hikes; Horse, the lanky son of a former coal miner and the first one of us to shave; Jug, a thick, pink boy with no edges; and strong-necked Stoner – Quentin Stone – who in street games shoved opponents around like a boulder.

Horsing around in the gym after school during the winter of my sophomore year, I joined the basketball players in their laps because Two-Bit was chasing me. Two-Bit and his brother Harley were cousins of Jug, all of them unreliable in a crisis. When I was thirteen they agreed to help me control a small fire I lit on the back yard terrace to burn weeds I was tired of cutting, but as soon as it got out of control they ran off, leaving me to call the fire department to put out the blaze before it whipped all the way up Ivy Hill and burned down people's houses.

In the gym, Two-Bit wasn't as inspired as he was when running away from the fire, so after three laps he flopped onto a bleacher seat. After ten laps I passed some of the players and was trying to catch up with Ricky Seals in front. Ricky was star guard for the basketball squad, quarterback of the football team and pitcher for the baseball team. Numerous girls liked him, but he was going steady with Lucille Potts. In the gym I was lucky to stay within a half-lap of Ricky, who didn't look like he was breathing hard. After that run, Coach Hays, a stout man with thin lips and light curly hair, pulled me aside and said I should come out for football.

"I'm in the band," I told him, though I wasn't good at trumpet, which I started playing because I heard buglers in the movies, and they made it look easy.

"You don't need to be in band. You need to be running."

"Do we have a track team?"

"The track team is whoever wants to run in the district meet in May. Usually it's a basketball player or two coming off the basketball season. You could come off spring practice."

So I quit band and went out for football in the spring of my sophomore year. Spring practice was like boot camp among friends, without the extra pressure of having to go to war anytime soon. Ricky yelled us through calisthenics and Coach Hays ran us through our routines. The second week we got to hit each other. The routine I liked best was running laps, which the heavy guys hated and the slim guys didn't love all that much. I had enjoyed running from the age of three when Mother raced me for short distances along the sidewalk and let me win. Then I moved on to playing with the neighborhood boys who didn't let anyone win anything unless they were setting some kind of trap. But in street chases I learned that if I could get a lead I could usually stay ahead over a long distance. Though I didn't think I was the quickest in short charges, Coach Hays said he wanted to train me as a running back.

When Chief or Stoner hit me in scrimmage they showed mercy as they took me down. Dozer, on the other hand, exploded into me with his short piston legs and long broad torso, setting off sparks in my head. Dozer had smarts but didn't work as hard on his books as he did on his game. Three years older than I, Dozer started school with his class of 1955 but in elementary school repeated enough grades that, by high school, he was in our class of '57.

Dozer at least did everything Coach Hays told him to do on the football field. That was more than could be said for the Keller brothers, Spud and Buster, medium-sized guys with round hairy calves. When scrimmages heated up, the Keller brothers started fighting – each other. Coach Hays rebuked them in a voice that ran up the scale, "STOP IT, girls!" If they didn't stop, Dozer or Rustbucket or Stoner pried them apart. Rustbucket was a six-foot-three, redheaded, freckled boy whose family moved from the Kitts coal camp to Harlan Gas on the southeast edge of Harlan. He came to practice only when he wanted to, which meant three or four days a week. Though he was supposed to be penalized for missing practices, Stoner told me that during football season Rustbucket kept his place as a starting tackle anyway because he was naturally strong. He was usually good for half a scrimmage before his smoking habit winded him.

"What do you think you're training for?" Coach Hays yelped at the Keller brothers as they were held back from each other. They liked being held back from each other for a respectable time. "What do you think you're training for? Boxing? Flyweight boxing?" When a word like *flyweight* came to Coach's mind, he knew he was onto an expression he liked. "When Lynch and Pineville and Bell County come to play, do you think they believe they're coming here to do *flyweight* boxing?" Coach's voice would come down a step. "Why don't we put all this *flyweight* boxing into something that might come in handy this fall – like blocking and tackling? All right, offense, call the play! Defense, line it up, LINE IT UP!"

By the last week of spring training I had gotten the hang of running into tacklers when there was nowhere else to go, though I preferred to run wide where it was less crowded. I carried the ball on wide runs with some success, but Ricky Seals took me aside to suggest that I run where the play is called because those routes were being blocked for me.

Late in the scrimmage, Ricky, a gentleman of an athlete, asked me, "This will be your turn, JJ. What kind of play do you want?"

"How tired does Rustbucket look to you?" I asked. Rustbucket was breathing hard now that practice had worn him down. Instead of charging through the line, Rustbucket merely stood up to grab any ball carrier conveniently nearby.

"He's a little winded," Ricky agreed.

"Hand off to me in a run through the right tackle," I said, aiming to get past Rustbucket with Dozer plowing the way for me.

Ricky huddled. "Slicer T-right," he ordered, "on three."

With the snap, Ricky pivoted and shoved the ball into me as I leaned in behind Dozer who shoved Rustbucket back so hard he fell in a blur as I cut through, zigzagged around the linebacker and then clacked helmets and pads with three guys who a second later were eight guys pushing me backward. One mass of boys trapped the bottom of my left leg as another mass pushed my upper body the opposite way until I felt my lower leg bend *forward* from the knee – *Crack!*

The mass settled down and peeled away to leave me on the ground with my leg bent the wrong way. To my surprise, the leg didn't hurt.

With Coach leading the way, Stoner and Jug carried me up the steps to Clover Street and the three blocks to Dr. Benton's office. An X-ray showed a crack in the femur an inch above the left knee. Dr. Benton, who had delivered me and had made all the house calls to treat me when I had been sick, ordered a plaster cast from hip to ankle. Mom drove me home. Waiting at the porch's screened door, Sarah sniffled until I said I was OK; then she phoned the news to all her friends.

At first I didn't see any significance to this leg fracture. I just thought life was happening to me normally – push a leg the wrong way in a clump of football players, break it, fix it, that's all. But if you pay close enough attention you come to suspect that life plays in stereo. One track plays what is happening inside you. The other track plays what is happening *to* you outside. You are in the middle, trying to figure out the wiring.

It turned out that the fracture cracked me out of a shell of sorts.

When Dad came home from work to find me in the cast, he smiled and patted me on the back, "You're doing fine there, son, doing fine." I think he saw me as gritting my teeth. I felt proud that I had been wounded in a manly sport. Putting up with a football injury like this was a lot nobler than enduring, say, bed-wetting, which I put up with until I was ten when Mom bought me an over-the-counter medicine that worked, Dry-Tab.

Four days after my leg break I was on the bed in the back bedroom reading *Reader's Digest* jokes when I heard Mother answer the doorbell. Mother's southern accent, which spoke "fourteen" as "foh-teen," contrasted gently with the other woman's accent, which spoke "fourteen" as "fowah-teen." Very familiar. Sarah, fresh home from school, exclaimed, "Miss Mira, Miss Mira!" which answered my question. Miss Mira pronounced her name Meer-ah. Until I reached fourth grade and saw her name spelled out, I thought it was "Miss Mirror."

Miss Mira was actually Mrs. Mira Crane, but she taught dance, so her students called her by the "Miss." Sarah was studying ballet, and I had taken ballroom dancing from Miss Mira two years earlier. Miss Mira moved her arms and hands in an almost liquid motion. When pointing to something, she held her arm and hand in such an elegant way that I watched her hand rather than what she was pointing to. After growing up in Charlotte, North Carolina, she studied dance in France, then married Herman Crane, who sold mining equipment. When Miss Mira reminded us in the dance class not to look down at our feet, I wondered if she missed Paris.

Mother came to the bedroom where I was seated against pillows and asked if I wanted a visit from Miss Mira. Sure. Sarah led Miss Mira by the hand down the hall on the hardwood floors that let you know who was coming if you paid attention to the footsteps. Mother had a heavier heel step than Miss Mira did, though the narrow oak flooring strips and the echo off the hallway cabinets softened all the sounds so you never heard a hard "clack," but rather a wooden sound between "clonk" and "clunk."

"How are you Jeremiah, darling?" Miss Mira asked, pronouncing my name as "dahling" and extending her right hand. Trim and of medium height, she was mother's age – in her fifties – but looked younger, with firm skin and few wrinkles. Even her light hair, blonde streaked with white, had a short, youthful cut that exposed a long neck one would expect of a ballerina.

"Not bad," I replied, "but I can't dance right now with this leg. I don't know how I'm going to get my britches on."

"We can solve that problem," she said. "Get some full-sized khakis from Powers and Horton, and if necessary, your mother can tighten the waist and seat."

Khakis sounded like a better fit than blue jeans I had bought when pegged cuffs were in fashion, for when I washed them I could hardly get them on or off, even without the cast.

"He's doing better," Mother offered, "but he didn't sleep well last night, and he isn't eating."

"How does your leg feel?" Miss Mira asked.

"It still hurts. I think it's partly because I can't bend my leg to move the muscles. I am waiting for the swelling to go down. But I haven't had to use as much painkiller today as yesterday."

Mother didn't like painkilling drugs because she had heard about people who got addicted to them. I had come to terms with painkillers, though. When I was twelve I read about how some people could control pain with the mind. I was convinced I could do this myself when I presented my dentist, Dr. Katz, with

17

four cavities, the work of Snickers and Almond Joy bars bought at neighborhood grocery stores along my paper route. I told Dr. Katz I didn't need Novocain. He obliged. That was the last time I tried that sort of thing in a dentist's chair.

Miss Mira sat on the bed at my left, her back straight, with a bangle of gold, copper and silver strands above her left elbow. Walking or sitting, she never slumped. She would even pick up her purse without curving her back too much. When she was around, I tended to straighten up some myself. "Give me your left hand, darling," she requested.

Sarah sat beside Miss Mira, looking up at her from beneath her brown bangs. When Sarah looked at anyone, her face mirrored any emotion, and her gaze at this moment showed delight as she asked Miss Mira, "Are you going to relax him like you relaxed Bessie?"

"Maybe it will help a little," she answered.

During a rehearsal for a ballet recital before Christmas, Bessie Harper, a friend of Sarah's, practiced leaps across a makeshift stage in the basement of the Harlan Baptist Church. Bessie was heavier than the other girls, and the stage was smaller than the regular practice area in the Lewallen Hotel ballroom, so when Bessie made three leaps across the stage her momentum took her into the wall and sprained her wrist. Miss Mira held Bessie's wrist until the pain subsided, then packed Bessie's hand in ice. By the end of the rehearsal, Bessie could move her wrist with only a slight ache, except she wouldn't take three leaps across the stage any more – just two.

Extending her tapered fingers, Miss Mira asked if I minded. I didn't.

Holding the wrist of my left hand, she used her right hand to press her thumb and forefinger, pincer-like, into a spot on the fleshy side of my palm. At first the pressure hurt, then throbbed and eased off.

Mother asked Miss Mira how her sons were doing. Miss Mira said that Michael, her eldest, loved his job as an architect and was adjusting to Lexington. She said Jack's construction business in Richmond was doing well, and that Casey was busy as an electrician in Harlan. Mother listened intently because mothers listen to each other's reports on their children as an exchange courtesy.

After that conversation, Miss Mira talked about a Fats Domino song she heard and asked Sarah about it. That impressed me, because no other adult I knew asked us about Fats Domino. It opened up Sarah. Then Miss Mira asked what song I liked.

I answered. "If I want to feel a little sad, *Autumn Leaves* does the trick for me."

"Do you ever want to feel sad?"

"Sometimes I like to feel sentimental," I answered, trying to figure out why I liked a melancholy song about missing a lost love. I wasn't thinking about Priscilla in that respect; she was a kid's daytime passion. By listening to *Autumn Leaves*, I figured I was mostly practicing sadness before I had a real reason to be sad, other than being sad from practicing. That was too foolish to explain to Miss Mira, so I said, "I think it is easy to like someone and miss them when they are gone. There is something sad about what time does."

"I think you are right," she acknowledged in an even but not pensive way as she eased her fingers into the indention between my thumb and forefinger. "There is something sad about time and what it takes away."

After about ten seconds, Miss Mira grinned slightly and lifted her eyebrows a bit. "I guess we have to figure out how to keep the better part."

She lightly placed her right palm on my palm. Shortly, her hands felt hot. I thought of how my palms sweated in my Priscilla days. Miss Mira's hands, though, didn't sweat the way mine had sweated. I felt relaxed.

Miss Mira patted my hand. "We'll leave you to rest, darling," she said, rising in my thanks. Though it was only six-thirty in the evening, I drifted off to sleep, and when I awoke the next morning, the skin on my upper thigh had shrunk away from the cast. The swelling had gone down enough to allow me to scratch the itching with a coat hanger wire.

During the two months my leg was in a cast I saw my abdominal muscles for the first time, grew an inch taller with more height on the way, and my old running dream, the one I had when I was seven, came back in bits and pieces, clearer than my other dreams that were odd and forgettable.

In the dreams I saw a Cherokee. Nobody said "Cherokee," because there was no one else in the dream, but I knew it anyway, the way you know in dreams. He wore a pair of light trousers. The sleeves of the broad-collared white shirt fluttered in the wind.

I could feel him running along a path in and out of woods, following the bed of a river to his right. As he rounded into the bend, he slowed to a walk and climbed up a short, steep rock path by a stream, along a bench of the hill to a low cliff with a niche like a sanded-out seat back, with splotches of grayish blue and webs of white. Here he sat, and over his head protruded a stone shelf anchoring the formation above it.

His view was eastward, the direction to which he was returning, which I knew because of the shadow of the sun. When he lifted his eyes, half-closed, toward the ridge of the mountain across the river, I felt his happiness and liked it.

The night after my cast was cut off I dreamt of the runner and the blue-streaked rock again. The following morning, with the sun speckling through the leaves outside, I stayed in bed long enough to replay the dream and take it in. In the clearness of the morning I saw what I knew – that as much as I enjoyed playing ball with my friends, I wanted to run in an open field.

5

Making the team

IT WAS HARD TO STUDY INDOORS WHEN THE OUTSIDE WAS ALL LIT up and warm, so I gazed out the window while Mr. Tuckles, my world history teacher, reviewed the dates of European wars. I could see all the way down Central Street. If I let my eyes go out of focus the way I learned from my friends in third grade, the rising street looked as if it ran into a green wall of stacked trees. If I did this long enough, the green would look so close that I imagined I could become part of it and understand greenness. I practiced my stare from the back of the room so I wouldn't need to turn my head in a noticeable way. Dozer also was gazing out, but he was so close to the window his neck was turned sideways. Mr. Tuckles stopped listing the wars in which France, Spain, England and Germany wrecked each other, and asked Dozer to share with the class whatever he had on his mind. Dozer didn't twitch, though his answer came slow at first. "I was wondering," he said, "if school a thousand years ago was any easier than it is now because there wasn't as much to know back then."

"And what do you conclude?" he asked.

"I conclude that since there wasn't as much to know back then, schools threw in the Latin and Greek. After there was more to learn, Greek got tossed out in order to make room for new stuff. Now there is even more to learn, and I'm betting that Latin is next to go."

Some students laughed until they realized Dozer wasn't laughing. "Very interesting," Mr. Tuckles acknowledged. One year after Dozer said this, Harlan High dropped Latin. This week, though, I was finishing up my second year of Latin, which

21

I had taken because French sounded too hard to pronounce, and I had been told Latin revealed the roots of many words. What I hadn't been told was that, in order to use these words in sentences, I had to – for example – do declensions of nouns by their cases: nominative, vocative, genitive, accusative, locative, dative, even ablative. Ablative!

Feeling relieved after my final exam in Latin, wearing fresh-creased khaki pants from Powers and Horton, I strode without a limp down the hallway to Coach Hays' classroom, which had emptied out with the final bell, leaving him enough quiet to grade his civics papers.

"How ya doin', JJ?" Coach Hays turned his head my way. "You're looking good. How's the leg?"

"My knee's still fat but I'm walking fine. In another week I'm going to start working out a little on my own a few days a week. I want to run track next year."

"Good, but I don't know if you heard the announcement. I've accepted a coaching position in Fayette County."

"What?" I said right out. Mr. Hays had coached in Harlan for as long as I remembered. "Why?"

"It's time for a change."

Fine time to tell me. "If I want to compete, how do I do it?"

"It's simple. Get in running shape. You won't run in any dual meets, but the new coach can sign you up for the district meet – you and anyone else you can get to join you. If you win or place in the district, you go to the regional. If you win or place in the regional, you go to state. What do you want to run?"

"The mile and half-mile."

"You would do well at distance, though most boys who have run for us have been sprinters. You know what you like, and what you like is what you do best. Are you going out for football this summer?"

"I think I can do better for the school in track. Next year I'm going to focus on that and see how it goes."

"You'll do fine," he said. "I'll order running shoes and send them to you."

I told him my size, thanked him and walked to the door. He said, "JJ?"

I turned. "Yes, sir?"

"You're the Harlan High School track team."

"Thank you," I acknowledged, impressed by the notion. "Thank you very much."

I headed downtown to sit with five guys perched on the coal monument at the corner of the Harlan County Courthouse. The view from the wall made it easy to see who was going in or out of Green-Miller Drug on the opposite corner of First and Central.

"How ya doin'?" I asked Rustbucket as I checked the granite cap of the wall to make sure it was clear of anything that could stain my pants.

Hunched over, glancing occasionally at the drug store door as he dangled his feet against the hard-sealed coal blocks, Rustbucket spat a brown stream of Mail Pouch chewing tobacco into a Coca-Cola cup. Bulls-eye. "Not bad, Jaybird. You?"

"Not bad. Not bad at all."

৩৩৫২

Sarah's diary – June 2, 1955

Jane wrote that she's returning to Camp Sochee. YEA!! She asked to be in my cabin. Maybe Billy Joe will be back at Camp Arrow, and we can meet him and his friends at the Rock Loop. Billy Joe liked Jane, but Jane didn't like how Billy Joe spit. I asked JJ why boys spit. He said some girls spit, but he couldn't name any girls who did. We only spit if we have something bad in our mouths, like a bug. The boys who play baseball like to spit. Baseball is so boring. Maybe that's why they spit.

6

Summer pursuits

To me, the wonder was that Sarah would go to summer camp at all, considering that there were no telephones in the cabins at Camp Sochee on the edge of the Smoky Mountains. At home she was on the phone so much that Mother's bridge-playing friends couldn't get through the line. Three years earlier, Dad had replaced the wall phone in the hallway with a cradle phone that Sarah could pull into the bathroom or back bedroom. She had spent a week at Camp Sochee in 1954, so she was confident that she could do without a phone since she would be talking with her campmates all day. Packed and ready, she gave me the footlocker I lugged to the car where Dad "supervised" – his familiar word – my loading of the car. We were a Dodge family. Our next-door neighbors, the Handleys, were a Buick family. The Baggetts, on the east side of us, higher up the street, were a Chevrolet family. Atop Ivy Hill lived Cadillac families, with Ford families further back.

"We're going to the filling station first," Dad reminded us as he drove us downtown to Main Street Super Service where he told Homer the attendant to fill up and check the fluids, and told me to "check the caissons," meaning the tires. After Homer put the gas charge on our bill, Dad edged up to Main Street, put his left arm out the window to signal other cars to let us out, then eased onto the street whether or not cars on the street slowed to accommodate us. Mother never relaxed entirely unless she was driving.

Walking with her to her assigned cabin, I warned, "Don't let the bugs bother you." Sarah couldn't stand any insect except a ladybug.

"I have the bug lotion," she said, patting her pocket, then asked a general question to anyone who would answer: "Will I be OK?"

"Of course," Mother assured her. "You'll have lots of fun with your friends."

"You will be fine," Dad said at his turn, leaning down to pat and kiss her. With a chuckle that came from profound satisfaction, Dad always welcomed Sarah to his side or lap, and would hold her as long as she wanted to be there. When Sarah was born, I was disappointed that I didn't get a brother to play with, but I grew into my role. That first required being nice to her. Once, when she was three and I was seven, Mom and Dad left her in my care while they went outside to check on some yard work. As Sarah climbed up the wide, dark walnut staircase in the center of the living room, I shouted at her about some little thing she did. Sarah didn't shout back the way my friends did when we played. She just sat on the steps at my eye level, bent herself into her cupped hands and sobbed, her little legs angled to the back of the riser, helpless. The sight of my hurting her that way blazed in me like slow lightning, voltage too heavy to crack into the sky and disappear. I knew as soon as it hit that this lightning was going to stay in me, burning where it came from. I hurried up the steps, apologized, held her to my side and vowed to myself that I would never again speak to her that way, and I never did. I had to learn a lot of things this way. It was pathetic, really.

After I returned with my parents from Sarah's camp, Chief picked up some Scout friends, loaded us into his father's pickup truck, and hauled us to Camp Sequoia by a lake in northeast Tennessee, where we worked the lakefront as lifeguards.

By now my left leg was strong enough for me to jog the trails and gravel road leading to the camp, always alone, for no one else had any reason to jog, especially not in the sultry heat of July that kept every tent door open and side flap rolled up. On the hottest days I drank enough water that I heard it sloshing in me.

25

By the time I returned from camp, Sarah was already home, listening to records. Some days she and her friends would swarm into the Cumberland Valley Music Store on Main Street, packing themselves into the wooden listening booth with the windowed door and swooning to the sounds that barely leaked outside.

The long days of summer floated bright and easy. On Mondays, Wednesdays and Saturdays I ran on the roads for an hour or so. To earn spending money I worked for Dad.

On the way home from Dad's office along Central Street I always checked the dusty display in the window of T.C. Hunter's store to see if anything had been sold. Mr. Hunter didn't move anything out of the window unless someone bought it. Since hardly anyone bought his goods any more except Mother, the windows featured the same items for years at a time. The two round straw hats were most familiar to me, since I remembered them from 1944 when I was barely tall enough to see in the window, but one of the two bowler hats had been sold recently, and in its place was a woman's black jacket with lace on the sleeves. The two open boxes of bisque dolls were the same as they were in 1953 when they appeared in the place left by the sale of black, lace-up women's shoes. Dad told me that T.C. Hunter, now in his nineties, showing bones on his body and peculiarity in his merchandise, once ran the shop as a top-of-the-line dry goods store.

Further up Central Street I stopped in the mellow coolness of Green-Miller Drug to see who was there. On a hot day, John Egred was a good bet to be inside, leaning against the cosmetics counter, holding his soiled gray coat against his tobacco-stained shirt and tie. If he was short of money, John motioned me to him and nervously asked if I could lend him a quarter. I could. Most times I could lend John a quarter, if I had one, and he always thanked me and told me if he ever could do me a favor to let him know, anything, any favor at all. A good bunch of the time John lived on tips for bringing someone beer or whiskey from the bootlegger, Mattie Burnall, in Clovertown near where John lived.

In grade school, on the playground, we enjoyed watching the sheriff's cars scream by to raid Mattie's place.

The fan magazines on the rack facing Green-Miller's front door mourned and analyzed James Dean's death. Interviews of those who talked with the ghost of James Dean kept us informed on how he was doing. By most reports James Dean felt fine as a dead person in 1955, though a lot of us missed him anyway.

By August, Stoner and I started making the evening rounds in his white 1952 Plymouth. First we went to the Youth Center three floors above the Modern Electric store across from Green-Miller. There we looked for someone to dance with; or, failing that, someone to talk to; or, failing that, someone to look at. Though Jug wanted to be with a girl, he went to the side room to shoot pool because that was easier. If we couldn't find girls, we piled into Stoner's Plymouth and headed to Jack's Drive-In on the south edge of town to see who was there. Usually we found at Jack's a car load of girls who had been at the Youth Center but were looking for someone other than us.

So we drove to Denny Ray's Drive-In three miles south of Harlan and ordered something from the carhop while Jug played the pinball machine inside. I saved a large cup of leftover ice to take on a drive through the Sunny Acres subdivision near Denny Ray's. Cruising along, I heaved the slush at a black, wiry-haired dog that chased us. These encounters offered a certain fulfillment to us and to the dog. We were all chasing something, hoping for a nice surprise.

SARAH WASN'T QUITE yet of the age to cruise Denny Ray's, but she was growing in that direction, closing the bedroom door more while talking on the phone, and repeating herself telling us about the endearing qualities of her classmate, Mike Dawson. The last time I had seen Mike was when he lined up behind me, with a quarter in his hand, at the ticket booth of the New Harlan Theater in January. I remembered him because his nose had let

27

loose some slickness near his lip and I wondered why he didn't wipe it.

One July evening I was having trouble reading in my room as Sarah played *Unchained Melody* for the eleventh straight time, so out of curiosity I knocked on the door of her bedroom across the hall. "Come in!" Inside, the sound waves almost made my shirtsleeves tickle. I was more aware of Sarah's loud music than my loud music, which featured Frankie Lane belting out *Rawhide* or *Moonlight Gambler*, men songs I could pantomime in the mirror, but Mother commented more on my loud music than Sarah's because Mother liked Sarah's gentler songs better. Mother also cut out articles on hearing loss and gave them to me.

Sarah was lying on the twin bed closest to the record player, smiling, eyes closed to the rose of the sunset glowing into the four windows as I plopped down beside her.

She asked, "How long do people in high school go together?"

"It depends. Some not long. Some for years."

"In my class," she said, "girls don't keep the same boyfriends for more than a year. Hardly even that long most of the time. They get all happy when they like someone else; then there is all this hurt because they break up."

After a pause, she continued: "I know what the songs say, but I don't think we love only *one* person forever, at least not in my class. We love lots of people. At different times, that's all. We take turns, unless we like two or three people at once, the way Willa Mae Cunningham does. When we get older, maybe we find out what it adds up to. Or maybe after we die... though that seems kind of late." She stared at the ceiling for a while, and then smiled to herself.

"So, what are you thinking now?"

"Nothing."

I could practically see Mike Dawson floating over her, all clean-nosed.

Sarah's diary 3 – August 1, 1955

I saw Mike at the soda fountain in Green-Miller!!!!! With his T-shirt sleeve rolled up he looks strong!!! When I sat in the booth with Willa Mae and Linda, WM said I should go up to the counter where he was, to order my Coke. I was too nervous. WM went up and ordered for me. I played "Sincerely" on the jukebox and WM said he looked over at me. Linda said she would ask Tony if he would ask Mike if he likes me.

7

The crack of doom

NEAR THE END OF SUMMER, AS I FINISHED PRINTING A MINE MAP ON the ammonia-smelling blueprint machine, Dad picked his hat off the rack and said we needed to check a mine at Lenarue along Martin's Fork, one of four waterways feeding into the Cumberland River near Harlan.

In his boyhood, Dad hiked the Martin's Fork road ten miles to attend school in town, long before the dirt road was widened, packed and paved into Highway 421. He enjoyed driving along this road. Better yet, he enjoyed being driven, now that I had a learning permit.

About a mile south of Lenarue, Dad gestured toward a stretch of exposed rock by the road. "You know that spot, don't you?"

"Where Big Steve was shot at?" Big Steve was my father's uncle.

"'At's right," he said in his deep voice, pronouncing "right" almost like "rat." I hadn't known our accent was unusual until Priscilla asked me why I pronounced "bike" like "back."

"Show it to me," I requested, parking off the road where we stepped into the heat. He led the way to an inverted corner of a rock formation. With his hands slightly trembling, not from emotion but from getting older, he pointed out a chip in the rock. The bullet that shattered the surface of the sandstone came through the brim of Big Steve's hat as he rode toward Harlan on the old trail there.

"When I was small," Dad let me know, "Uncle Steve would take me for protection. But I wasn't with him on that day."

"What kind of protection?"

30

"No one would shoot at a child, so if I was behind him on the horse, nobody would shoot Uncle Steve in the back."

"That was a serious chance to take with you."

"That was a smart chance to take with me. He did with me what I would want him to do." Dad studied the spot. "A rock doesn't show bullet holes the way wood does. That's a good thing about rock." After rubbing the cliff side with his left hand, he added, "But what a rock gets, it keeps for a long time."

"How long do you think this cliff will be here?"

His hat shaded his full-lidded, sky blue eyes as he scanned the hill. "This cliff started getting laid down by the inland seas about three hundred million years ago, I would reckon. If left to nature, this mountain will be worn down in thirty million years, if man doesn't take it down first."

"Where do you think we will be in thirty million years?"

"I hope someplace where it's not too hot."

I laughed.

From there we turned around and drove to the coal camp commissary at Lenarue. Fred, a short, stocky, former miner who worked at the store, stepped out the side door stoop. "Howdy," Dad greeted him. "How is the missus – Mary Ann?"

"Doin' fine, Little Steve," Fred replied. "How you doin' there, JJ?"

"Doin' OK," I said as I waited for Fred to make a wisecrack.

"JJ, make sure your mother feeds you enough." He said that because I wasn't as fat as I was when he saw me last. He patted his gut hanging over his belt.

Remembering the words of the song, *Sixteen Tons*, that Tennessee Ernie Ford was making popular on his TV show, I asked Fred, "You don't owe your soul to the company store here, do you?"

"Not hardly," he said. "I owe that to the Lord Jesus."

31

That stopped my wisecracking. People took their religion all kinds of ways. Some politely listened to sermons that reasoned with them before they headed to Sunday lunch. A few preferred preachers like those who stood beneath the World War I doughboy monument in front of the courthouse, hoping to save someone lost in the crowd waiting for a VTC Line bus to an outlying town or coal camp. Some Saturdays I stood near the cedar-whittling men on the benches to listen to the preacher who pressed his right hand against the side of his throat as if to hold in the veins as his voice swelled his neck red into a rhythm – "and YOU, huh, and YOU, brother, huh, are CALLED to the Lamb, huh, AMEN, huh, before the CRACK of doom comes down on you, huh, you are CALLED, huh, out of the FIRES of hell, huh, AMEN, huh, hallelujah, huh!" I was fascinated enough to pick up the style, but when I was asked to say grace at supper, Mother said I couldn't use the crack-of-doom speech, that it was not appropriate for blessing food, to which Dad added, "Don't act a fool."

Fred opened the side door for us to enter the commissary building and into the office of Brandon Lee, a mine operator who lived with his wife and two daughters in one of the newer homes on Ivy Hill. Mr. Lee's office, like Dad's office and all the other mine offices I visited, had furniture built to last even if a fight broke out – heavy metal desks and tables, dark vinyl couches with stainless-steel arms, sturdy filing cabinets with drawers easy to slide open or shut. The chairs were made of oak or steel painted green.

"How are you doing on the Harlan seam?" Dad asked.

"We should have at least four more years left in the Harlan. Then we could go to the Darby or maybe the Kellioka."

"Kellioka would be a better seam," Dad offered. "Its roof is not as flaky and thin as the Darby's, you know."

"I would be happy to stay long enough to finish the Harlan seam here," Mr. Lee said. Looking to be around forty, Mr. Lee's

32

light brown hair matched his work clothes. "Harlan County had forty-two mines three years ago. Look at what we've lost. You saw the *Enterprise* report. We're down to twenty-eight."

Even coal-fired steam locomotives that pulled the coal were being replaced by diesel engines, which Mother resented, though in our own home we had switched from coal to fuel oil in 1954. So had a lot of families, despite fretting they were turning their backs on their industry. Switching from a coal furnace to an oil furnace made cleaning easier for mother and our part-time housekeeper, Miss Becker, who mumbled a lot about soot. The new oil furnace also made life easier for me because the coal furnace stoker had to be shoveled full and my chore was to fill it – every day in the dead of winter. For me the fun of tending the coal furnace had been removing the wreath-shaped clinkers from the firebox and dropping them into the galvanized tub. Sometimes I poured water on the clinkers to watch the steam mushroom upward. One Saturday afternoon, when I was alone in the house, I thought it would be interesting to cool off the clinkers with my own bodily water. I had not properly calculated the odor or how thoroughly it would penetrate upstairs. I had to open windows and boil onion soup to camouflage the smell before my family came home. I had to eat all the soup, too, because nobody else would.

Rising from his swivel chair, Mr. Lee asked if we were ready to go to the mine up the road. Yes, we said, and packed ourselves into the cab of his pickup truck. Passing fifty yards of L&N railroad cars lined up at the tipple, the truck bounced and crunched up to the mine head where we strapped on our belt batteries and helmet lights and lowered ourselves into the steel bottom of the "man-trip" car latched behind the locomotive where Mr. Lee whirred us into darkness of the main, as the central tunnel was called. The deeper we went, the more I thought about the mountain on top of us and how much it must weigh. "How far we going?" I spoke up loud enough for Mr. Lee to hear.

"About half a mile. We're going to the face," meaning the coal being worked. The mine had two tunnels carved out parallel to the main. The ventilation fan of the tunnel on the left brought in the air; the fan of the tunnel on the right pushed it out. The lights of the locomotive and our hats skimmed across the columns of coal and the brattices that covered corridors in order to direct air across the face. Inhaling on one side, exhaling on the other, holding still in the center: this is how a mountain breathes when it is being mined.

The locomotive yanked right into a corridor, then, after a distance I could no longer calculate in the hypnotic shadows, arced left on the rails, following the noise of heavy grinding. We rumbled in the coolness until our lights zigzagged across a crew of miners hustling in crouched positions, one of them adjusting a cutter with protruding, chainsaw-like blades that sliced under the coal layer.

After shouting back and forth with a supervisor about the work, Mr. Lee pulled us in reverse out of this corridor into another tunnel and let the motor whir to a halt, allowing us to pull ourselves out. I kept my head bowed to avoid hitting the sandstone top, but Dad, being shorter, stood upright to unroll his blueprint and consult with Mr. Lee about where to cut next.

Pointing to a section of coal still in place, I asked if the column would be left there.

"Until we are ready to retreat and rob," Mr. Lee said. "Then we will put up timber supports and take out the columns."

"What happens when the supports rot?"

"The roof falls. That is what it is supposed to do. The mountain settles."

I thought about the Harlan County miners who had been killed in mines like these – fifty or sixty men a year from the 1920s through the '40s, more than a dozen men a year in the '50s, mangled by machines, blasted by dynamite or methane gas, crushed by rock, some entombed alive too long to save.

"How do you like it here, Jeremiah?" Mr. Lee asked.

"I don't know, sir," I replied. "I see those roof bolts holding up the ceiling rock, and I don't know."

Dad said, "You have to respect a mountain if you expect it to keep you alive while you are taking from it."

Mr. Lee's lamp flashed across my face briefly as he told me, "Outside, you may be more likely to get hurt, not because it is more dangerous, but because you don't remember it's dangerous, so you get careless. You can get hurt anywhere."

"Yes sir, but on top of the ground I can stand up. This is a powerful place, but I like to be where I can run."

Dad informed Mr. Lee, "Jeremiah is going to run track for Harlan High next year."

"I didn't know Harlan had a track team," Mr. Lee said. "You fast?"

"Not fast enough yet, but I'm faster outside this mine than in it."

"If you heard the top cracking toward you," Dad chuckled, "I bet you could move fast inside a mountain."

"Record time, probably," I admitted. "The crack of doom can do that, I suppose. The crack of doom at midnight." I went on, though not as spirited as the preacher man, " – midnight here no matter what time it is." With my hand quivering at the thought of the mountain caving in, I concentrated on the light from my father's head so I wouldn't notice so much the dark all around.

❧

Sarah's diary – August 5, 1955

Tony told Linda that Mike thinks I'm cute!! I told Linda to tell Tony to tell Mike that I like him. Willa Mae, Samantha, Linda, Jenny and I are going to swim at the pool tomorrow afternoon.

Linda lent me the latest Nancy Drew mystery, *The Scarlet Slipper*.

JJ asked me to turn down my music. Why? He plays his louder than I play mine sometimes. He has his own room. I turned it down anyway.

August 6, 1955

Mike came to the pool with Tony, Pokey and Kevin Bentz and they said hi. Pokey and Kevin tried to splash our hair wet. So immature! Mike didn't try to splash us. I like that about him. He's the quiet type.

I'm halfway through the Nancy Drew book. Jenny said I might like *Anne of Green Gables*. She's going to lend it to me.

Linda said she heard that Kevin likes Jenny. That's an interesting bit of news. On Sunday he took Jenny to see *Love is a Many-Splendored Thing*, but today at the pool Kevin cannonballed her. Jenny looked surprised. Kevin should ask me for advice. We're not in sixth grade any more. We're in junior high.

8

Fall, 1955

"YOU'RE BACK IN SCHOOL. IT'S TIME TO THINK," DECLARED MR. Cobb, our bone-thin biology teacher, as he wrote with clicks of chalk across the slate blackboard, "All summers come to an end," the first day of class, 1955.

Dozer raised his hand. "On the blackboard there, what do you mean, all summers come to an end?"

"Life on earth runs in cycles," Mr. Cobb explained. "Plants and animals live and die. Civilizations rise and fall. Seasons rotate. Summer goes into fall and winter."

"That's just the summer here, isn't it?" Dozer inquired.

"What do you mean?" Mr. Cobb smiled with a quiver. Sometimes Mr. Cobb acted as though he had drunk several cups of coffee and had to giggle or fidget in order to handle the caffeine.

"Summer in the United States runs June to September," Dozer explained, "because of the way the earth is tilted, or something like that. But at the equator, it's like summer pretty much all year, ain't it?"

"The sun's shifting angle doesn't have as great an effect on the weather at the equator as at the poles," Mr. Cobb acknowledged.

"Right," Dozer said. "So, if you live on the equator, summer doesn't come to an end. The most that changes is the names of the months."

"But there would be change. There is always change," Mr. Cobb insisted, scratching himself. We couldn't tell if Mr. Cobb was aware of where all he scratched himself – standing up, even.

"Sure, there's change," Dozer went on. "You know better than we do, but around the equator summer doesn't end the way it does in Harlan. It's a matter of where you are." Dozer leaned back and tapped his pencil on his book a few times before sticking it behind his right ear, finished.

"OK, class," Mr. Cobb said, "what do you think? Do all summers end?"

Some students said they agreed with Dozer, causing Mr. Cobb to quit the topic. He outlined the work and papers due for the first six weeks, followed by an announcement:

"We have a special student who will join our class tomorrow – Jenny Lee, an eighth grader who is gifted." With a giggle at the sarcasm he was about to let loose, Mr. Cobb said, "I hope you can keep up with her."

Jenny Lee – I knew her as the daughter of Brandon Lee, the coal operator at Lenarue, and as Sarah's friend, and as the younger sister of Barbara, who was Miss Mira's best dancer. Twice when I waited for Sarah outside the studio room in Miss Mira's house, Jenny sat across from me waiting for Barbara, who was assisting. Miss Mira called Jenny "Sister" and not only talked to her but sat to talk with her. Jenny had a reputation for being precocious and independent, which Sarah's friends viewed with curiosity and some unease.

Mr. Cobb continued, "Miss Lee has finished courses at her grade level and has permission to take this class. I expect everyone to be respectful and helpful to her."

After class, Lois Ann Smith, a cousin from somewhere on my paternal grandmother's side, spied me coming into the library for study hall and waved for me to sit by her. Blonde and soft-faced, Lois' lips were full and her mouth was expressive. She had to restrain herself to keep from being heard by the librarian, Miss Posey.

"I hear you're out running on the roads."

"Yeah, training for track."

"On roads?"

"People are talking about *that?*"

38

"People talk about everything."

"I guess."

"I hear Lucy Giddon likes you."

"I've never met Lucy Giddon."

"That doesn't matter, you know that."

Yes, I did know that, come to think of it.

"Oh, there she is," Lois gestured toward a shorthaired, sturdily built girl entering the library. "Do you want me to say anything?"

"No, please, but keep an ear out for me."

"OK, sweetie."

Sitting vigilantly behind her librarian desk, Miss Posey stared pointedly at us through her horn-rimmed glasses before striding to the far end of the library to quieten Jug, whose happiness was causing him to laugh loudly, not allowed. School had begun.

The next morning Sarah gave a quick rap to my bedroom door to hurry me up for breakfast so I wouldn't be late. Downstairs, as I turned in the living room to go down the hall, I saw Dad standing in the bathroom, which he called "the closet." Looking dizzy, he put down his razor and staggered toward the door. I froze. After steadying himself against the doorjamb, Dad lowered himself to the floor. I ran to him as Sarah dashed from the kitchen, crying already, with Mother close behind her.

Sliding my hands under Dad, I asked Sarah to cup his head as I lifted him into my arms and, with Mother's help at balancing, stood straight. Dad's eyes had a confused look.

"I'm taking him to the hospital," I said.

"No," Mother said, "put him on the bed. I'm calling for an ambulance."

She grabbed the phone and told the operator to call a funeral home to send an ambulance to the James' yellow brick home on Ivy Street, three houses up from the corner of Second.

After waiting a long fifteen seconds, I said, "The ambulance is not fast enough and our car's in the shop. I'm taking him. I can get him there quicker." Harlan Hospital was only a block and a half away, about a hundred yards downhill.

"Carrying him may hurt him more; we don't know," Mother protested.

"How long will that ambulance take?"

Dad finally spoke some words about his left arm, so I asked him, "Do you want me to start carrying you, or do you want to wait here?" I still didn't hear sirens. When I had set the back yard on fire, the sirens came on even before I hung up.

Groggily he ordered, "Start." With mother opening the front door and Sarah opening the porch door, I moved carefully down the steps to the first landing, then quicker along the stretched, almost horizontal steps by the terraced area as the siren finally wailed.

As I reached the sidewalk the ambulance screeched around the corner and up the hill, braking beside me in the street where two men jumped out, told me I should have waited for them at the house, *easy for you to say*, strapped Dad onto the gurney, backed down the hill and hustled into the ambulance bay where I met them because it was quicker to run than ride.

As Dad was rolled to the emergency room, Dr. Benton whisked in the door, asked questions and ordered medications intravenously. A nurse ushered us out of the room to the hallway. At the nurses' station, Mother phoned Harold, who soon appeared with Uncle Clyde.

On a bench we sat in a row, talking low and intermittently about the circumstances. Nurses on their rounds traipsed past us as the minute hand climbed up and down the mountain of the wall clock face while we waited, helpless.

Finally, Dr. Benton came to us. "Steve had a stroke. A clot stopped the blood flow to part of his brain. His left side is paralyzed, but if he gets physical therapy he might bring back some of his movement."

I asked, "What happens after this? What are his odds?"

"We work for a long life. We will give him medicine to reduce the risk of clotting as best we can."

"Good," Mother exhaled, holding Sarah in her arms and patting my hand, "then we have time. We have time."

I felt reassured, though I knew the time we had was not the same as it had been an hour before. I felt as though a thick glass wall had come down across my life. Through the clear divide I could see the past, as close as ever, but I couldn't move in it any more, and death was on the side that I was on.

◈

Sarah's diary – September 21, 1955

Daddy fell with a stroke in the hallway, the most awful thing of my life. JJ carried him to the ambulance. It tore me to see my daddy carried. Daddy always carried me. Now it's getting all backwards. In fourth grade Della Baxter lost her father in a mine accident at Three Point. I cried in the restroom when that happened, and I didn't even know Della that well. Della said her mother told her that God wanted her father in heaven with Him. Why? God is everyplace. I'm not. Keep my daddy where I can see him.

9

Rain walk

THE MORNING AFTER MY FATHER FELL, I GOT OUT OF BED ON TIME to walk with Sarah to school, remembering the October afternoon in sixth grade after Miss Becker killed my parakeet, Charley, by letting it out of the porch screen door while everyone else was gone, though she denied doing anything. I couldn't stand for Charley to be kept in a cage, so he was let loose in the house where his favorite space was on the fireplace mantle where he loved himself in the mirror. The only problem was that he left ringed droppings on the mantle and I had to clean them up to keep mother from getting too disgusted.

Miss Becker must not have liked cleaning up after Charley – or me, for that matter. In those days it was hard for me to pick up my clothes, I don't know why. Miss Becker was a tiny woman with white hair pulled back tightly in a bun. Her gums had shrunk with age, but that didn't slow down her talking to herself. She was bothered by just about everyone except the late Franklin D. Roosevelt, whom she liked because he started Social Security. Mostly she would tell people off when she was alone in the basement ironing clothes. I should have listened. She probably was telling off Charley for leaving droppings on the mantle, and telling me off for leaving underwear on the floor.

As if that weren't enough, the year before losing Charley I found my dog, Biscuit, dead in the yard with white crust on his mouth and flies all around. Two years later Mother found out that Mr. Tundrell, a wiry man who lived several blocks away and had a big smile like Teddy Roosevelt's, poisoned Biscuit with strychnine. Mother found this out from Mrs. Tundrell, who sought Mom's help because Mr. Tundrell was threatening her. The problem got solved when Mr. Tundrell suffered a fatal heart

42

attack while lifting a casket at the funeral home where he worked. I had never heard of anyone dying more conveniently than that. I had always thought of Mr. Tundrell as friendly. He showed me around the mortuary and showed me the first corpse I had ever seen up close, on the embalming table, covered with a sheet. It was an interesting coincidence that the second corpse I saw was Mr. Tundrell's, when I went with my family to pay our respects to Mrs. Tundrell, who seemed to get past the grief pretty fast by moving to Myrtle Beach.

As I went to school the morning after my father's stroke, I remembered how depressed I had been in sixth grade, and how a friend came to me in the rain. I had been walking home alone, saddened by the loss of Charley. Stepping into the downpour, with no raincoat or umbrella, I didn't care if lightning struck me – I could think that with no lightning actually around – though I didn't want my hair to be shocked so straight that Mr. Tundrell wouldn't be able to brush it down in the casket. At that moment a girl's voice shouted my name from behind. Laura Green ran up to me, pulled me under her umbrella, and locked her arm in mine to lead me to a porch until the thunder let up, all without a word of chiding.

Five years after that rain walk, here I was, still alive, though in another kind of rain. Passing Laura on my way to biology class, I waved to her and said, "Thanks."

She paused. "For what?"

"For being nice," I said.

"Oh?" she said, trying not to show too much puzzlement – "You're welcome," and flowed on.

Leaning against the opened classroom door, Mr. Cobb said hello to us as we entered the lab room. My mind was elsewhere, so when I got to the table I was surprised to see in my chair+ a girl with neck-length black hair – Jenny Lee.

"Oops," she acknowledged as I reached her side, "Is this your seat?"

43

"Not any more. I'll take the one across the table."

"I'm sorry. When I came yesterday, it was empty, and Mr. Cobb didn't move me. We can switch."

"I like this seat over here," I said, sitting down and facing her. I had seen Jenny earlier in the month from a distance when she stood with Sarah and her friends atop a float they were decorating for the Black Diamond Festival parade. Seeing her up close now, with a narrow waist and filling bust, she didn't look as childlike as I remembered her.

"Welcome to high school," I said. "What happened in class yesterday?" I had been at the hospital.

"We were told to read the first chapter and learn the classifications."

"I'm going to have to catch up."

"By the way," she added, "I am sorry about your father. I hope he is recovering well." *Recovering well?* Sarah and her other friends didn't talk like that.

Boot-clunking through the door before Mr. Cobb closed it, Larry "Zorro" Baines strode to our end of the table, dropped himself onto the stool beside Jenny and, in the style he was known for, asked, "Who are you?" She told him. In the fifth grade Baines moved to Harlan from a coal camp near Brookside where he was a friend of the Scraggs brothers, Luther and Shelton, who lived at the bottom of the hollow. A school bus started its route at the Scraggs' place, so if snow was forecast and the Scraggs wanted to stay home, they hosed down the road the night before to ice it up. When the bus driver couldn't get up the hill, the driver would call the superintendent who would cancel school because of bad road conditions. All the boys in class, especially Baines, liked the Scraggs brothers, but the brothers moved to Hazard in the eighth grade, leaving Baines to himself, watching too many Zorro and Lash LaRue movies. It was during that period he took to wearing black pants and long-sleeved shirts, even in warm weather, which raised a sweat on him the last month of classes because the school didn't have air-conditioning.

Mr. Cobb tapped his pencil on the edge of his desk to get our attention. He told us why scientists made up Latin names for science and asked the classification order.

Dozer raised his hand and was recognized. "We start with the plant and animal kingdoms. From there, everything divides up, down to the species."

When it became clear that Dozer had finished, Mr. Cobb said, "That's right," and asked if anyone knew the other categories. Not getting a response, Mr. Cobb looked around until he settled his gaze in our direction. "Jenny?"

Jenny hesitated, and then listed them.

"Good. And would anyone happen to know an example of a phylum?"

Nobody answered.

"Miss Lee, would you like to try that one?"

Not sounding enthusiastic at being singled out, yet not wanting to displease Mr. Cobb, Jenny listed three examples.

"Thank you," Mr. Cobb said as a twitch of satisfaction snapped his chin up a notch and went on to explain the Latin roots of arthropoda as Zorro leaned way back in his chair, cocked his head sideways, and took a long look at Jenny.

After school, Sarah and I went to Dad's room in the hospital where we talked until our older half-sister, Marci, with her husband Alexander Garos, a wholesale grocer in Knox County, arrived. Being twenty years older than I was, Marci seemed more like an aunt when I was small, but as I reached my teens, I thought of her more as a sister who always treated me kindly. Because Marci had eloped with Alexander the year I was born, I never had lived with her, except when she came to Harlan or we visited her in Barbourville. Marci's wavy, light brown hair and light skin contrasted with the dark hair and olive skin that

45

Alexander inherited from his parents who emigrated from Greece after World War I.

Until I heard Marci play a violin solo at church I had never cared much for string music. I had gotten numbed by all those movies in which the violins swooned in every time someone got sad or fell in love. I didn't know how violinists could stand it.

"Papa Steve," Marci greeted him with a kiss, "are you behaving, with all these nurses around?"

"Yes," he chuckled. "My left side doesn't work."

"I'm going to stay with you now," Marci said, "so Mama Elizabeth can go home and get things done."

Taking our leave, Sarah, Mother and I walked home. I knew Mother hurt, but she rarely cried in front of us. She said the hardest parts of her life were losing her father and her first baby. Mother told me that, when she was having a difficult time, her father came to her in a dream and told her not to worry, that everything would be all right. This reassured her deeply. The surprise to me was not that her father came to her from beyond this life, but that she had trials that had weighed on her so heavily.

It was two years before I was born that my brother, Daniel, died at the age of nine months. Mother never said what his ailment was, but Miss Becker told me Daniel had a defective heart evidenced by blue lips. When Daniel got sick, Mother carried him to the hospital where Dr. Benton gave Daniel castor oil and told Mother she could take him home. Mother refused, so Dr. Benton put Daniel in a room where Mother could watch him. In the night, Daniel stopped breathing and Mother called for help, but Daniel couldn't be saved. The service for Daniel was held in the living room while Mother stayed in bed upstairs.

Dad's stroke laid on a new burden. Mother sat Sarah and me down on the couch at the east end of the living room, and we agreed on what do to. Mother would manage the finances, Sarah would help with chores, and I would assist with Dad.

46

When we brought Dad home from the hospital two weeks later, we hired Homer, who worked part-time at the Gulf station, to help with Dad and drive him around on school day afternoons. I took over in the evenings. At night I put Dad to bed and read *The Upper Room* lesson to him.

Twice a week Homer took Dad to physical therapy. I helped Dad practice walking in the evenings. With Dad's left shoe heel anchoring a brace that buckled around his upper calf, he held onto me with one arm as I pulled him up from the wheelchair. He swung the left leg forward and put a little weight on it. Methodically we walked in the living room that handsomely spanned the front of the house, back and forth, day after day.

On the last Saturday in October, Dad said he wanted to try walking with his new aluminum cane topped with a wrist support. After taking a while to balance, Dad let go of my arm, positioned his cane, took a step, steadied himself, and moved a leg.

"All-righty," he said. Looking forward, he took another short, cautious step. "I want to go to the porch to see the weather."

He lifted his foot over the threshold and onto the new plywood ramp slanting down to the green concrete floor. Easing up to the waist-high brick wall, he gazed through the screen toward the valley where the mountains folded into layers of fading blue in the gray of the rain.

"Pretty soon we're going to have you running out there," I said.

"I got my fill," he replied. "It's your turn." Satisfied with the view into the mist, he turned by degrees to line up for his slow journey back inside.

Sarah's diary – October 1, 1955

My moods have gone up and down all week. After dance class Miss Mira asked me to stay. She asked how I was doing (fine) and showed me a swing routine. That made me feel so much better!!! I taught JJ how and danced it with him at the Youth Center tonight. Mike, Brad, and Tommy danced with me. I also danced with Booger when he asked me, but I felt embarrassed. Booger is a good dancer, but that's such a yucky nickname. I told him he ought to have smacked whoever started calling him that. He's big enough. His real name is Teddy Booker. Even Horse is a better nickname than that.

10

Trick or treat

On Halloween Sarah interrupted my homework at the kitchen table and asked if I wanted some candy. No. "I want some candy," she said.

"OK."

"Then go with me trick-or-treating on Cumberland Avenue."

"Where Mike lives?"

"I need to trick-or-treat the Dawsons."

"Mike's dad is a sheriff's deputy. How are you going to trick him?"

"I'm going to hide my identity."

Sarah trotted upstairs to change into her white dress. She also wore a black mask over her eyes, like the Lone Ranger's.

In the living room Mother uncrossed her legs, rose from her chair and advised us, "Be careful what you eat out there."

White cloth sack in hand, Sarah pulled me out the door and hiked down to Cumberland Avenue, which was flat. Only the streets near the river were flat from one end to the other.

We turned onto a side street toward a white frame house with cheap curtains that were always closed. A group of costumed teenagers huddled behind a nearby hedge.

"You can forget going to Mrs. Hacker's house," I told them. "You're not going to get anything." I used to deliver the newspaper to her. Any time I came to collect, she refused to answer the door. She still owed me $18 from three years previous.

"We can try."

"Her mind's not in a good way," I tried to explain. She had a hard spell when her son was killed in Korea, and then her

49

husband died. I heard she was stingy before she was widowed, but being alone made her worse. She filled up her rooms with old newspapers and junk. Each spring her cousin Herman Crane worked to persuade her to let him clean out her rooms. Mr. Crane gave the newspapers – the ones she didn't pay for – to our Scout paper drive and helped us haul them. Mrs. Hacker's papers filled a pickup truck. As Scouts, we liked her.

One of the stouter boys behind the hedge moved toward Mrs. Hacker's porch carrying a paper sack with a twisted top he was trying to light with a match.

I intercepted him. "What are you doing?"

The voice from the Dracula mask explained, "Mush fire." We made a mush fire by filling a sack with manure and setting a match to it. The purpose was to get somebody to stomp out the flames and smear the manure all around. These activities never stopped us from writing essays about how we were the leaders of the future.

"Don't do it," I objected.

"Don't tell me what to do." Four more boys came from behind the hedge toward us.

"I'm asking you," I said, aware that I had my little sister with me instead of Stoner or Horse. "If your mother was all alone, would you want someone setting a fire on her porch?"

"She ain't my mother," Dracula said.

A costumed boy whispered loudly, "Pokey, do it or don't do it – we should get out of here." So that was who Dracula was – Pokey Giddon, a strongly built sophomore with some acne problems, and the brother of Lucy, the girl that Lois said liked me.

I said, "You aren't supposed to start a mush fire on a wooden porch. That's arson. Go put that thing on the Dawson's stoop if you want to. At least it's concrete."

"No!" yelled Sarah.

The four boys surrounded Dracula protectively. One of the costumed girls waiting at the hedge yelled for the boys to stop, but Dracula and his friends scampered to the door, plopped down the burning sack, knocked on the door, rang the doorbell, then ran down the street with the girls fussing after them. I jumped on the porch and with one foot slid the sack onto the grass where it burned open. From the smell I could tell that the boys had used cow manure. I knew they had gone to a lot of trouble for this, but I thought pig manure would have stunk better.

We made our way to the Dawson house where I waited on the sidewalk as Sarah rang the doorbell, talked to Mrs. Dawson, received a treat, and ran back to me. "Guess what Mrs. Dawson said. She said Mike went to the Halloween program in the gym and that he might be looking for me."

So we quickstepped to the gym where school clubs had set up booths and games. Sarah left me so she could chatter with her girlfriends and be seen by Mike Dawson. I walked over to the Kissing Booth. For fifty cents a guy could get kissed by one of seven girls, including Lois, whom I asked, "Why don't you have boys in there, in case some girl wants a kiss?"

Standing beside Lois, Gretchen Ames, a hefty classmate with thin-plucked eyebrows, exhorted, "Give us Ricky Seals!" In fifth grade Gretchen pressed a paper-painted tattoo onto her upper thigh and let me see it.

"Girls don't have to pay for kisses," Lois explained. "We get them free."

Gretchen insisted, "We'll pay Ricky Seals!"

"But why are you charging so much?" I asked Lois. "Fifty cents a kiss?" I could get a cheeseburger and milk shake for that.

"We're raising money for the Musettes," she explained. They were all members of the girls' choral group.

"What does fifty cents get me?"

"A kiss on the cheek," she answered.

"Cheek? Is that what Jeff gets?" Lois dated Jeff Ketchum, who played the tuba in the band. I heard that on band trips Lois and Jeff rode in the back of the bus.

"Jeff is special."

"And I'm not? I want someone else."

Gretchen grabbed the dollar out of my hand and went full-lipped onto my mouth for about – I don't know – five seconds. I took a deep breath and asked her for my change. She came at me again for nearly as long. After that I knew I wasn't going to get any money back.

ↂ

Sarah's diary – October 28, 1955

Gretchen kissed JJ twice at the Musettes' booth. I don't know what he was doing over there, paying good money for that. She almost killed him.

11

Interesting time

MOUNTAIN-SWEET, THE NIGHT AIR SETTLED IN CRISP AND COOL around the bright lights of the last football game of the season the Friday after Halloween. As soon as the band played the National Anthem and pranced off the field, Lois split from her fellow majorettes and headed to me on the sidelines where I stood with Scotty Lanier, a neatly dressed friend who had stayed fairly clean even in the dirt days of our childhood. Wearing a red and white scarf draped down the front of his leather bomber's jacket, Scotty looked like one of those clean-jawed, rich-looking, wavy-haired guys in fashion ads that make you think that if you buy the clothes you will look like him, but you won't.

Her cheeks pink from marching around in the cool air with nothing on her legs but pancake makeup, Lois mentioned that Lucy Giddon had a hard week because her brother set a sack on fire on Mike Dawson's front stoop and Deputy Dawson caught her, gave her a talking-to and let her go. I told Lois that sounded terrible.

Feeling guilty, I followed Lucy and a friend of hers named Verna to the bleachers, sat in front of them and made pleasant remarks through the first half of the game, but they didn't respond much. It felt cold back there. So, at halftime I left to buy popcorn and sit with Scotty, who in fifth grade set off firecrackers with me outside the Greyhound station, and we got caught and ended up in court. At least Lucy didn't have to go before a judge.

Scotty had been a promising running back on the football team the season before. As we watched the bands perform at halftime, he told me he didn't return to the squad because players weren't allowed to drink water during August practice, and he didn't like being thirsty, so he went to the coast of Maine over the summer to wait tables for the tourists. "You should go up there with me."

"I'd like that, but I have to work for my Dad."

"Think about it."

As the players jogged back to the field, spectators ambled back to their seats. With Sarah and her group of friends was Jenny Lee, who looked up at me and waved. Pleased, I waved back. At Jenny's side walked a thin boy wearing a suede jacket.

I asked Scotty who the boy with Jenny was. Scotty would know because he was Jenny's first cousin – his mother and Mrs. Lee were sisters.

"Kevin Benz."

"Her boyfriend?"

"Recent boyfriend. Now just a friend."

"What happened?"

"I don't think he's old enough for her."

"How old is he?"

"Fourteen."

"That sounds old enough to me."

"In Kevin's case, not old enough."

Curiously, those words, "not old enough," echoed in my head the following afternoon as in preparation for my workout I limbered up on the west end of Ivy Street, the only level part. Accelerating down the runway, I crossed Second Street with a thrust that lifted me past the Handleys, past my house and the Baggets', around the belly of the hill, then steeper to the humped center of the hairpin curve where I circled for a breather and then hooked and pulled sharply up the grade until the rise of Ivy Hill road eased off to a more human angle with a view of my green-shingled roof through the trees. Swirling leaves in its wake, a car rounded toward me and moved to the center of the road to give me ample space at the edge of the sheer drop. As I headed alongside the small cliff on the bulge of the first curve, a voice called my name, leading my eyes to Jenny Lee, sitting on the brow of a rock face about twelve feet up from the road.

Whoa. "What are you doing there?"

54

"Just sitting." She rested her chin on her hands, elbows propped on her knees, looking relaxed. "How far are you running?"

"From the first flat to the second flat a few times, then back down."

"Have fun."

"Maybe I will see you then."

She waved goodbye with a shy arc of her right hand, and I took off again around the forested curves, past the larger homes on the crest, then quickly down to the first flat, a clay-packed clearing where my friends and I had played softball in the summers. Wanting to finish this run promptly, I sped past the final row of houses and the gravel road dipping east of the hill and rising to the second flat where I made two loops around the ridge.

Upon my return to the sandstone outcrop I slowed to a walk and searched for Jenny, but she was not on the rock where she had been. Disappointed, I jogged on around the curve until I heard her voice from the south face where she sat in the same manner as before, resting her chin on her hands.

Pausing to gauge her elevation, I made a short run up the rocks by the notches familiar from childhood climbs, and with a few grabs, steps and pulls reached her side.

"How was your run?"

"Nice, after I got up the steep part at the start of the hill," I answered, pulling my sleeve to wipe my face as I took a seat a few feet from her. For a moment her brown eyes, rayed with bronze in the iris, liquid clear, fixed on mine with an alertness that reached out.

I asked if she ever thought of what it would be like if she could go back to the time the cliffs were formed.

"I'm not sure I would like to be standing here in person at the end of the Paleozoic era – "

Paleozoic era?

"— but I would like to see it as a movie kind of thing," she said. "Can you imagine, six miles of earth crust shoving up?" Part of Pine Mountain's 125-mile long ridge stretches along Highway 119 from

Pineville eastward to Harlan, with strata slanting up in one road-cut of mountain, down in another, warping here and there.

"I wonder if Pine Mountain got shoved up by a lot of little earthquakes or a few big ones."

"I think it would have to have been a bunch of movements with some big shifts mixed in, wouldn't you?" Jenny replied. "If geologists haven't figured that out yet, they will. Science is good about that. That's what's so fun about science."

"It would be quicker if we could travel back in time and check that out. Did you ever read H.G. Wells' book, *The Time Machine*?"

"No."

"In the book this guy went way, way out to the future. It wasn't good. The working class was underground and the leisure class was on top of the ground. The working class folks came aboveground at night to kill the leisure people."

"Why?"

"For food. They ate them. Like cattle."

"Ugh."

"The movie was better. It had a more romantic ending. At the end, the movie made it clearer that the guy went to the future to get back with this leisure-class girl who liked him."

"I hope they didn't get eaten."

"We'll never know. Wells never wrote the sequel."

"You should write the sequel."

"I should. I should write what the guy did when he found the girl again. He could bring her here to 1956. Settle on Ivy Hill. Check out the Cold War."

"Would you want to go to the future?"

"No, I'd rather see the past."

"Why?"

"Because that could explain some things to me – what people knew in the old days, those prophet folks and mystics. I would like to go back and find out. I don't care as much to see the future, because in the future, I will be dead."

56

"You wouldn't be dead just by seeing the future, would you?" she asked, holding a slightly crooked grin above the dimple in the center of her chin as she looked at me sideways.

"I wouldn't be dead, but I would be seeing a time my *body* would be dead."

"If you were seeing the future, you wouldn't need to have your body there, would you?"

"I would have to get used to the idea that I was alive seeing a time when my body was dead. Wouldn't you feel a little strange seeing the future where you might read your death notice?"

"Maybe," she admitted. "If that happened, I would know I didn't need my old body. I think I would wonder mostly about time – about what time is."

"How old are you, Jenny?"

"Twelve. How old are you?"

"Almost sixteen. Sixteen in November."

"Well, I'm almost thirteen. Thirteen in February."

"Then you're closing in on me, Kid," I said.

Mrs. Lee's cheerful voice in the distance called Jenny to supper. She didn't move. We talked a few minutes more until Mrs. Lee called again. I said, "I think she wants you."

"I enjoyed talking to you," she said politely, rising to leave.

"Thanks. I'll see you in class tomorrow."

"In the future," she pointed out.

"That's right," I agreed as I edged down the rocks sideways. "I look forward to it, because I expect to be alive then."

"Same body?"

"Same body."

"Good. Me, too."

All the way down the hill I repeated the conversation to myself, to make sure I understood what we said.

Sarah's diary – October 17, 1955

Tony said Booger likes Willa Mae. Booger has to do something about that name. At the moment, Willa Mae likes Bill, Wilfred and Bongo. I'm sure she can fit in Booger.

I lost another pound. Mother said I couldn't get up from the table until I ate the peas. Nothing is yuckier than peas. I threw them up. Mother thinks I threw them up because I want to be thin. I threw them up because peas make me sick. So do green beans.

I asked JJ if he thought I was too skinny. He said I looked good. SEE!!! He also said I should eat more. Dad doesn't complain about me. I can sit on his lap without crushing him. I'm glad he can walk again!

October 18, 1955

Miss Mira asked me again if I could stay a while after the dance lesson. She took me to the sunroom study off her living room and asked me how the family was doing. Why do I get weepy at the wrong time? What's worse, my nose got red from wiping it. I COULD HAVE DIED!

On the shelf by her desk Miss Mira had a cross and symbols of the different religions of the world. She told me what the symbols meant and talked with me until I felt good.

October 24, 1955

In the cafeteria Friday I called Ted Booker "Teddy Bear" and hugged him. He turned red when everybody laughed and called him Teddy Bear. After lunch I told Teddy to take on this Bear name because he shouldn't be called Booger if he wants to have a girlfriend. I hope it works. He still likes Willa Mae. Some girl will like him when he's not Booger.

12

Driver

I PASSED MY DRIVING TEST AND BECAME INDEPENDENT TO THE EXTENT that my parents would let me use their car. The first weekend I could drive without my mother in the passenger seat, Jug, Stoner and Horse asked me to take them to the Wayne Drive-In to see *The Birth of Twins*, a documentary playing between the main features. We didn't invite girls along for this because of the partial nakedness involved.

Through the years Horse had shared with us a few nudist magazines, whose stated aim was to serve "health" interests. These magazines usually featured people playing volleyball, though they did not look particularly athletic, and playing volleyball this way looked risky, unless naked people played with more care than we played on Ivy Street. As it turned out, the film was no better. The twins were delivered by caesarian. None of us had ever seen an abdomen sliced open by a scalpel before, with babies plucked out of the blood and fluids. We drove off halfway through the second feature, a romance of some kind.

When not driving friends to Denny Ray's, I chauffeured Dad through the mountains. The more comfortable I became at driving, the faster I drove. The faster I drove, the more Dad ordered me to slow down so he could see things. When Mother drove with me and I was listening to the Top 20, she told me to turn down the radio.

Eating at a booth at Howard Drug with Stoner, I complained that our parents didn't understand us.

"How much do we want them to understand us?" Stoner asked with a smile that was always genuine but usually brief.

"Enough for them to know why we feel the way we do."

"Are you kidding?"

Hmm.

A few days later, in biology class, Zorro clunked in with his boots and took his seat early. I asked him if his parents understood him.

"Yeah, my mom and stepfather understand me some."

"What do you mean, 'some'?"

"They know I'm strange."

"Strange how?"

"Lookit," he said, holding his arms wide. "Nobody else here in black."

As Jenny Lee sat down, Mr. Cobb tapped his pencil on his desk to start the class and told us to organize into small groups and take a biological inventory of an area of our choice.

Jenny, Zorro and I agreed to check out a stream at Mason Pond, where Uncle Clyde owned an old family cabin on Black Mountain, north of Harlan. Sarah asked if she could come along.

"We're looking for bugs and things," I let her know.

"I didn't know Jenny touched bugs."

"You've never played with Jenny outdoors?"

"We walk outdoors. She'll go places with us, and to movies; not a Three Stooges movie, but other movies."

"Come along and see how she does. Larry Baines is going."

"How did you get to know Baines?"

"He sits by me in biology."

"He's always by himself. He doesn't smile."

I offered to pay her 50 cents if she made Zorro smile, a deal.

On Saturday, as Zorro ambled to the car, his mother bent out of the screen door enough to order him to be careful. "OK, mom," he answered in a passive, nasal tone without turning around.

"This your car?" Zorro asked me as he closed the back seat door and set his bag beside him.

"It's my parents'."

"You should ask them for a Jeep. You could drive through the woods."

"I'd rather walk in the woods."

60

Pointing to Sarah in the front seat, Zorro asked, "Who are you?"

I introduced them. Zorro nodded.

The Dodge hauled us around the steep curves of Black Mountain and, halfway up, onto a long dirt road leading to the cabin.

"Cool," Zorro commented as I parked. We crunched across the leaves to the cabin and unlocked the screened door to the porch facing the quarter-acre pond. The cabin smelled fruity from the wood, stale from being closed. With our tools and notebooks we walked to the head of the small stream that bubbled out of rocks on a slope a short distance away, and measured off a ten-foot radius in which to take our inventory. Jenny agreed to write the list. I said, "We can look up the classifications later."

"Yeah," Zorro chimed in. "We'll look them up later. Here's a Daddy Longlegs."

Jenny said as she wrote, "I think we'll find that under Phylum Arthropoda, Subphylum Chelicerata, Class Arachnida."

In the stream, Sarah jiggled a rock and shrieked "crawdad" as the creature scooted for new cover as Zorro attempted to catch it without slipping off the stones.

Jenny spoke almost to herself as she scribbled. "Crayfish, um, Arthropoda, Crustacea, Malacostraca. This is the arthropods' day."

Zorro said, "Maybe we shouldn't wait to look up the classifications. We'll just figure them out as we go along."

After a few hours chasing crayfish, Zorro declared, "Let's have some action."

He pulled from his sack a bullwhip, tipped with two strands of leather like a snake's tongue. Moving to a cleared spot, Zorro whirled the bullwhip over his head and snapped it loud as a firecracker. Smiling in satisfaction as the echo hinted of return fire from a gunfight, he whirled the whip in a pattern, cracking it in front and behind.

"Very good," I said, enjoying the sound and patterns he commanded from his slight and unimpressive body. He bent in a slight stoop, as if he were leaning forward to go somewhere, though most of the time he wasn't moving.

He jumped onto a hip-high rock near a tree. Pointing to a thick branch about ten feet from the ground, Zorro announced, "Here's how to swing if you are in trouble." With an over-arm thrust, he wrapped the whip over the branch and swung off the rock in Tarzan fashion, landing loudly on the ground where his boot heels dug in and nearly made him trip. The whip dangled from the tree. Zorro took a minute to unwrap the whip from the branch by throwing the handle over the limb in a hit-and-miss fashion. When the whip finally fell into his hands, he said, "That's how you do it."

"OK, Larry Boy," Sarah said suddenly, "let's see how good you are," and ran shouting. "See if you can beat a little girl to the cabin."

Splashing in his boots across the shallow stream, Zorro chased after Sarah who shrieked as he got closer to her. Sarah was a fast little runner but Zorro overtook her at the cabin and slapped the corner post first, with a laugh.

"Made you laugh! Made you laugh!" Sarah shouted, laughing herself. I owed her 50 cents.

Turning to Jenny, I took the notebook and tools from her hands and told her, "I can beat you."

Jenny bolted ahead. I caught up with her and grabbed her waist from behind, pulled her back, let her go, then ran until she grabbed my shirt to slow me down so she could touch the cabin first.

With Zorro breathing harder than the rest of us, we filed into the porch, dropped our gear on a bare table where I could almost smell the food that had been served for our family picnics – baked beans, potato salad, poke sallet, barbecued chicken, lemonade. Today the fare was simpler: pimento cheese sandwiches and Nehi sodas, orange and grape.

"Jenny," Zorro asked as he took a chair in the semicircle facing the view beyond the screen, "how does it feel to be so smart?"

62

"Hey," Sarah interjected. "I'm smart."

"Cool," he said, "but Jenny's the one in my high school class."

"Yep," Sarah allowed, "Jenny's smart."

Blinking her dark eyelashes, Jenny looked past me at Zorro, with a grin that took a few seconds to steady itself against the surprise. "I'm regular."

"You ain't regular," he said. "You're – what? – three years younger than we are. You know stuff. How does that feel?"

"I feel regular. I'm interested in things. I study."

"You got a boyfriend?" Zorro asked.

Unfazed, she replied, "No."

"Do you like someone?" he pressed on.

I looked at Jenny.

She gazed forward as she rocked, then raised her chin with an exultant giggle as the crown of her head pressed against the wicker back of the rocker. This was the youngest I had seen her act. Shifting back to a smile, she fixed her eyes on Zorro again and blushed. "You sure ask a lot of questions."

"I want to know."

"I don't know that I want to tell that. Everybody has secrets. Even you, I bet."

"Yeah," Zorro admitted, rocking in his chair.

Sarah requested, "Tell us one of your secrets, Zorro."

"Which kind?"

"A small one."

"Like what?"

"Why you wear black."

Zorro kept rocking, with the expression of satisfaction he showed when he cracked the whip. "It feels right. Sometimes life is dark."

"Yeah, it gets dark," I jumped in. "It gets light. Look outside here." I restrained myself from breaking into my crack-of-doom sermon. "Here we are, friends, on the porch of a quiet cabin on a mountain. We have a life ahead of us. Shouldn't that count?"

"It counts," Zorro said. "But this will all pass. You will die, and so will I."

"Well, sure, because nothing here stays still – that's how we get born. When does it not feel dark to you?"

He thought it over before he replied, "When I'm driving on a rough road. Four-wheel drive. Moving. Fast. Unstoppable."

I asked, "Are you going to someplace or from someplace?"

"I'm not thinking about that," he said. "I'm just driving." He pushed his rocker back and forth.

ॐ

Sarah's diary – October 22, 1955

Zorro is a strange boy, but I can handle him. I think it is the way our personalities fit. I can joke with Zorro.

Jenny likes JJ, though she doesn't say so. JJ likes Jenny, but he thinks I don't know that because I'm 13. HA!

13

Talk about feelings

I LOOKED FORWARD TO THE WALK TO THE SOUTH END OF MAIN Street to pick up Sarah from her dance lessons at Miss Mira's before joining Mom and Dad for Christmas shopping. I thought Barbara Lee might be assisting and maybe Jenny would be waiting for her, giving me another chance to talk to her.

As soon as I reached the unscreened porch of the Cranes' red brick home squatting on a sloping yard near the base of Bailey Hill, Mr. Crane opened the door and invited me to "go on up" to the second-floor dance room. In the hallway at the top of the steps I plopped into a soft chair, alone – no Lee sisters. In the cream-colored studio room with a mirrored wall, Sarah and a half-dozen other girls softly clomped in and out of view until the music from Miss Mira's record player scratched to a halt. Miss Mira's voice said, "You have the posture right, Bessie darling and Sarah, but move from the inside out, remember; from the inside. You are – " she pronounced *are* as *ah* – "thinking of the rules."

"Yes," Bessie's voice admitted.

"You are thinking outside. I want you to feel that motion inside as you bend your right side and turn. First, imagine yourself doing this. Wait until you have an image of yourself and then try it."

After another round of music, Miss Mira asked them how their movement felt. A bubble of voices, some of them sounding ready to go home, said it felt good.

"We'll keep working on it," she emphasized. "That's all for the day."

Sarah filed out the door amidst her friends, shepherded by Miss Mira, clad Christmas-like in green slacks and blouse with a red scarf. I trailed the ballerinas down the stairs.

Mr. Crane laid his *Look* magazine on a side table and arose to tell us goodbye as the dancers bustled out the door with us, their leotard legs moving like sticks beneath the bulk of their coats.

Upon reaching the sidewalk I asked Sarah, "What's all this stuff about working from the inside out? She never talked about that in ballroom dancing."

"That kind of dance isn't as advanced as ours is," Sarah explained.

As we ambled across the bridge and up Main Street with the crowd weaving in the glow of the streetlamps and store lights, I asked Sarah, "How's Mike Dawson doing?"

"I wouldn't know."

"Why not?"

"He wouldn't talk."

"At all?"

"He would say stuff sometimes," Sarah acknowledged, "but it was usually about his baseball card collection or something like that. He never would talk about feelings."

"Feelings?"

"I heard he liked me, and he heard I liked him, but – "

"How do you know he heard that?"

"I had Willa Mae tell him. He told Willa Mae he liked me."

"Oh."

"But he wouldn't talk about feelings."

"How do you know he wouldn't?"

"I said to him, 'Let's talk about feelings.' He wouldn't."

"You mean you outright told him, 'Let's talk about feelings'? He's a guy, you know."

"Guys like girls, don't they?"

"Well, sure, but – "

"That's a feeling, JJ. Girls talk about feelings all the time."

"You girls talk to *each other* about feelings, but how many of you talk to *boys* about feelings?"

66

She turned to me incredulously, "You mean to say you could like a girl and go out with her, and you wouldn't let her know what you felt?"

Sensing the tables turning on me, I insisted, "If I were going out with a girl, if I talked to her ten times, she would know if I was a friend or if I liked her more than that."

"How would she know?" Sarah asked, as we stopped at the door of Forester and Spillman's clothes shop where we were to meet Mother and Dad.

"By the way I act," I said. "Boys and girls know when one likes the other."

"Not each time," Sarah insisted. "I didn't know what Mike Dawson really thought. Or maybe I caught on that he didn't really like me much, on account of how he wouldn't talk about it."

Inside Forester and Spillman, Sarah took Dad's hand to encourage him out of the chair where men sat while the women shopped for their husbands longer. The clerk said, "I hope the coal business picks up. We don't need a down cycle now." Dad agreed, arose from his comfort, put his arm on Sarah's shoulder affectionately and, with a limp, led us out the door.

Mother said she wanted to buy some porcelain dolls for her sister, Aunt Betsy, who sold antiques in Vicksburg and collected dolls to display. So we walked to T.C. Hunter's store, which had so many coats of badly cured yellow paint outside that the wood was webbed like alligator skin. The corner frame of the window outside the door was smudged where Mr. Hunter leaned against it on warm days. On this evening, Mr. Hunter sat almost hidden in a rocking chair behind the counter. Four bulbs hanging bare from the ceiling lit his shadowed form in a white shirt with a soiled high collar and striped suspenders.

Near the cash register some boxes of dusty candy – brands I never saw anywhere else – looked very hard. Across from his counter stood a mannequin dressed with a woman's blouse, jacket and plumed hat that reminded me of a photograph of women on the Titanic. A hand-written sign propped against the mannequin said, "HOT DEAL."

Dad greeted Mr. Hunter, "You look like you are doing the same, T.C."

"Doin' the same, Little Steve," Mr. Hunter replied without a smile as he stood. The fact that Mr. Hunter used cordial words meant he liked Dad. Otherwise Mr. Hunter might be abrupt or not talk at all. He refused to sell wares to people if he disliked something about them, even if what he disliked was a mystery. However, Mother always spoke kindly and respectfully to Mr. Hunter about his merchandise, and Mr. Hunter was always happy to sell to her. Mother usually bought something at his store before the holidays to give him some business, though I wondered what Mr. Hunter would do if we bought a lot, because nobody was manufacturing these goods anymore, except maybe the belts.

Dad asked, "Remember ol' Armageddon Cornwell, who gave away his earthly goods and went up Black Mountain in '51 for the rapture?"

"His little woman came down madder'n a wet hen, but he stayed a while," Mr. Hunter recalled with satisfaction "I think he was feared of her."

Actually, I got anxious about the end of the world myself in 1954 when I was fourteen and found a big, slick-paged Bible prophecies book in the glass-door bookcase in our upstairs hallway. One of the chapters on Revelation told how the symbolism referred to dire events. I got more and more concerned as I read along, wondering if I would finish high school before Harlan got burned up. I was relieved when I got to the part that said the end would come in 1945.

Mother paid for the dolls with bisque legs and arms that clacked together and Mr. Hunter opened the large National Cash Register machine with a caSHEENG so loud against the deadness of the store that it made me jump and made Sarah emit a little scared sound like a high-pitched "uh". Taking her change, Mother told Mr. Hunter, "I hope you are feeling well this holiday season."

"Couldn't feel better," he said. "Business is good."

Mother and Dad walked to another store as I took Sarah with me to Pennington Grocery. Sarah rarely wanted to shop for food, but Bernie Cole, a freshman, was working as a delivery boy during the holiday break. Now that Mike Dawson had flamed out of Sarah's heart, Bernie was looking good.

At Pennington's I promptly filled my basket with ingredients for Mother's holiday tea – frozen orange juice and lemonade, a can of pineapple juice, and tea along with cloves and cinnamon. Sarah commanded me to slow down as through the door came Bernie, a lanky boy with a big Adam's apple and brown hair plastered back in a ducktail. Sarah led me to the checkout line where he bagged groceries.

When Bernie looked up, Sarah said, "Hi, how are you doing?"

"Fine," he said in a raspy voice. "How are you?"

Sarah said she was fine, too.

When I paid and picked up the bag, Bernie said, "See you later."

"See you later," Sarah closed.

Outside, I concluded, "He can talk. We know that much."

"Oh, yes," Sarah rolled her eyes skyward for a moment. "And what a nice voice."

"Wonderful voice," I told her. 'What do you think he feels?"

"I don't know," Sarah said. "Isn't he gorgeous?"

"Gorgeous," I nodded.

WITH THE FRAGRANCE of Mother's punch sweetening the house on Christmas as we sat by the tree, I unwrapped the gift from my parents, a green windbreaker running suit with white stripes, the colors of Harlan. I hugged Mother, who worked so hard to give me what I wanted, and thanked Dad, happy that he was alive with us, his cheeks veined pink by the medicine that thinned his blood. When Dad learned to walk again I packed the worry of his dying somewhere in my mind, but some nights I awoke at three in the morning, as if from a nightmare I couldn't recall. I would tell

69

myself to quit being anxious, to remember that my parents were with me, to go back to sleep. In the mornings I followed the low voices to the kitchen where they sat in the welcome of waffles, and I found as much comfort in the sunrise as in the sleep. On December 25, 1955 I had made it to another Christmas with the family complete – the first Christmas I counted that way.

My present to Sarah was a box of diaries from Bissell Office Supply. She kept them in a large drawer with hundreds of letters and notes, almost everything that had been written to her, papers packed so thick it was hard to open the drawer without scrunching the top layer.

Mother received the most presents. Years before, this surprised me, because Mother wasn't a kid. But Mother was the spirit of the season, the gift-wrapper and gift-giver. She tended to relatives and friends. Throughout December she kept the house festive. Dad relished the activity that Mother organized and sparked, but if he had been the only parent in the house, on Christmas Day he would have said he loved us, given us U.S. Savings Bonds and driven us to Harold's house to eat – that would have been it.

Dad looked forward to the family coming in – first Harold, Judith, and their new generation of Jameses: Rollie in his tenth year and familiar with the names of dinosaurs; and Linda four years old and never tired of riding on my back.

While freeing himself of his coat, Rollie told Dad, "Guess what we learned in Sunday school?"

"What?"

"We learned where heaven is."

"Where is it?"

Rollie pointed upward, "Up there. That's why Jesus raised His eyes."

Harold asked, "What if you are at the South Pole, where our up is their down?"

Judith intervened. "Don't confuse them, Harold. They're little."

Smiling in his own satisfaction, Harold took his family's coats down the hall to the back bedroom. Every once in a while the humor chuckled out of the shyness of this gentle, finely featured man nobody would suspect had killed at close range or had taken a Nazi bullet in his left side in the Battle of the Bulge. He didn't have a need to talk about it. If anything, he talked about the real estate he was selling, and not even much about that. So unassuming, he was pleasant to be around, a good brother.

When I tired of carrying and swinging Linda, I fetched my electric train from the attic and laid out the track on the far end of the beamed-ceiling living room while the adults sat and talked by the fireplace.

Marci and Alexander joined us for the long afternoon meal, then everyone herded back to the living room. "Marci," Dad announced from his easy chair, addressing the rest of us seated in a circle, "we would like to hear you on the fiddle."

Obligingly, Marci unpacked her violin and tuned it. "OK, Papa," Marci said as she straightened herself in her chair. "This is a piece I am composing myself. It's not done, so you won't hear the real end of it."

As we fell quiet, Marci closed her eyes, paused to hear the music in her head, nodded a slow beat, and began with long notes, distant and soothing. Taking hold of my mood, the music picked up volume until she stopped with dramatic, guitar-like plucks of the lower notes, like a bass.

Withdrawing reluctantly from the easy rise of the tune, I asked her when she would finish it.

"As soon as it comes to me," she said. "It's taking its time."

THE DAY AFTER Christmas, The Platters sang *Only You* over and over to Sarah in her room. I didn't feel like running, so I lay on my bed wondering what Mr. and Mrs. Lee would think if I called Jenny. I wondered what Sarah would think. I wondered what I would think.

71

The phone rang. Mother's voice from the foot of the stairs said the call was for me. I picked up the extension that had been installed in my room after Dad had his stroke.

"Hi, this is Jenny."

What's happening here? "Jenny?"

"Did I interrupt you?"

"No, no. How are you doing? What's up?"

"You said you were interested in rocks. Miss Mira brought some quartz pieces from North Carolina. I wondered if you would like to see them."

What's happening here? "I would. When?"

"Now, if you want to," she sounded a little tentative, "or some other time if you are busy."

I wasn't too busy, and I wasn't going to tell my family where I was going. I reasoned that I was being nice to a classmate, though I knew I wouldn't be standing outside Sarah's eighth-grade homeroom door to meet Jenny, not with everybody looking on. Age-wise, I should be seeing her sister Barbara, but I never thought of dating a girl in a class above mine, it seemed so unnatural.

After I hiked to the Lees' house and checked to see that my hands weren't sweating – they didn't perspire that way much anymore – Mrs. Lee opened the door and welcomed me in an animated way as if I belonged there. In the family room, Jenny waved me over to a shelf where she stood with Barbara.

"Lookit," Barbara said, gesturing to dozens of stones spread across the shelves. Some were colorful river rocks, worn shiny smooth. Others were more dramatic – a few of them cracked open, revealing sparkling and colorful insides.

Jenny picked two clumps of quartz, looking pleased to present them. One held a cluster of glass-like, five-sided spears about a half-inch thick sprouting from a flattened white bottom. The other piece was a hefty spear of quartz about five inches thick.

I said, "So you told Miss Mira you liked rocks."

"We talked about it at her studio." Jenny handed me the thicker piece. "What do you see when you look at it?"

72

Recalling how I stared out the classroom window to understand the greenness of trees, I gazed at the stone in a distantly focused way to let the edges sparkle until the reflecting light filled my field of vision. I did not do this very long because I did not want the Lees to see how strange I could look, all blank-faced. "What I see," I answered as I sharpened my focus on the piece, "is stone within a stone. A crystal within a crystal."

"That's interesting," she commented.

"What do you see?"

She inspected the quartz as Barbara and Mrs. Lee left the room to go to the kitchen nearby. "Chemical forces."

Trim and tall, Mrs. Lee brought in a tray of cookies and a pitcher of punch and placed them on the coffee table in front of the couch. "Help yourself," she smiled. Then, to my surprise, she left.

Jenny asked, "Want to sit?"

"That would be nice." I sat on the couch.

Jenny asked if I would like some music. Sure. The first track was *Autumn Leaves*. I could practically hear the lyrics in the music as it started out, but in case I didn't remember all the words, a chorus came on. I knew the singers weren't bouncing or even swaying. They were standing real still, singing on behalf of a guy remembering this girl whose sunburned hands he used to hold, gazing at the leaves outside his window bringing winter down on him. I asked Jenny why she played it.

"I like the album. It's mother's. That song was on it. It reminds me of – "

"What?"

She pondered a few moments. "Fall."

"Then let's play it again."

With the music in the background, Jenny sat on the couch beside me and talked about the tone of Emily Dickinson's poems and read some stanzas to me. I talked about Thor Heyerdahl's *Kon Tiki*, and how that raft trip showed that people of ancient times could sail between continents.

73

After more than an hour there, we got up and hiked through the woods north along the ridge toward Baxter, a trail our Scout troop used on some outings, and during the conversation that was running through me like a telephone wire all tickly clear, we agreed we would like to take more walks together on Sunday afternoons. She rested on a boulder, and I took the space beside her, with my arms touching hers, and she didn't move away.

On the way back we said little, leaving me to reckon with the spin of my head, rotating from unease about her age to the freshness of being next to her, a little like the way I felt as a kid when I did too many somersaults across the lawn.

When I returned home I shuffled through the open door of Sarah's room as The Platters finished singing *Smoke Gets in Your Eyes*. Placing her pen in the crease of her open diary, Sarah began to rise from her bed to restart the record player. I let her know, "The Platters are tired. They need a break."

She lay back down on her side and inquired, "What you been doing?"

"Walking."

"So, what's going on?"

"What do you mean?"

"You've been looking all satisfied lately. What's going on?"

"Not much," I said.

"Boys," she shook her head.

Sarah's diary – December 26, 1955

JJ has this little dilemma. He likes Jenny, who is smarter than most seniors but is my age. Boys think they have a hard time, but they don't know what girls go through. I liked James Dean as soon as I saw him in "Rebel Without a Cause," but by the time the movie came out he was DEAD. That's what we go through. I love my brother, bless his heart.

74

14

Relativity

IN BIOLOGY CLASS MR. COBB SHOOK OUT A GIGGLE-TWITCH AS HE declared that the winter was making us too dull and our minds needed stirring up. In that cause he proceeded to perplex us with the theory of relativity though the theory had nothing to do with biology. To illustrate a point, he told us how a person traveling near the speed of light would return to earth younger than a twin who didn't travel that fast.

Dozer asked, "If someone is getting paid for going on a three-year trip near the speed of light and comes back only two years older, would he lose a year's pay?" When Mr. Cobb said, "No," Dozer asked, "Why would he get paid for three years' work if he only worked two years?" Mr. Cobb said pay was based on time as measured by the employer.

That January I wished the law would work both ways, that it would slow down for my hours with Jenny but on her birthday thrust her through the hidden realm of physics with a skip through the calendar, a year older yet unchanged. But February carried her the same and closed in on me as I trained longer, harder, six days a week on the football field at Huff Park behind the Presbyterian Church. I ran alone. Nobody else had any business on the cold crust of the field in the dead of winter. Running had been a release for me. Now I went up against the pain several hours a day, hearing only my breath and conversation with myself to keep me going.

I felt the speed increase and the loneliness weigh down with the layers of clothes beneath my windbreaker. I missed seeing people on the roads and streets, but I couldn't run wind sprints there.

Nor could I expect Mother to hunker down on the Huff Park bleachers in the winter wind to keep me company, though she would have if I had asked. She was busy. Wearing a brace, Dad walked to the office and back without a cane, more than enough to expect of him.

Standing near the goalposts after a workout in mid-February, I said to the quiet, "I would like a little company down here."

A week later, as the Eagle Laundry whistle signaled its 4:30 shift end, a dark-coated figure climbed to a bench in the center of the bleachers and leaned back to watch.

After a few wind sprints, I approached the stands. It was Zorro.

"What are you doing here?" I asked.

"Just watchin'."

"You didn't tell me you were coming."

"I just thought of it."

"Well, it's good to have company."

"When you finish, I have a question for you."

"Why not ask it now?"

"I don't want to mess with your practice."

"Go ahead."

"It's strange, man," he said, sitting up to bend forward. "I need some advice."

"OK."

"Your sister Sarah," he said. "She was fun, that time we went up to your uncle's cabin. I've been thinking about that. But she's young. Eighth grade, you know. What would you think if I talked with her?"

My mind reeled. "She likes to talk, but it depends on what you tell her. She likes you as a friend. She likes another boy right now, Bernie Cole."

Zorro nodded. "That's what I heard. That's cool for her. Yeah. That's all I wanted to say. I'm going to watch you run if you don't mind."

I didn't mind.

76

Back home, Sarah was lying flat on her back reading her English paper when I came to her door. I didn't plop myself onto the empty twin bed this time, because I didn't want to stay long. I informed her, "I talked with Zorro this afternoon. I have news. He likes you."

Like a spring-loaded toy, Sarah flipped up to a sitting position. "Zorro?"

"Yep."

She fell back. "He's a little out of my age group, don't you think?"

"It all depends on how you want to see it, I guess."

Sarah's diary – February 15, 1956

I didn't feel like eating supper, but I ate some of Miss Becker's tuna salad. Mother thinks I want to slim down because I gained two pounds over the holidays. I told her I couldn't eat because I was nervous over what Zorro said yesterday. What if he asks me out? I don't want to hurt his feelings. I want to keep him as a friend, even though he's kind of old. JJ said he told Zorro I was going with Bernie. We need to find another girl for Zorro. I can't imagine who that would be. Mom says, "God makes them and they get together."

15

Move it

THE LAST FRIDAY OF FEBRUARY I DIDN'T FEEL LIKE RUNNING, SO I walked the first hundred yards down the desolate football field under dingy skies. Beneath the goalpost I leaned forward for a minute, head down, arms propped on my knees, and whispered, "Move it." I was beginning to remind myself of Miss Becker, except she talked to herself louder. My body heard me and moved.

By now my feet knew the cushion of the grass and hardness of the sod in every part, wet or dry. By now I was a friend to the shadows of the place, grateful when there was enough sun to bring them out.

On difficult days, the afternoons I grunted bending down to tighten my shoelaces, I had to imagine the future in order to get to it. When my body felt drained and heavy, as on this day, I imagined the race in May. I thought: *People will be there to watch. Nobody will care how I got to the starting line. Nobody will care about preparing for that day. Only the result will matter. And the matter will be simple: win or lose.*

This thought cycled through my head every time the drabness weighed upon my will. I knew that these times, the winter days before the race, were the real days of my judgment.

I was pushed by the wish to win and the dread of losing. Yet I also knew that beyond the repetition and pain was a special pleasure. I first felt it – an electric lightness – in the image of the Cherokee who ran through my dreams. He glided with ease and power in a harmony of movement. On a mission to someplace, he strode with a gait so smooth that he blended into the beauty of it.

By this late February day I had twice felt that dreamlike charge lifting me. Both those times stood distinct from the workouts that otherwise blurred together.

I first felt the current on an August run when I didn't have to summon strength through effort. I simply had to measure out the force that banked up so abundantly in me it had to be released.

In early November the silken thrust came through me by surprise – from below the heart, it seemed – in the middle of a half-hour endurance run around the field. To make the power last, I fixed my attention on the enjoyment of it and rode it five miles into the dusk.

This steady, moving surge didn't feel like the caffeine charge I got from Mother's morning coffee. It didn't feel like the adrenaline that trembled my hands when I gave a speech in school assembly. It didn't race the heart. It had no fear; it came on full and sure and ready. It didn't want to eat or sleep or study. It wouldn't even be satisfied to dance a fast beat all around, as glorious as that would be. In me this power had to run.

Slogging around the field with my breath fading white against the chill, I didn't feel this driving lightness, didn't know where it went, didn't know why it stayed away so long. But I feared that if I stopped, if I quit preparing my mind and body for it, I would lose the connection to whatever it was; I would lose the chance to go wherever it would take me.

16

Elvin

SARAH'S YELL INTERRUPTED MY HOMEWORK. "JJ, COME HERE, YOU'VE got to hear this. Hurry." Leaning away from her mattress, she turned up the volume knob of the radio on the night table.

"WELL, IF YOUR BABY LEAVES YOU!" the voice rocked out. A new voice.

Sarah informed me, "Heartbreak Hotel."

The singer had a thrusting emotional style that didn't break down in tears the way Johnny Ray did in *Cry*. "Who's that?" I asked.

"Elvis Presley."

"What's that? *Elvis?*"

"Shhh. Listen," Sarah closed her eyes.

The singer had a catchy style, enough to get me to buy the record, I agreed. When the song was over, I left Sarah so she could contemplate it.

Before biology class settled down, I asked Jenny and Zorro, "Have you heard the song *Heartbreak Hotel* by Elvin Presley?"

"I think it's Elvis," Jenny corrected me.

"Cool, man," Zorro nodded deeply. "He drove a truck in Memphis. He's got it." Zorro moved his right arm above his head as if he were cracking a whip, providing the "whack" sound with his voice. "He delivers."

"Truck driver, huh?"

"Truck driver for Crown Electric, used to be. He's been out there. You heard him. He delivers."

After class, Zorro leaned over and told me in a private way, "Your sister is a cool friend."

"She's good."

Zorro stood and sang briefly in a low, whiny voice, "down at the e-end of Lo-onely Street." Bobbing his head to the tune as he left the room, I couldn't tell what he was feeling, other than that heartbreak was sounding popular these days.

At the end of class I invited Jenny to walk with me Sunday. As I made my way out the door, Dozer walked beside me and inquired, "You're not robbing the cradle there, are you, Jaybird?"

That stunned me. I couldn't think of anything to say, so I just looked at Dozer and walked on, worrying: *Have I done the right thing?*

In study hall I took my usual seat beside Lois. Before Miss Posey rapped her ruler to order silence, I asked, "What's the latest?" I wondered if people had seen me with Jenny.

"About who?"

"Me."

"I heard Lucy Giddon likes you."

"That's out of date. I tried to talk with Lucy at the last football game. She hardly spoke."

"I don't know. That's all I heard."

Lois's report gave me a little relief, but Dozer's words stuck like a splinter in the brain waiting for talk to move across it the wrong way.

From the day of Dozer's remark until Sunday afternoon, all I could think about was whether I was doing the right thing and what people would say. But when I reached Jenny's house and she came out the door in a shapely blue blazer and skirt, all those questions lost their grip in the pull of her presence.

We hiked east of Ivy Hill along a dirt road that branched up and around to an old, unfenced cemetery. Near the top of the narrow burial ground I pointed to a dip in a grave. "See this?"

"It looks like the coffin caved in," she observed, leaning over, "except the hole is not long. Maybe only the top part of the coffin gave way."

"Yeah, the old wooden coffins cave in, and people think that's awful. But why not let the body return to the earth? We could start running out of graveyard space after a while."

81

"Zorro should be here," Jenny mused, using her foot to gauge the indention of the ground. "He would like this conversation."

"Actually, this wasn't caused by a coffin caving in. In the fifth grade our Bumblebee Club tried to dig to the casket."

Jenny pulled her foot back from the dip. "What were you doing digging in a colored graveyard?"

"Colored?" I asked. "How can you tell? Some of these sandstone markers have nothing on them."

"Maybe the words wore off," Jenny reflected. "Look at that one made of concrete. The cement isn't as hard as granite, but the words punched in it will last longer than the ones in sandstone. These people were poor. The government must have paid for some of the cement markers. I hope so. See the inscription for this gentleman?" Jenny pointed to a line: "6 U.S. Cld. Cav." and said, "He fought in a colored cavalry unit – World War I, I bet."

I read aloud a cement marker roughly engraved:

J. D. BRIGHT

✞ BORN ☆

SEPT. 18, 1895

DIED JUNE 29

1922 IF I COU

LD ONLY HE

AR MY MOTH

ER PRAY AGAIN

And another nearby, with the last phrase "on the sea of time" thinly scratched, as if the cement had dried too fast to punch the letters deep:

D. K. BRIGHT

BORN Oct. 8 ✞

1865 Died SEPT.

1, 1924 DEATH

IS ONLY A DRE-

AM ☆ ON THE

SEA OF TIME

Jenny asked, "Now, who was in this Bumblebee Club digging around up here?"

"Horse, Jug, Two-Bit, Harley and me."

Jenny raised her eyebrows.

"We formed it in the Whitman's empty garage on Ivy Street. The garage had bumblebees in it; that's how we thought up the name. Horse got to be president because a bumblebee had stung him. He said that qualified him, and that sounded reasonable to us. He was also bigger than we were."

"You needed some girls in that club."

"No. We did boy stuff." I didn't bother to explain that our main activity was picking up cigarette butts from the sidewalks, bringing them to the garage, and smoking them. Late in the summer Horse bought a cheap, dry, foot-long cigar for us to pass around. That caused us to throw up in the garage. It took three weeks for the smell of the vomit to fade enough to use the place again. By that time school had started, so the club dissolved into the open play of recess and street games.

"Some girls like boy stuff," Jenny said.

"Not our boy stuff."

"Digging in graveyards?"

"We had been to a horror movie and wanted to see a coffin, and maybe even some bones."

"You dug up the bones from here?" Jenny scanned the grave.

"No, we dug a knee-deep hole and hit something hard. Jug jumped out of the hole and ran. That scared Two-Bit and Harley enough to make them run off, too. Horse thought Jug might squeal on us. Jug can't help talking when he's excited. So we filled in the hole and hurried home with our shovel and pick-axe before it got dark."

Jenny alternately looked at the gravesite and me. Then, holding her skirt below her knees, she knelt before the inch-thin slab of brown stone and ran her hand across the top of it, as if to feel what was in the marker. Then she brushed her hand across the inscription, barely touching it:

JERUSHA BELL TESS
Born Feb. 17, 1842
Died Oct. 21, 1899
TO MEET AGAIN

Jenny said, "If she had any family, I hope they didn't come up here with flowers after you tried to dig her up."

"Not just me," I corrected her. "We."

"You were a curious little thing, weren't you?"

"Jenny," I asked, "You know that I enjoy being with you. What do you think of the fact that I'm so much older than you?"

"That was fast," she said more shyly. "I thought we were talking about the Tess lady buried here." She shrugged in an I-don't-know way.

I explained, "If people see us, they are going to start talking. Pretty soon the whole school will wonder why you are walking around with someone like me."

She shrugged again.

"I'll try to be cool about this," I said.

She cocked her head sideways with a grin. "Cool like Zorro?"

"Nobody is as cool as Zorro," I said, feeling my control of the mood slipping. "Except Elvin, maybe."

"Elvis."

"Yes, yes, I mean Elvis." I repeated the name, "Elvis, Elvis, Elvis."

Jenny giggled a quarter-second note – sent it right into me, unaware.

❧

Sarah's diary – February 28, 1956

JJ is usually a pleasant person, but tonight he was so pleasant he made supper for everyone – bean soup with all the fixings. This is not normal.

84

17

Welcome to Rosenwald

By March the sun stayed up long enough to let me run longer and still finish in daylight. The football team gathered on the
field for spring practice. I had company at last, for a few weeks.
After the team finished its calisthenics, Horse waved his helmet as
he shouted, "Get your butt over here, JJ, and run laps with us!"

"Make them run!" the new coach, Billy York, ordered me.
Coach Hays would have said, "Make these girls run!" I missed
Coach Hays. But Coach York – strong-jaw handsome at 30 and
nicely dressed with creased shirts and pants – said he would sign
me up for the district track meet.

I joined the clumpy herd in a ten-lap warm-up. When the
strung-out team regrouped itself in the center of the field to do
short drills, I kept running, feeling more secure as time went on.
After an hour and a half, the football players finished and walked
up the steps to Clover Street, some of them barefoot, some of them
clacking their cleats on their way to the high school gym two
blocks east. I kept working out until I was alone, and then some
more. That was the only way I knew how to run against the
unknown.

The day after the football team finished spring training, I was
alone again, wishing for company, but not too hard or out loud,
because the last time I asked for company I got Zorro, whose real
interest was Sarah. On my way home I stopped by Green-Miller
Drug, nearly empty except for Rustbucket on a stool at the
counter while Elvis for a dime sang *Love Me Tender* out of the
Wurlitzer jukebox. I ordered a milkshake and slid onto the green
vinyl bench of the front booth as Scotty Lanier sauntered in with a
smile on half his mouth, ordered a chocolate soda, sat opposite me
and asked how I was doing. I told him I would be racing in May.

"That sounds interesting. Maybe I should do that."

"What?"

"Run in the meet."

"You should," I said.

"Yeah, that would be interesting. I like the idea of going a mile."

"That would be good. You might want to start training now."

"I have time," he said dismissively. "I would only run one race."

"You can work out with me after school."

"When's the meet?"

I told him the date in May.

"I'll show up sometime."

"I'll have Coach York put you on the sign-up list then?"

"Yeah, sign me up. I want to try that."

I had a racing partner. *Didn't I just ask for company?* I thought, *if I'm getting what I'm asking for I had better straighten out my life some.* For starters I would pick up my clothes.

Near the end of a late-March workout at Huff Park, exuberant voices bubbled from the parking lot. Bringing the sound forward, a dozen boys streamed onto the field. From the red of their shirts and the brown of their skin I knew they were from Rosenwald High, home of the Red Devils, on the eastern edge of town. Behind the squad strode a young man of medium height I took to be their coach, wearing a brown fedora like my father's favorite hat. As I finished my sprints, the coach ordered his squad to stretch and warm up with a light run.

I loved three colored adults. The first was Mrs. Betsy, a hefty older lady who cared for me as a child when I stayed with Mother's relatives in Mississippi. Each time I arrived on a visit and ran to her, she would say, "Lawsy, you have grown into such a big man," words that made me feel powerful.

The second was Louie Felker, who took time to talk with me when he did construction work at our house. He let me play with wet cement when he built our steps, and he told me to call him Louie. When he left Harlan to fight in World War II, I prayed for

86

him each night and helped mother pack cookies to send to him. He wrote me letters from his ship on the South Pacific, and when he came back he resumed his construction work. I was always happy to see him and hear his husky voice with a smile in it.

The third person I liked a lot was Mr. Brace, a strong, wiry man with white-streaked hair. Mr. Brace did yard work for us and took me on Ivy Hill to pick blackberries for Mother.

Once Mr. Brace brought along his grandson Harvey to pick berries. Harvey and I competed to see who could pick the most, but both of us together couldn't pick half what Mr. Brace picked. Other than that, I never played or talked with anyone but white children, and never thought anything about it. Some colored people lived in the Georgetown section, west of the river downtown, and others lived in Stringtown, which stretched by the road and river on the east end of Harlan. Some of the colored houses looked poor, but so did some of the white houses along the road and at some of the coal camps. At the movie theaters, a balcony section was reserved for "colored only." I never thought about that either. I figured that each race was different and liked to do different things, and that the races were happy amongst themselves.

Warming up in their jog around Huff Park, the Rosenwald runners didn't try to catch up with me. They were having a good time talking. When I stopped at the goalpost, the coach introduced himself as Wally Odell.

"Track coach?"

"Track coach, basketball coach," he let me know in a cordial voice.

"I'm Jeremiah James. Most call me JJ."

"What you running, JJ?"

"Mile."

"A distance man."

"Yessir. How many milers do you have?"

"None. This year we're running the 100-yard dash, the 220, the 440, some low hurdles, mile relay. We're doing the shot put and discus. And the javelin."

"Running in a state league?"

"No, the Southeast Kentucky Conference's got no place for us. We set up meets with Negro schools – in Benham, Lynch, several in Virginia. You can join our practice if it suits you."

"Thank you, but I'm not a sprinter."

"I'll run these boys a distance or two," he nodded toward them. "You'd be welcome."

As he said this, a crack crinkled on the glass of my mind. When as a child I swam with friends at the old city pool next to the bridge to Georgetown, little boys from the Georgetown side perched in trees or stood outside the fence to watch us, causing me to think, *What pleasure it must give these kids to see how much fun we are having in here.* Nobody thought of inviting them to join us.

Coach waved to a runner who had finished his laps. "Lamar, come over here."

Lamar sauntered to us, his muscles outlined through his light-brown skin.

"Lamar," Coach Odell said, "this is JJ. He runs the mile for Harlan. Lamar runs the 220 and 440. He's as close to a distance man as we have this year. If you want a quick pace, key on him." He ordered his team to line up.

"Thanks. I might take you up on that some day," I said.

Lamar said to Mr. Odell, "He's white, Coach, much as pink don't count as colored. Don't get him in trouble."

Coach Odell nodded toward me. "Whatever he wants."

I felt challenged, not by the run, but by the idea I could get in trouble if I ran with Lamar. I asked, "What's next?"

Coach Odell said, "Two-lap run."

"Let me do that with you before I go." I lined up beside the boys and requested, "Don't kill me!"

One boy shouted, "Barbeque time!"

88

Another: "Peanut, you gotta wiggle your legs fast if you want to keep Loretta. She don't care for nobody in last place."

"Loretta would run her fingers through my hair if I was so far last I didn't finish at all, just lying down."

"Peanut ain't got it anymore! Loretta's on that finish line waving at ME. Lookit what she's waving!"

"Her sweet lips calling – she's calling me, 'Bobby Joe, come home to mama!' "

"TWEET!" Coach Odell blew his whistle. The whole dozen boys fired off and left me. "LORETTA!" some of them shouted, which also surprised me because I never thought of shouting during a sprint when my lungs worked hard enough to breathe, much less talk. Curving around the field after the first hundred yards, some of the runners slowed and I began closing the gap. On the second lap I passed more and picked up my pace, but I strained barely ahead of a boy in fourth place; I couldn't gain on Peanut in the second spot because he would speed up just enough to keep me from passing, like a tease; nor could I gain on Lamar ten yards ahead. When I finished third, a worry flashed through me. This was my first race on a field, and I had lost.

Catching his breath, Lamar walked near me and said, "For a miler, you're good at a two-lap."

"I'm trying," I replied, grateful for some reassurance. "You got Loretta, huh."

"Would have, except there ain't no Loretta, other than in our heads – good a place as any. The only girl around here is white," he said, nodding over his shoulder toward the sideline, "putting the eye on you."

I looked to the sideline where Lucy Giddon strolled past the bleachers with her brother Pokey. Sure enough, they looked our way as they proceeded to the parking lot. I thanked Coach Odell and walked out the gate as the squad lined up for another set of sprints. From the fading shouts I could still make out the name "Loretta."

Sarah's diary – March 31, 1956

Another interesting bit of news: Teddy Bear took Willa Mae to the Sunday matinee of "The King and I." GO, TEDDY!! WM also likes Ricky Seals, but two other girls I know of in my class like Ricky Seals even though he is a senior who is going steady with Lucille Potts and doesn't know any of them are alive.

At the movie I asked Jenny to sit with us. JJ ate his popcorn in little bites and chewed with his mouth closed. I bet he thinks I didn't notice that. Bear took his popcorn by the fistfuls. I got a bag myself but I don't stuff it in my mouth before I have finished chewing what is already there. When they pop popcorn with that butter smell during the "coming attractions," it always ruins my diet.

18

Lying in wait – the first dance

"I'll tell you what I like about Harlan," Rev. Boswell exclaimed from the pulpit with a wave of his robed arms before our washed faces. "I came here from a big city. In the big city, the worst criminals had high-priced lawyers. Those lawyers weren't content to simply plead 'not guilty' and make their case in court. Those lawyers would tell the newspapers, tell the TV, tell the radio that their client was a kindly man, much misunderstood, even if their man had a police record as long as your arm for threatening his wife whose body had been found in his basement freezer. When a business got caught in a scam it got its publicity outfit to make the company look nicer than a church kindergarten. In that kind of value system, deceit is not a wrong; it is a goal, bought and paid for. In that kind of environment the truth means nothing.

"Harlan is different. Oh, we have some mean people here. We have some dishonest people here. We have some real doozies. But at least in Harlan everyone knows who they are and what they are. People will tell you outright that 'So-and-So is mean as a snake.' Or, 'So-and-So is a crook.' This is a hard place to pretend to be something you aren't. That's one thing I like about the people of this town."

Did this mean I should tell people I liked a girl thirteen years old?

Rev. Boswell looked my way and said, "If you speak only part of the truth in order to mislead someone about what you did, and you are not doing this to protect someone else from harm, that is a lie. That is deceit. That is the way of a coward, a moral coward."

I nodded yes to let him know I agreed. I didn't want him to have the wrong impression in case he did, somehow. As I followed my family to the vestibule on the way out, I shook Rev. Boswell's firm hand and told him, "Good message."

That night the *Ed Sullivan Show* finished with a trick dog act good enough to make Dad lower his *Harlan Daily Enterprise* and watch the dogs through the upper part of his round wire-rim glasses. During a commercial for toothpaste, Sarah scooted to the TV and turned down the volume, silencing a ditty about the dental benefits of chlorophyll. Sarah needed our attention. Bernie Cole had asked her to a school dance at the Harlan Country Club on Saturday. Could she go? Mother and Dad both knew all about the Coles, who owned a store in Loyall three miles west of town. Upstanding folks. Mother said yes, but how would they get to the country club, since Bernie was too young to drive? Sarah said one of Bernie's friends would take them unless I wanted to. I said I would.

I would rather be with Jenny, but I didn't want to stir up talk. So I called Laura Green, my childhood friend who pulled me out of the rain in fifth grade. I knew she would go as a friend; she dated several boys, none steady. Laura consented. On Saturday I picked up Laura first, then Sarah, then Bernie on the way. Dressed up tighter than I had ever seen him, Bernie filled the car with cologne that made me crack open the triangular ventilator window some. Though Laura was the top student in our class – we knew she would be the valedictorian – she was not full of herself. She talked easily with Sarah. Bernie commented when he could, to keep from being left behind.

After a short drive past the Lenarue coal camp, we twisted up the road to the country club and entered the big room where The Pastels, a dance band of Harlan High boys, filled out a Glenn Miller tune. Sarah and Bernie left us to sit alone on the opposite side. Laura and I danced a fast piece together, then danced separately with other friends. As The Pastels paused, a boy entered the main room. He looked like Zorro except he had on a blue suit and cream-colored shirt with the collar turned up a little. The boy edged through the crowd. It *was* Zorro.

"Hey," I stood.

Sarah walked up to him and asked why he had a light shirt on.

"Like it?" he asked.

"Of course," Sarah said. "It makes you look good. It looks like the one Elvis wore in that picture of him with his guitar."

"Cool," Zorro nodded as the band launched into *Rock Around the Clock*. Zorro pulled Laura into the frenzy of the music while I sat and concentrated on the way everyone on the dance floor bounced, the way I concentrated when I watched *American Bandstand* with the sound turned off.

On the next slow dance I pulled Laura to the center of the floor and shuffled methodically – and there Jenny was, entering the porch. Caught by surprise, I tracked her through one window after another, her dark hair accented by the red of her dress. On the dance floor I rotated Laura in a way that I could watch Jenny as she flowed into the main room, took some punch and cake, and sat with Bessie Harper. I could tell that when Jenny saw me with Laura she stopped eating.

I waited for the next song to see who would dance with Jenny. No one. I danced with Laura again. When the band finished, Jenny's chair sat empty. I sat through another number. Still no Jenny. Worried, I excused myself and searched through the clubhouse until I found Jenny at the end of the porch, gazing out the window toward the putting green lit by flood lamps. Coming to her side, I said, "Hi, there."

"Hi," she replied politely.

"I'm glad you came."

Forcing a smile, not working too hard at it, she nodded yes.

"What's the matter?"

She looked at me point blank, hurt-fire rising in the pool of her eyes. "You came with Laura."

"Yes. You know I'm trying to keep you from being talked about, that's all."

She looked down for a few moments, expressionless, thinking. "It's not what people say that hurts me," she informed me. "I care about other things."

In my head the stage lights went on, the curtain parted, and there was my act, revealed – to me. What could I say? I asked Jenny if she would like to dance.

Hesitating, she did not raise her voice. "What about Laura?"

"She's a childhood friend. We dance with whom we like."

"OK," she said, and walked with me inside, to the center of the crowded dance floor.

The Pastels played *Only You.* It didn't sound the same as The Platters singing it, but who cared? The world closed in with the ease of the lid of our Maytag washer as the gentle cycle mixed and moved us back and forth, skirts and slacks in water. Zorro asked Sarah to dance, Bernie asked Willa Mae, Horse asked Laura, and I held Jenny Lee for the first time.

AFTER THE DANCE, Sarah and I dropped off Bernie and Laura and parked in front of our house. As I pulled the key out of the ignition, Sarah asked, "So, how was the dance with Jenny?"

I could see Rev. Boswell behind the pulpit, looking at me, speaking for God Almighty. In as nonchalant a way as possible, I told Sarah, "I have to admit I like the way she dances. I like the way she thinks."

"Do you kind of like her?"

Cliff's edge. Don't look. Jump. "I kind of do."

Sarah thought about it. "That's good. She's nice. Very smart. Very pretty. She's different from any girl I know."

"She's young," I added, bracing.

Sarah shrugged. "So what?"

I didn't know what to answer, because somebody somewhere had dialed me into a TV program where everyone younger than I was also happened to be smarter than I was.

94

Sarah's diary – April 7, 1956

What a sweet brother. He confided in me after the dance. He told me he liked Jenny and listened to my opinion. I was so HONORED. He probably worries that, once it's out, people will talk, because he's older than Jenny. OF COURSE. My friends always talk. I wish I could tell them myself. It's all so exciting.

19

Breath of fresh air

LOIS LAID HER HAND ON MY FOREARM IN STUDY HALL AND ASKED IF I was OK because, she said, I was taking short breaths. I hardly realized it. My attention had squeezed down on the need to train, study, go to bed by ten and figure out the best way to race, and I felt restless when I wasn't doing any of those things.

"Do you want to know how your popularity is?" Lois asked.

"Oh, brother – what?"

"Lucy Giddon doesn't like you."

"I figured she stopped liking me way back."

"Not stopped liking you. She dislikes you. That's what I heard."

"What did I do to make her dislike me?"

"What did you do to make her like you?"

"Nothing."

"Maybe that's what made her not like you."

I didn't have enough free space in my head to think about that. By the end of the school day the attic of my brain had turned stuffy on its own used air, like the steamy dank of the Brewster's' coal shed that Jug and I hid in one blistering July afternoon in sixth grade after we, along with Two-Bit and Harley, pushed a waist-high boulder off the edge of Ivy Hill near Jenny's cliff, not expecting we could loosen the boulder because for years we had pushed on it and couldn't budge it. But now that we were able to rock it back and forth, we thought it would roll only twenty yards into the trees that would halt it, but after the boulder disappeared into the woods and we walked away, we heard more trees crunching and glimpsed the huge rock rumbling out of the forest picking up speed toward the Bingham's house, *oh lordy, don't hit it, don't hit it*, across the Bingham's yard, *stop stop stop*, down to the street, *oh no*, smack into the side of a sheriff deputy's cruiser parked on Marsee Drive, slamming glass and metal as loud as a prison sentence chasing us down the hill where we leapt into the metal coal chute and slid not fast enough into the coal pile where we hunkered for four hours sweating until we thought it was safe to sneak home to wash up and stroll to the cruiser where husky workers jack-hammered the boulder and talked about how the rock must have come loose with the rain a while back, *must have*, we agreed, *GOLLEE, CAN YOU BELIEVE* – , *must have*, and in church the next Sunday I dropped my whole allowance into the collection plate.

Today only my brain was in a coal shed, with no need to be there or stay there as I walked up the incline of Williams Street in front of the school past students boarding a yellow bus. Lo, at the corner Jenny stood holding her books while talking to Bessie Harper. When Jenny finished and came my way, I asked if I could walk her home, and with her acceptance we headed to the spot where the round boulder stood five years earlier. She invited me to sit with her on her small cliff across the road, and I asked her to talk so I could hear something besides the same thoughts going around and around pointlessly, like my old electric train.

"Let's see," she began as we settled down. "What comes to my mind is that you would like to be in Florida."

"How did you know?"

"Sarah told me y'all liked Naples."

For spring vacations from my fourth through eighth grade years, when the coal business was good, Dad drove Sarah, Mother and me out of the black and white of winter into the color of Florida. On the way through southern Georgia we stayed in my favorite motel with cabins shaped like teepees. Dad always asked to see the room before he took it, though the rooms always looked the same, like concrete teepees. In the little Gulf Coast town of Naples, Mom and Dad fished on the pier while Sarah and I played on the sand bars and white beach. Even the briefest thought of this brought back the refreshment of the water on my feet.

97

"A winter vacation in the sun is nice," Jenny went on, "but I like to live in the mountains. I would rather have it cold outside than hot. I like the brightness of the snow. I like dry snowflakes, though they don't make good snowballs. I enjoy watching the dry snowflakes that go a long time in the wind, sideways and upwards outside my window. I think the scientists are wrong saying no two snowflakes are alike. Imagine how many snowflakes there are. Zillions. Zillions of zillions. And each crystal is hexagonal. At some point snowflakes have to run out of new designs. One of these days science has to admit that."

"You're ahead of your time."

"On that one, yes, I am. And do you know what's funny? I'll bet at least a million kids are ahead of their time, but they get talked out of their questions. Kids know that at least two snowflakes have to look alike, but they're told that can't be, so they stop asking the question because science is right about so much. On the other hand, some people hardly trust science at all."

"Some of those people don't bathe," I offered. "They don't believe what experts say about germs."

"I enjoy landscapes of Wales. I like spicy foods, but not meat so much. I appreciate people who don't talk down to me. I wonder about a *Ripley's Believe It or Not* feature I read a while back. It told about a three-year-old child who spoke and understood languages he never heard from his parents or anyone around him. Far-away languages, too – nothing close to where he lived. I wonder how that happened. That's what comes into my mind. Is that good enough?"

Good enough.

At home I plopped sideways in one of the two easy chairs separated by a lamp table so I could hear Dad tell me something. Dad was sunk into the other easy chair, reading a *National Geographic* story about squid. "Dad," I asked, "in the meet, I don't know how fast the other guys are. What would you do if you were me?"

98

He thought about it. "No matter what fix you find yourself in, don't get beat in your mind." Though I knew this, I was sure I needed to hear it, because I asked, and a parent's answer sinks in deeper.

I doubted Scotty Lanier was worked up about the race or asked anybody anything because he didn't show up at the field until a week before the meet.

"Where are your friends?" Scotty inquired as he sat with me on the Harlan Green Dragons' bench, loosening his sweat pants.

"What friends?

"From Rosenwald."

"They will be here in a while. How did you know about them?"

"I heard it at school."

"Heard what?"

He grinned: "That you'd rather run with Rosenwald runners than with whites."

"Who's saying this? Lucy Giddon? Pokey?"

Scotty stopped adjusting his socks and sat up. "I'm just playing with you. It's no matter to me."

"They are my friends. What other whites am I supposed to run with?"

Scotty opened his palms upward. "Me, I guess."

"That's right," I went on as I tightened my shoelaces, a little heated in my forehead over that school talk. "Tell anyone who's interested that I'm running with a white folk, now that you're here. Tell 'em I'll run with anybody black or red or brown or yellow as long as that person wants to do what I'm doing. I'll run with any girl, though girls aren't given a chance at track, which makes no sense to me." I sat up. "Tell 'em that: I'm here to run."

"OK."

"Are you ready?"

Scotty was ready to do half a workout the first day, with longer practices the next few appearances. He did well in the sprints but declined to run longer than a mile in any given drill, explaining that "it's just a race," and he was saving up for Friday.

On the Wednesday before the meet, Coach Odell waved Scotty and me over to his squad of Rosenwald runners as they stretched. "This is our last hard practice," he said. "We'll work out light tomorrow and go to Benham on Friday. That's our last meet. You boys might want to go light tomorrow, too, to save up for your meet."

I thanked him. "Then we will sprint some with you today."

"There you go," Coach Odell nodded. He lined us up and whistled us off on the first of ten 100-yard runs. At least half the runners beat me each time, beyond any chance of my getting Loretta's respect. Scotty stayed impressively close to the front. In a walk back up the field to line start another sprint, I moved alongside Lamar and asked his advice. "Pace yourself," Lamar suggested. "Don't blow yourself out at the gun. You might not know how the others will run, but you know what kind of runner you are. Run on that."

"What do you mean, what kind of runner I am?" I reflected that I was asking the advice of someone who wasn't allowed to go to school with me.

"I don't know what you folks call different kinds of runners," Lamar explained. "I call them pacers, trackers and kickers. The kicker can hang back until the last because he knows he can close with enough speed to pass in the stretch. The tracker has some speed left at the end, though not as much as the kicker. So the tracker doesn't want to fall too far behind; he wants to keep close to the leaders until he makes his move. The pacer doesn't have a sudden kick at the end, but he has steady speed. He wears down the others by setting as strong a pace as he can hold and by getting far enough ahead that the trackers lose him and kickers can't catch up."

"What do you do?"

"The shorter the race, the less strategy I find in it. In the 100-yard dash I just eat dynamite and let the gun set it off. In the 440 I run as steady and fast as I can without locking up, so I have something left to hold off the kickers."

"What would you say I am?"

"What are you?" Lamar rubbed his sweaty cheek. "I'd say you're mostly pacer and tracker at this point. You have endurance. You warm up your motor with a long run and then go for the kill. Don't let anyone draw you out early; that's not the way your body works best, from what I can tell. If you overdo it too soon, you could lock up. You also have some of the kicker in you, but wait to see what kind of speed you develop. Any style can win as long as it's the fastest and you don't let your mind mess you up."

At the supper table, in the tangy humidity of tomato soup, I tried not to slurp while eating. When Mother asked how my day was, I told her I was thinking a lot about the race, but that a guy named Lamar, from Rosenwald, gave me some good advice that made me feel better.

"Rosenwald?"

"Yes," I said. "A colored friend."

Dad, Sarah and Mother said nothing for a while. The windows were steaming up from the simmer of the soup. Mother asked Dad if he would crack the back door a little. He obliged. Then she asked me, "How long have you known Lamar?"

"About three weeks. Rosenwald practices on the field before I finish. Sometimes I join them."

"Join them?" Mother asked as a concern steadied itself in her head of pinned-up hair with a silvery blue tint.

"I run wind sprints with them sometimes. Lamar is their best runner at distance. He helps me."

"What else do you do with them?" she inquired.

"I get beat."

Dad laughed, "You're not fast enough, huh?" His laugh made Sarah chuckle with relief.

"Not against Peanut or Lamar, and I'm two days from my reckoning."

"Well," Mother said finally, "it's nice that Lamar helped my son."

20

First call for the mile

LIKE THE "ON" SWITCH OF A FINAL EXAM, TIME CLICKS ME INTO THE present tense as Mother drives Dad, Sarah and me through Barbourville, down College Street past Union College's red brick, Georgian-style buildings fronted with white-column porches, set back on a grand lawn of stately trees. Dad, out of navigational habit, motions his hand left toward Marci's house in the row of picturesque homes facing the college.

With a smile that holds as she walks to the car to kiss Dad, Marci hugs the rest of us and takes us inside where Alexander welcomes us with caramel ease. Marci offers us breakfast refreshments – not much for me, as I talk on the surface of the conversation, a water bug on the pond. The time is 10:30. The mile run is at noon. I need to get ready, so I put on the green shorts I bought to show my school's colors, though I prefer the feel of the white cotton shorts I wear in practice.

Alexander bids us goodbye and drives off to Lexington for a weekend trade show for grocers as the rest of us head across the street onto the campus, around the three-story classroom building with "Union – 1907" over the doorway of the center tower entrance. Behind the building, across a parking lot to a gentle slope topped with bleachers overlooking the freshly striped cinder track, I survey the oval and glimpse Scotty strolling among the athletes gathered loosely in groups.

Approaching the bleachers, we spot Mr. Lanier a third of the way up, a sociable prospect because he and Dad can talk about construction and what is going on in Harlan County. Climbing, Dad collects both feet on each riser so he can step with his stronger right leg, and Mr. Lanier scoots over to give Dad the aisle seat.

I descend to the field and walk with Scotty whose words are cheerful though his tone isn't as confident as it was when he had talked about how he didn't have to train much for this event. We mostly think to ourselves.

To sign in, Marci leads me to an official standing behind a table that supports a shiny banner: "Southeast Kentucky Conference – District Track and Field Meet." Marci introduces me to him – Deke Sands, Union's track coach – and tells him I'm registered for Harlan. Mr. Sands' squinting blue eyes and grin suggest he could do mischief, maybe not digging up a coffin, but some mischief. He checks me in for the mile and half-mile as a loudspeaker blares, "First call for the mile."

I ask, "Who are the good milers around here that you know of?"

"Bobby Dodd of Knox Central here in town has done well. He's pretty strong, consistent." He gestures to a lanky, light-haired boy with a strong, clean, country-boy look, running slowly with a teammate in their blue uniforms with a broad gold stripe from the left shoulder to the right waist, fancier than my Fruit-of-the-Loom cotton T-shirt.

The loudspeaker names winners of the discus and shot put and gives the distances of their throws, then announces the final call for the start of the high jump on the opposite side of the field. Marci says she will wait on the grass by the bleachers and keep my suit and road-running shoes. After stretching, I join Scotty in a slow run on the track for the first time with my spikes. The track feels easy – level, clear, with a snappy grip.

The loudspeaker announces the second call for the mile, prompting Scotty and me to return to the swath of slope where Marci waits. As Scotty and I strip down to our shorts, shoes and shirt, I remind Marci and myself, "This is it. If one of us doesn't come in first or second, this will be a short track season for Harlan High," and I leave with Scotty to join a group of milers shuffling around in the grass near the starting line, trying to stay limber. I'm getting pumped with adrenaline, gasoline begging for an engine.

103

Loudspeaker: "Third and final call for the mile!"

As we gather on the track, a young woman with a clipboard checks off our names. A man lines up the dozen of us by schools, placing Scotty and me in the sixth lane. I tell Scotty he can stand in front of me at the line. He does what I tell him.

The crowd shouts a babble of cheers and commands. In a monotone voice, the official instructs us: "Don't step over the line before the starting gun. If there is a false start I will call you back with an additional shot. Shift lanes whenever you want as long you don't interfere with the runner in the lane you are entering; otherwise you can be disqualified. The gun will mark the first runner to reach the final lap."

The starter backs off the track onto the grass inside the stretched oval. "On your mark!" We crouch as the starter raises his blank-firing pistol.

"Get set!"

Silence in the crowd.

"POP!" Motion eats the fear whole as Scotty jumps forward and everyone else swarms ahead of me. Twenty yards off the start, thirty yards, I roll in a controlled gait, feeling a live wire and uncertainty as the stretched-out pack in front of me folds like shuffled cards into the three inside lanes. I am in last place. *Rosenwald!* I hold onto Lamar's advice to run my own race and not get drawn out early. My legs spin almost on their own as I follow the knotty string of boys around the first curve. With the angle of the bend I gauge the positions of the runners curling around and glance over at Scotty charging into second place behind a racer in blue and white, colors that could be Barbourville High, or could be Bell County; *yes, it is Bell County out front.* Scotty glances back over his left shoulder to see where I am on the curve – surprise flashes worry across his face as he spots me at the tail of the line. I wonder how long Scotty and these other guys can keep up this speed, but I'm sure I can run down most of them before this race is over – this track is long, and we have seven more turns to make as we unwind from this first curve.

Ahead, legs churn beneath a mix of bobbing heads and pumping elbows – down the backstretch – into the second turn where I close in on some lagging runners and glide past them at a pace still easy as I roll out of the bend and onto the straightaway behind boys moving in three loose clumps. We head toward the midfield starting line where the voice of an official blurts out the time – "ONE-FIVE! ONE-SIX!" – which means little to me because I never ran against a clock, and I am not racing against a clock now, only against runners, ten ahead of me, some way ahead, thirty yards it looks like.

SECOND LAP: Past the stands I think how good this feels, not as good as the electric lightness that could move me smooth as ice on ice all day, but good enough so far, easier than practice, easier than running alone. Swinging around the third curve I see that I am closing in on the line. A runner from Williamsburg – orange, blue and white – passes Scotty, who settles in at third place. Bobby Dodd is at fourth behind Scotty. I'm not tiring. I tell myself to hold steady, that I have a long way to go, and the speed of this crowd isn't as fast as it was on the first lap.

On the straight course I watch only the runner ahead of me. We slant into the fourth curve, rotating our view again. As I come out the other end I restrain myself from passing in front of the spectators who are not as loud as at the start. The crowd doesn't roar as one voice anyway, but shouts at different runners as they come close – I hear some mother shrieking – *that has to be a mother* – shrieking at a boy named Buford, and I think, *Bless you, Buford, you and your family, but whoever you are – no offense against your mama – I aim to wear you down the same as you aim to do to me.* The pace is still good, too early for me to open up: I don't want to burn this feeling out too soon.

THIRD LAP: Holding on, with all of us looking straight ahead like zombies in fast time, we push past the stands. Some boys ahead of me change positions and tilt around the fifth curve where I gauge the spread and see I am closer to the leaders now, within twenty yards. Bobby Dodd passes Scotty to take the third position. Showing strain, Scotty doesn't look back to see where I am on the turn. Another runner in front of me slacks suddenly, so I bump out to avoid him, then hug the inside lane again. Someone in gold and white, Middlesboro colors, overtakes the Bell County pacesetter.

I need to get closer. Flinging out of the curve and into the back straight, I edge out to the second lane as I see the middle group falling back – closer, closer. The momentum is mine. I pass one. I pass another. I pass until the middle group is behind me. Scotty is dropping back, too, away from the lead group. He slows toward me, his head back, chest out, legs tightened into shorter strides. Pulling up beside him, I want him to stay loose, easy for me to think because I am not loosening up. Between breaths Scotty huffs, "Let's do it," but he slows more as I move ahead.

In turn number six I begin my chase of the three out front because if they are kickers I need to wear the kick out of them soon, for I don't feel an all-out sprint in me, only a steady speed with some reserves. I see Bobby Dodd in second place, looking ready to make a move on gold-and-white at the front. I keep the reach of my stride long though I am breathing harder to feed the piston work of the muscles that have burned off the high octane of the start. I tell my legs, *you're doin' good, guys, doin' good. Give it to me, give it to me; one and a half laps is all I ask now; give it to me.*

Out of the sixth curve I overtake Bell County at number three to get close enough to move in on the front pair. Bobby Dodd passes gold-and-white to take the lead. *Dangerous, dangerous.* I can't give up any distance or momentum now, so I begin the rundown, pass gold-and-white and pull alongside Dodd. We barrel into the spotty yells of spectators who, except for my family and maybe Mr. Lanier, are cheering for others, but that doesn't weigh against me – I ride the noise because I know I'm one reason they're shouting – I'm taking on the last of their favorites and my body has more to deliver, not so easily now, but I take the pressure as a friend because the pace is picking up and I still feel strong in it.

FOURTH LAP. Final lap gun. I slip ahead of Bobby Dodd and see nothing in front of me but track, straight and clear, open territory, and what little running I hear is behind me. On the seventh curve I glance sideways to see Dodd slipping, *good, good, good, hold on, keep it up* as on the back straightaway I feel the strain seeping into my torso like fresh-poured concrete that I can't allow to set before the finish line. The only spikes I hear are mine, but I know Dodd is behind me somewhere, and if my cement hardens, he'll roll past me easy as a boulder down a hill with no tree left to stop it. On the last curve I glance back to see him five yards behind, but I can't trust that – I don't know what kick he has. Coming out of the final curve I glance over to see Dodd giving everything he has. I tell my body that we are desperate, to keep it up, it's almost over, he can't catch me – I shove into the noise, down to the finish line enlarging – I break the ribbon and let the pain close in and do its business on me quick while I walk and catch my breath – *not so bad, not so bad.* I walk over to Bobby Dodd and, when I have enough breath, tell him he ran a good race, and the same to gold-and-white.

Scotty trails in fourth from last. Half-stumbling to a stop, he leans over to catch his breath while I slap his moist back as the loudspeaker announces: "In the mile. First place, Jeremiah James, Harlan..."

I savor the words, but mostly I want my family to hear them. After I pick up the medal from Deke Sands at the officials' table, Sarah runs to me, jumping, and Marci embraces me with relief. Relaxing with my family in the stands, I review the sequence of my run – it all happened so fast, as if in a speeded-up movie that has to be watched first and figured out later.

HURDLES ARE PLACED on the track. The next set of racers goes to the ground on hands and knees, adjusts to the starting blocks, rises to the "get set" command and punches ahead with a bang. Hurdlers from Williamsburg and Barbourville High don't jump raggedy like the others but glide over the hurdles with a running-split leap, their shoulders streaming level to the eye. The satisfaction of the mile run whirs inside me like a flywheel, spinning my appreciation out to what I see.

After two more hurdle events, the track is cleared for the 440-yard run, one time around. A spindly boy, about five-feet-eight, from Corbin, bursts into an early lead and stretches his legs out as long as the stride of his six-foot-tall pursuer, and holds him off.

Drinking orange juice that mother has squeezed for us, we watch the 100-yard dash, taken by a fiery sprinter from Pineville. Then Scotty and I stroll closer to the pole vault area to watch as the competition whittles down to three. A pole-vaulter from Benham clears the bar with a rise that almost hangs in midair before he curls to the other side and drops.

The public address system puts out the first call for the 880. Though Scotty isn't running the half-mile, he warms up with me on the infield from which we watch an 880-yard relay whip around the track. Barbourville takes the lead. The baton passes. Knox County takes the lead. The baton passes. Bell County takes the lead. I can't take my eyes off it until the relay zips to a finish, allowing me to reflect harder on my next race as the movie of the outside world turns remote and out of focus.

At the second call for the 880, Sarah descends to the grassy sidelines. She wants to hold my suit and shoes for this race and let Marci stay with the family in the bleachers.

On the final call for the 880, I am back at the starting line with Bobby Dodd, with the gold-and-white runner from Middlesboro, with a bunch from the mile race, plus three new runners. I am up against the unknown again, but not as much as before because I figure that Dodd is one of the best competitors in this group and I have just outrun him. On the other hand, this is a shorter race than the mile, and I am better at longer distances; plus, I have no tactic other than to run quicker sooner and try to hold out. Anticipation dials up the heartbeat. I breathe deep to pack more oxygen as we line up.

The starter instructs us. Quiet. "Get set." The gun.

Move it. The other runners burst ahead as I fold in behind the tight string at a steady, quick tempo into the curve where I pass two because they are not fast enough, and I have to stay closer to the lead runner, which I see is Bobby Dodd, *so what is he up to, going out front this early?* Coming out of the curve I shift to the second lane, certain that I will pass someone before the end of the straightaway because my legs are wheeling faster this time. Halfway down the backstretch I see Dodd threatened by one of the new runners – maroon and gold, Pineville colors. I think maybe this maroon guy is a kicker, like Peanut and Lamar, so I pull up tight in the middle of the pack and, around the second curve, slip past a runner to stay within ten yards of Dodd and maroon-and-gold. The strength is coming, but I have to breathe deeper and press ahead, pushing and loosening at the same time, feeling for the maximum my muscles will do without succumbing to their acid, enjoying the quick pace we are keeping, like a shared power, except that none of us wants to share anything in the end.

We tear across the lap line for the final circuit and keep our positions down the straightaway and through the curve as we tighten up the slack. Three boys run short of steam and drop behind me as I take aim at the front four gliding in a single line onto the far straight where I watch their backsides. *Move it,* I tell myself, *move it,* enough to overtake the fourth-place runner and advance until I reach the side of the third-place runner in red and white, Corbin colors. We run step for step, like dancers out of a slingshot. I try to pass. He holds me off – a race within a race. I stretch my legs further. He does the same. Because I am in an outer lane I want to pass him before the turn that would force me to run more steps than he does just to get around the bend, an extra distance I can't afford because this guy is strong. Loud, we are chopping cinders loud, we are synchronized so close together, shoulders nearly touching, close enough to hear him grunting little umph sounds in his breath, maybe in my breath too. I don't know how long red-and-white will keep this up, but I'm pushing as long as I can – I think of what Dad told me, not to let the mind break, *not break, not break, not break.* With twenty yards of straightaway left before the final bend, the red-and-white runner slows a little, a sign he's at his limit, pushing on the wall, the breaking point, a sign that triggers in me a wild-dog-instinct and blanks my pain with frenzy – *Grandpa Dannon, is that you?* – I press for the takedown – he falls back – I leave him and wrap to the inside lane as I slant into the final curve in pursuit of the final two with maroon-and-gold easing into the second lane to pass Bobby Dodd, but maroon-and-gold can't do it – Dodd fights him off – Dodd's got the wild dog in him now, and extends his lead. I haven't enough time or breath to cuss as I fling outward to get around maroon-and-gold because I need to get into second place and within striking distance as the hand of the clock ticks down with no pause that can stop it with seventy yards to go.

Halfway through the last turn I grind past maroon-and-gold and push up to Dodd a half step at a time until I edge around him at the end of the curve and drive hard, breathe hard, ache hard into the final stretch because I don't know what Dodd has left in him. *Oh, brother* – I hear something of what Dodd has left in him – fast footsteps sounding closer to me. I hear nothing of the crowd, only rapid-fire chipping in the cinders. I don't look back because whatever I see won't make me go any faster, even as I lose the sound of his spikes, *push it, push it, push it* – I snap the ribbon with my chest... I slow down...I look back to see Dodd five feet behind – deadly close, but not close enough.

I walk to catch my breath and take the grip out of my abdomen, and say a word or two to Dodd and maroon-and-gold from Pineville, and tell the red-and-white Corbin runner he was tough. He seems to take some pride in that before he waves in acknowledgement to the woman screaming, "Buford!"

The public address system sounds my name and the name of Harlan as I look to Mother, Dad and Marci in the stands. Sarah jumps up and down in the grass. I know the world doesn't care, but this is my world, this is my world, giving me the chance to never be the same again.

110

21

New life

To celebrate my wins, Stoner treated me to lunch at Pop's Café with Jug, Two-Bit and Harley, then headed back to Central Street where we stopped in front of the Baughman Insurance office at corner of Second and lingered to look at the latest *News Photos of the World* laid flat along the waist-level base of the plate-glass windows. One photograph showed a smiling man in India standing at the edge of a grave beside an opened coffin. The caption said his coffin had been packed six feet underground and protected around the clock by armed guards of the maharaja who had challenged him to prove he could live without air, food or water for sixty days. The caption said that when the coffin was dug up and opened, the Moslem fakir looked asleep and pale until he came back to life.

"That's a long time to go without a toilet," Jug observed.

"Gollee, buddy," Two-Bit exclaimed. He was short enough that I could see the top of his head and how he parted his hair crooked. "Shoot, man, ain't nobody going to git me in one of them caskets, not even above ground. Remember that guy who cooked up this plan with his wife to let her play dead and get buried in order to get insurance money, and then the husband would dig her up that night, and they buried this woman, but the husband died of a heart attack at the graveside service – 'member that? – leaving his wife in the ground there where nobody could hear her?"

Harley corrected, "That was in a *Tales of the Crypt* comic, Two-Bit."

"It could have been true."

"But that was a comic book story."

"It could have been true, like that guy in the picture there. Hey, remember that grave we tried to dig up behind Ivy Hill?"

I asked, "What do you mean, 'we tried to dig up'? Jug hit a rock and y'all ran off, leaving Horse and me to put the dirt back in, just like you ran off and left me when I set that fire in my back yard."

"You don't know that that was a rock," Two-Bit protested.

Harley added, "That could have been that woman's casket."

Two-Bit went on, "Back then, we was little. It was scary being around dead people. Lookit what that guy in India did – he was alive all the time he was down there. What if that woman buried on Ivy Hill – "

"Jerusha Tess," I said.

" – What if she was alive, like that – whatchamacallit – FAY-keer?"

I said, "That Indian man knew what he was doing. He didn't get himself embalmed, you can be sure of that."

"How do you know that Tess woman was embalmed? They didn't always embalm people back then. Sometimes they didn't even know for sure if they was really dead. They put mirrors up to their noses."

Stoner spoke up, "Is everybody here crazy?"

I answered that one, "Pretty much."

Unable to sustain interest in this conversation any longer, Stoner moved along the window to see another *News Photo of the World*. I gestured Jug, Harley and Two-Bit closer to me in a semi-circle. "Guess what."

"What?"

"Jerusha Tess could be alive."

Harley said, "We ain't in fifth grade no more, JJ."

I pointed to the fakir in the photo. "Look at what's possible."

Jug laughed and punched me. Harley said, "Pssh." Two-Bit looked at the photograph some more.

THE NEXT MORNING, out of a sleep drugged by the mountain air through my windows, Mother loudly declared from the bottom of the staircase that the kitchen would be closed for breakfast at nine, which my Big Ben alarm clock showed was ten minutes away. I calculated that I could get dressed in seven minutes, giving me three more minutes to remain motionless in bed and to think of Jenny and how I would like to see her this Tuesday, a school-free day because of a teachers' conference. Though the warm weather had turned off the coal furnaces and the street-cleaning truck had sprayed down Ivy Street, I had to clean the wallpaper in the living room, and I needed to practice running a few hours and write a term paper. I wondered how Jenny came out of nowhere and took hold of me. I wondered what my parents would think if I brought to my home a girl who last came to our house the year before to Sarah's giggly seventh-grade summer dance party on the porch. I asked for a sign, for a clue about what to do when, CLACK, Miss Becker stormed into my bedroom, without knocking, as usual, not the kind of sign I had in mind. As noisily as possible, Miss Becker strode over to pick up my clothes, except I already had my pants and shirt folded neatly on the padded rocking chair, part of my effort to reform myself. Miss Becker didn't really want to clean up. She wanted me to get out of bed and, having succeeded in busting my reverie, swished out. A minute later, Sarah tapped my door and pattered downstairs to meet the deadline, so I jumped out of bed and dressed. Clump, clump, clump down the steps while buttoning my shirt, I rounded through the dining room and slid into my kitchen table seat with two minutes to spare.

"I beat you," Sarah pointed out.

"Not by much."

"Did, too. I'm faster than you. Girls are faster than boys when they want to be." Sarah wanted some mental action, a change from an evening of listening to the Four Lads singing *Moments to Remember*.

"Sure enough," I agreed. I didn't want mental action. I wanted food.

After breakfast, Mother sang as she and Sarah cleaned wallpaper in the bedrooms. Mother didn't have a singing voice, but I liked to hear her anyway. Once, when I was in fourth grade, she sang *Red Sails in the Sunset* while driving to Knoxville. From the back seat I imitated her in a mocking way. She said that was hurtful, and turned quiet, but didn't get after me. I apologized over and over, but she wouldn't sing in the car after that. I never mocked her again. In my lucid moments I thought of how, if she had wanted to, she could have cut me down to size but didn't. Now, at least, she was singing in the house. She liked songs of the 1930s through the early 1950s but stopped at the border of rock and roll. Dad never sang solos – hymns in church were enough for him – though he got a kick out of listening to Little Richard scream *Long, Tall Sally* when I caught it on the radio. He had never heard anything like it. Neither had I.

I cleaned the living room walls with my globs of Walvet, light green dough that got blacker as I wiped with it and kneaded the soot into the glob that smelled like the play putty with which I made snakes in kindergarten, almost as memorable as the scent of crayons. I had just wiped clean the living room and dining room late in the morning when Dad entered from the porch. Dad had gone to Creech Drug for breakfast with Uncle Clyde and the regulars before making a stop at his office. Mother speculated that Dad was enjoying Creech Drug breakfasts more at this time because he could shake salt on his eggs and slather butter on his grits without any of us nagging him about blood pressure and cholesterol. He probably ate bacon there, too, crunchy crisp the way he liked it.

Dad didn't take his hat off as he came through the door, which was rarely locked unless we were out of town. "Jeremiah, I need you to go to the Lenarue mine with me to check a survey."

"Right now?"

"Now."

"Daaad," I protested. "Do we *have* to do it today?"

"Are you with me or not?"

"Well, phooey. I need to run, and I wanted to do other stuff."

"Run to Lenarue, then," he said.

I thought about it. My oatmeal didn't feel heavy any more. I agreed to make the nine-mile run out and back.

In my white shorts and T-shirt I set off through town, three miles to Sunny Acres where I looked for the wiry, car-chasing dog, but he was trapped yapping inside his two-story house, click-scratching against the picture window. Leaving Sunny Acres, I crossed the road to Denny Ray's where Dad stood beside his car, his hat shading his eyes. He didn't wave me to come over; he just waited.

I asked him what he was doing there.

"Up ahead half a mile," Dad nodded southward "three big dogs were chasing cars. Do you want me to take you past them?"

"I'm not worried about dogs."

"Fine," Dad said right away, "but before you get around the bend in that next hollow" – he pronounced it more like 'holler' – "get a stick. If a dog comes toward you, walk. Don't look at it, and don't act afraid. If they can't scare you, they get second thoughts. Some day you won't need a stick."

"You ever fought off a dog?"

"No, because of what I'm telling you. Don't think that it will come to having to fight them off. Don't blink and don't sweat. Don't give 'em even the smell of fear."

Taking that advice, I jogged to the curve, picked up a smooth branch piece, broke it into a two-foot-long club, and headed around the bend. Near Gray's Knob, five miles from Harlan, three large dogs barked their way up from the riverbank of Martin's Fork. As they ran up behind me, two separated, one out into the road and one behind the guard rail. "Bunch of chicken dogs!" I said aloud but without staring at them because if they lit into me I wouldn't be saying this. After passing, they trotted ahead less noisily, and then crossed the road to scamper into the hills as Dad returned in his car to check on me without slowing down, soon coming from behind me again on his way to Lenarue where I met him in the parking lot of the commissary.

As he pulled himself out of the car, looking satisfied, I thought of how, when I was small, he wanted me to be able to take whatever pain came my way. I could take pain now – some, at least – and I shared with him the satisfaction of willpower, though I knew it was yet a game to me, not to him.

We wove our way through the commissary to the door of the back office where Mr. Lee told us to come on in. Off to the side, at a green table, penciling numbers on a ledger sheet, sat Jenny, and I wondered how God did it. She turned to see us and I asked her what she was doing there.

Mr. Lee answered before Jenny could. "She's working on my tonnage reports. She helps out sometimes when Irma is off – my assistant. Steve, you remember my daughter, Jenny, don't you?"

Jenny arose and said hello to Dad.

Dad looked pleased. "You square the tonnage figures, do you? What kind of coal did you ship most this month?"

"Mostly stoker, some block. That's usually the case."

Mr. Lee said, "And you, JJ – it's good to see you again." He turned to Dad. "We enjoy having JJ come by the house every now and then."

116

Dad didn't look surprised. "Good company for him, if he talks to this young lady."

Jenny said, "Thank you."

Mr. Lee asked Dad if we were ready to check a site for a ventilation fan. Dad said we were ready. Mr. Lee told Jenny she could come along and help if she wanted to. I could tell he liked having his daughter around him.

Dad and I followed the Lees' mud-splashed GMC truck past the mine head, around a rock road along a bench of the mountain at the level of the Harlan seam. While Dad and Mr. Lee spread a blueprint map on the hood of the truck to "get our bearings," as Dad said, I opened the trunk of the Dodge to gather the surveying equipment. As I pulled the transit out of its case and picked up its tripod, Jenny came around and took out the leveling rod and measuring tape.

I told her, "I didn't know you worked at the mine office."

"I don't much. I just help out a little a few times a year."

When Dad pointed to a spot to set up the transit temporarily, I kicked away some large sandstone rocks to make a more level base, exposing red stones, and I told Jenny, "There's some pretty rock for you."

She lifted a small, smooth stone and declared, "Red dog."

"No Latin in that name."

"None at all. Look how red this one is. It's burned slate." She handed it to me.

"It looks redder than the clinkers I used to pull from my furnace; heavier and smoother, too." I rubbed it some and passed it back.

"A different chemical composition might not come out as red as this," Jenny said. "This red dog came from the slate off the conveyor belt to the tipple. It caught fire by spontaneous combustion."

"Spontaneous combustion?"

"Some of the slate had a lot of fine coal mixed in it. Sunlight warmed it, and the heat built up in the heap after a long time. They use it for fill."

"So it just caught fire by itself, huh, and made itself into some nice-looking rock?"

"Yeah, pretty much by itself, it got a new life when it got back to air and sunshine," she said, slipping the stone into her jacket pocket. "Pretty much by itself."

I thought that could be a sign, of something. Or maybe an Elvis song. Heat in the slate pile. Rock on fire.

ೂ∞ల

Sarah's diary – May 15, 1956

Jenny came up to me in the cafeteria. I was hoping she would say something about JJ. Instead she said she had read *Pride and Prejudice* and said she thought I might like Jane Austen's work. I checked P&P out of the school library. I need to do one more book report anyway for Mr. Larkin. He had recommended *The Last of the Mohicans.* Can you imagine?

22

Phantoms of High Noon

WITH THE WEEK CLOSING IN ON THE REGIONAL MEET, IT DIDN'T matter any more that I trained alone because I was crowded enough with the memory of Bobby Dodd and the expectation of winners from other district meets who would face off against me. On practice runs I imagined racers around me. I stretched to pass the phantoms and fend off the runners at my side without looking for reassurance or peace of mind. I imagined threats, talked to them, defied them – friends, really. They were my best hope against the real thing – a miler from Somerset who had finished ten seconds faster than I did, the fastest time in the state so far, and I would face him in the regional.

To take a break from studies and concern about the race, I ate lunch mid-week with Jug at Howard Drug and then walked with him to the Greyhound bus station so he could play the pinball machine. When he was in junior high, Jug spent a lot of time playing pinball at the VTC Line bus terminal near the river. One summer afternoon a gunfight broke out in the station and a man fell dying against the machine Jug was playing, causing it to "Tilt!" After a month of not playing pinball at all, Jug shifted to the Greyhound station where he never saw anyone shot. Though Harlan had a reputation for being rough, only Jug, among all my friends, actually got to see a shooting, which gave him something to talk about and a few weeks of popularity.

As Jug won games in the peace of the Greyhound terminal during our lunch hour, I spotted Lamar, resting on the bench in the section marked "Colored Only." Happy to see him, I sat by his side and asked where he was going. He was heading up to Kentucky State in Frankfort for an orientation for incoming scholarship students. He said he wanted to become a math teacher.

Lamar nodded toward a station employee coming our way and warned I might be asked to leave. I kept talking to Lamar until the bent man in a white dress shirt, with a Veterans of Foreign Wars button on his cap, gestured me to the corner and told me I was in the colored section. I told the man I was saying goodbye to a friend going off to serve his country and paying a steep price for being an American. At that, he nodded approvingly to Lamar and shuffled back to the baggage room. As Lamar boarded, I thanked him for helping me, and waved goodbye, sad to see him go.

Jug had twenty-three free games left on the pinball machine that day, but we had to hustle back to school.

At the end of biology class, I leaned over the table and talked with Jenny briefly before she left. As I gathered my papers, Dozer swaggered by and in a low voice asked how the cradle was doing. I told him the cradle was too small for what was in it, and I was trying to rob it. He said, "I don't blame you," and left.

What? After all that? "I don't blame you"?

After the final bell, Sarah met me outside the school so we could walk to The Quality Shop to pick up a blouse she had ordered. Zorro caught up with us at the street, so we let him come along. It would be a new experience, getting Zorro inside The Quality Shop, stocked with nice suits. Halfway downtown, at the corner of Second and Central, two boys – Birdseed Craxton and Pokey Giddon – stood facing us. Birdseed was a wiry, scruffy street kid whose plainly clad parents walked with him in the middle of Ivy Street, rarely on the sidewalk, on their way to or from odd jobs. One time Mother hired Mr. Craxton to cut the grass, giving him free access to our basement where the lawn tools were stored. The next day our grass clippers and a wrench set were missing.

"Hey, Jaybird," Birdseed called out, standing like a gunslinger who might be looking for Gary Cooper in *High Noon*, except he was smaller and scruffier than the man in the movie. "I read in the *Enterprise* how you were a fast runner." Pokey stood aside, keeping his eyes on me as Birdseed went on. "I'm fast. Let's race."

I'm in the scene. "I don't want to race you. You don't run what I run."

"What do you run?"

"I run the mile."

"If you can go that far, you can run a block. Let's run a block."

"What are we running for?" I demanded to know, then turned to my companion. "Zorro, what are we running for?"

Zorro shrugged, "I don't know. To see who's fastest?"

"Birdseed's fastest. He already said as much. I don't have any quarrel with that. I'm not a one-block runner."

Birdseed said, "The newspaper said you're the best around."

"The newspaper didn't say that. It said I won a mile race and a half-mile."

"Oh, c'mon," Birdseed pleaded, "Please, let's do it. I want to race."

"Ooookay," I consented. "Let's line up. Sarah, you go up to Mound Street and see who wins. Zorro, start us when the street's clear." Sarah walked to the corner of Mound Street and waved her arms. Zorro took his position, legs apart, his right hand arced slightly away from his hip at the place where his whip would hang if he were at Mason Pond. After Zorro nodded for us to get ready and sent us off, Birdseed scrambled ahead, pumping his arms high. I passed him halfway up the block, breathing hard because I hadn't warmed up.

121

At the intersection, when Birdseed got some red out of his face, he huffed, "I ran pretty good, didn't I?"

"Too good." I said. "I don't want to race you again."

That seemed to satisfy Birdseed; Pokey, too. Even Zorro. Sarah – she just looked at us. Feeling peaceable again, Zorro, Sarah and I moseyed on down to The Quality Shop.

23

Second call for the mile

PRIMED FOR THE SHOWDOWN, I AM FILLED ENOUGH WITH A JELLY - sweetened biscuit and a cup of hot chocolate, a fraction of what I usually eat. Sarah can hardly eat that much, her stomach having swayed with the curves for an hour on the daybreak ride along Highway 119 to Pineville, straightening out more along U.S. 25-E past Flat Lick and Stinking Creek to Barbourville. Marci's living room offers a homey resting place but not much rest of mind as the sunlight spreads white in the sheer curtains through which I can see at the end of College Street the white columns and spire of Union College's brick chapel.

I tell the women and Alexander I will see them later. I want to go to the field early. Dad isn't here. He is at an emergency meeting with some Harlan business leaders to see if there is a way to persuade the owner of a mine up Yocum Creek to keep from shutting down his operation. Dad isn't optimistic about this. He says the meeting is more like a wake, getting together to adjust to the passing. In Harlan a slogan declares that "coal is king", but Dad says the coal market is the king, and a market doesn't care about Harlan or any other place it draws from. When the market price for coal goes down too far, too long, the mine work stops, the tipple is left to die on its timber legs, the coal camp empties, and businesses choke and fold. The workers head out to places like Dayton and Detroit. Still, Dad says, a person has to try to get past the tight times, work hard and hang on in case the tide comes in again.

Out the door of Marci's house, I take my time, strolling onto the campus, weaving around the sidewalks to the field. The place is familiar to me on this second trip. I don't have to figure out where to register, where to find water and the toilets. I am free to put my mind on the race.

In the parking lot, track teams roll in carefully and spill out of station wagons, cars and school buses. Some grown-ups tote seat cushions and picnic coolers. Stepping down to the field, I see more school colors than before. I am struck by how small some of the runners look, as distinct from the field athletes – football types – who throw the shot put, javelin or discus.

At the registration table I say hello to Union's track coach, Deke Sands, who greets me by name and checks me off the lists. He tells me, "You ran a good mile last time. What are you planning for this one, if I may ask?"

"The standard stuff, I guess – set a pace, try to get within striking distance on the last lap. But I don't know how the race will develop."

"If you're fast enough, and if you're steady enough in the head, you have a lot to work with."

"I saw the Somerset miler's time in his district. He was faster than the guy from Male High in Louisville. Bobby Dodd is back. He was hard to shake loose last week, and I don't know what he's done since."

"He's worked, I'm sure, but you've worked. Your time usually improves as the season goes on."

"Mine had better improve," I agree, "and it had better improve more than Dodd's or that Somerset guy's."

"If I can ever help you out, I'd be glad to."

"Too late for this race, I guess."

He chuckled. "Yeah, well, you'll do your running for yourself. But if I can do anything for you here at Union, just let me know."

124

"Thanks."

Loudspeaker: "First call for the mile!"

Mother, Sarah, Marci and Alexander step up to the bleacher platform, so I accompany them to seats halfway up. Sarah rocks back and forth before she gives up sitting and says she is going to the field with me to hold my gear.

We choose a spot for her, but she still can't sit. I lace up my spikes and jog onto the track with other boys. After a lap, we clear the lanes as another race is announced and set off. When the winners are declared, the loudspeaker puts out the second call for the mile. I look at the runners here and there on the field, anticipation all around. After stretches and two sprints to give my body notice of what's coming, I walk to keep limber.

"Third and final call for the mile!"

A dozen milers assemble at the starting line where we are given lanes based on our district times. Knox Central's Bobby Dodd in lane three looks the same – smooth, honest, country-strong, not to be underestimated. On the outer side of Dodd in lane four is a miler from Red Bird, shorter than I, heavier, a linebacker type. I am placed in Lane 2. In Lane 1 beside me I see for the first time Somerset's Bradshaw Perkins, wearing a gold uniform with purple trim and lettering. I look at Somerset just enough to get a fix on him – wiry legs compared to mine, a little taller, a long face, serious. *Fast as a fox, too, that boy.*

Just run your race. Don't think of how fast Somerset is.

I have to think of how fast he is. He's the guy to beat. He's the target.

He's everybody else's target, too. You're the underdog. That should take some pressure off you.

If I had a choice, I'd rather be the favorite.

You got this far. If you can get at least second place, you can make the cut that takes you to state.

125

Failing that, I have another shot in the half-mile.

You do better in the mile than the half-mile. Put it all out here. Run your best race for sure and survive if possible.

Survive, survive. I've got speed and endurance to work with. That's how I got here... Of course, that's how they all got here.

Think of yourself. They can think of themselves.

Yeah, think of myself. Lord, help me do my best. Here I go.

I pause the sound of the talk in my head. The starter recites his instructions with the same rat-a-tat voice as last time. My concentration on the race switches on high, loading my circuits, making the starter sound as if he is in a room somewhere off to the side. I know the rules. The only reason I need to keep track of the instructions is to know when they are done.

"On your mark."

Quiet around us.

"Get set."

At the crack of the starting gun we ride the flash flood out like critters in the rapids, positioning ourselves to avoid hitting each other, enjoying the rush that leaves pain in the wash and gushes us into the scenery, free to let loose and settle in to a race with four laps ahead.

The fast start puts me three-fourths the way back, not dead last like the first time, maybe ten yards off the lead as we reach the first curve, all of us close together three lanes thick except for some in front who are pressed into two lanes with the little Red Bird runner out front spinning his thick legs. Halfway through the curve I spot Somerset in the middle of the pack, Dodd at his side.

On the back straight a Clay County runner rifles past me on the outside, but I don't challenge him – I keep my eye on Somerset and my mind on my stride, which feels smooth and easy. Into the second curve, a blue-and-white runner from Oneida Baptist High sails by me. *What is this guy up to?*

126

Don't let him pull you out.

We straighten into the front stretch. Two ahead of me trade positions, but I keep my place in line because the pace feels fast, and the pack isn't too stretched out.

As we stream past the starting line, the official calls out times. "SIXTY-ONE! SIXTY-TWO!" So far, I am running faster than in the first race, and I look forward to moving up. In a spark across my brain I glimpse the Cherokee. *Are you there?* Gone.

In the clutter ahead of me, Oneida Baptist passes another boy and follows close on Dodd, who is at fifth place, Somerset at fourth, as we round into the third curve.

Keep your pace.

Out of the bend we unfurl again. The Red Bird runner tires back from first place to second, leaving the lead to a miler in green, Jenkins High. Clay County passes Dodd. Dodd doesn't like this; he passes Clay County to stick with Somerset. Dodd knows what he is doing. As my middle clump slows, I pass a runner and wrap back to the inside lane going into the fourth turn. Out of the side of my eye I see Red Bird straining in the front group. Looping out of the curve and onto the straightaway, I see backsides and can't gauge placements well, just speed.

Crossing the line into the third lap, half the race gone, I reckon myself to be fifteen yards behind the lead, with Somerset positioning to pass and take third place – I see that much. I can't afford to lose ground. I want to hold some reserves for the final lap, but if I don't pick up my pace, Somerset could put too much distance between us, and I don't know what these other guys in front of me will do. So, coming out of the fifth curve I pull the throttle out easy so the body can adjust without clenching in on me, and move past Red Bird. Breathing heavier along the back straight, I roll train-like past one runner of the middle group, then another, then another until I come up on Oneida Baptist who has given this a good run but is burning out, so I move ahead of him into the fourth position.

Somerset shrinks the gap between himself and Jenkins High while Dodd follows with the same momentum, so I need to get close to them or I will be out of this game. *There it is* – he makes his move – Somerset passes Jenkins and has nothing ahead of him but a runway cleared for takeoff. Dodd tries to keep on Somerset's heels by passing Jenkins on the curve but can't get around him and is forced to run wide at his side. I pull up on the rail behind Jenkins and Dodd. I'm the tail of the front group, with the rest of the field lost behind us. Pounding out of the bend behind the three of them on the way to the officials and the crowd and the last circuit, I work against the increasing tightness in my gut.

The gun pops Somerset into the final lap with no slowing down. I am seven yards back from him as I shift to the second lane to pass Dodd.

Dodd fights me off before we get to the curve. I am hurting earlier than I expected, given the speed, but I want this chase, down to my lungs and bones I want it, and I hear no cheers or footsteps or anything else outside the mind-sound of my desperation.

Across the seventh bend I see Somerset pulling away from us. Jenkins moves a few feet further ahead of Dodd. *These guys are serious, serious, serious!* I can't just keep a strong pace and expect to run down Somerset. I have to kick now, whether I'm a kicker or not. I drive the legs harder against the tension, relieved only by the machine feeling of speed itself as I come up to Dodd, closer, closer, and pass him not easily but by inches enough, and start my advance on Jenkins at second place. Halfway down the back straight I overtake Jenkins and edge over to the inside lane, wondering how much Somerset has left at this pace. I don't even know how much I have left, my body is wrenching so, from the legs and gut on out, but *I have to go after Somerset*, six yards ahead, now down to five, with Jenkins and Dodd chopping close behind me, all of us in a wild pack after each other with Somerset at the point.

Into the last curve I sense the slight centrifugal force of the lean and take from it enough hope to pull closer to Somerset. Halfway around the bend I ratchet up to within five feet of him, the closest I've been to him since the starting gun set him off without so much as a wave goodbye. We sweep onto the last straight where I push with what I have left, if I can just lighten the heft of armor forging in my chest and legs – *Move, you guys, move; stay with me.* The strangling of my thighs and calves tells me that my legs cannot do more, so I ask them to not let up, at least not let up.

Somerset glances at me and grinds on. We sprint, but I'm not gliding. I'm wringing the movement out of me, willing it, begging it out of the clench and hurt and burn because I see Somerset unyielding, and I hear what's behind me, closing in. Dodd, my fellow predator, pulls alongside me for the kill. I ask but can't command any more speed out of my legs. My body does all it can to keep from slowing down as Somerset breaks the ribbon five yards in front of us, and Dodd steps ahead of me to finish second.

Across the line I let the stiffness brake me to a stroll and let go. Like a wave from a heavy magnet, disappointment bears down through me with the weight of a future falling inside and out and taking me with it until I lift my gaze and see Sarah jumping and my family standing, shouting, letting me know I'm alive, I'm here, full of heat and fury-spent and loss, and I cannot escape. With the whirlwind left to spin itself down in my head, I walk from the raceway into the crowd where I hear the voices again, some calling me by the name of "Harlan."

24

Brahms' way

WITH THE DEFEAT FRESH AND THE HALF-MILE RACE AGAINST Somerset and Dodd two hours away, I tell Mother I'm taking a break. "Take this," she offers me a cup of limeade cold from the Thermos. I savor the drink plus a refill and ask if anyone wants to walk around the campus. Marci says she will go with me and stop by her office. Not Sarah. Sarah wants to watch a Benham boy jump the high hurdles because he said "hi" to her when she waited for me near the track.

Marci and I weave out of the crowd, around the back of the high-windowed 1907 building and over the arched brick breezeway to the library, to the front side of the campus where we drift off the sidewalk into the shade of the leaves. Marci asks how Dad is doing. I brace at the question but answer that he is walking well, with a small swing of his left leg. In the distance a "pop!" triggers a race and a scream-spiked mess of cheering.

From the canopy of the trees we angle to the sidewalk in front of the Pfeiffer Hall dormitory and to the back of the chapel where we enter the Fine Arts Building. As Marci unlocks her office I wander upstairs and down the hall. Through the window of a music room I spot two kettledrums waiting for me, just as the unused timpani waited for me in the equipment room at Harlan High after band practice. The door is unlocked so I slip in, take the soft-ended drumsticks and tap the drums, tightening the rim knobs until I get a vibrant pitch. Striking a few times and leaning my ear close down, I enjoy the hum until it fades off the drumhead.

Marci appears and leans against the doorframe. "You should learn to play the timpani."

After another tap disappears beyond my hearing, I rest the sticks crossways on the drum where I found them. "I played the triangle in the third grade rhythm band, but that doesn't qualify. I'm not a natural drummer."

"How do you know?"

"I've heard true drummers and watched their hands. They're born with something. Like you — you're a natural at music." I step into the hallway so she can close the door and walk with me down the staircase. This day she seems closer to me than usual, because of the empathy she put into my race, I believe.

She explains, "I work at music."

"You work at it because you like it and pick it up fast. Where did that come from?" Dad said Marci loved to play the piano and violin when she was in first grade and never had any doubt about what she wanted to do. After earning her bachelor's degree at Union, she went to Indiana University for her master's and doctorate. She also said she learned some Hebrew and Sanskrit – harder than Latin – to do her dissertation on word-sounds common to different religions. To me that research was a long way from playing a violin, but she said she enjoyed it.

"Genes, I guess." She smiles at the string-bean pun she is about to make. "String genes."

"How did the music get in those genes?"

"The same way running got in yours, I daresay."

In her office, where three posters of her concerts line the wall across from her desk, Marci studies sheets of paper, places them in a folder in the filing cabinet and locks it. "This is one of my works-in-progress, the piece I played at Christmas. It has been more work than progress, to be honest. It has been very difficult to get out."

"Composing must be slow business."

"It usually develops pretty quickly for me once I get the theme in my head."

"Do you ever hear sounds in your dreams?"

"Sometimes."

"What do you do with them?"

"Nothing. I can't remember them when I wake up, hard as I try. Some composers have gone into a very concentrated, semi-trance-like state and *perceived* music coming through them, but that is different from dreaming."

"They hear music coming from where?"

"Johannes Brahms says it is from Spirit, the soul."

"I bet that was a nice surprise the first time he heard it. The prophet gets the future, and he gets a concert."

"It was grandeur to him. He put himself into a state of awareness he called the superconscious. The book – it's here somewhere – let me find it." Marci turns to the wall of bookshelves across and beside her desk, leaving me with the view of the back of her wavy, almost frizzy hair, inherited from her mother.

She tilts a book forward, the way Jug as a kid looked off the end of the high diving board at the city pool to see how far it was to the water. The book makes a short tumble, hardly scary at all, into her certain hands. She passes the volume to me – *Talks With Great Composers*, by Arthur M. Abell. I leaf through it and hand it back.

As she returns the book to the space where it will stand at attention until called on again, Marci goes on, "Brahms said he went into a contemplative frame of mind and prayed for inspiration to compose something uplifting. He sensed vibrations that formed into images and themes – whole compositions. He had been moved to do this after finding out how Milton, Tennyson,

132

Goethe, Beethoven and others said they were inspired to do their works."

Following Marci out of her office as she fishes in her large purse to find her key, I ask, "Have you ever heard music coming through?"

"I imagine parts and put them together, but not like Brahms – I don't actually *hear* a symphony playing front to end."

"Tell me when you do. That sounds very handy to me – getting yourself a free symphony, or maybe a song, do you suppose, like *Long Tall Sally*?"

"I don't know if *Long Tall Sally* answers a prayer to uplift mankind."

"It uplifted me."

"You weren't aiming very high."

"I needed to laugh and dance."

"I'm pleased to know those needs in you were fulfilled."

"Even so, I would like to hear what Brahms heard."

"Apparently one has to know how to listen the right way," she concludes, adding a "thank you, sir" as I clunk the crossbar of the exit door and push it open.

"That's the trick, sounds like."

SHORTLY AFTER WE rejoin the family in the bleachers, the announcer makes the first call for the 880-yard run. Sarah descends with me to the slope where I lace on my spikes and limber up in the grass beyond the first turn until a hurdle race finishes and workers clear the way for me to walk in the cinder grip of the track again.

"Second call for the 880."

I half-resign myself to the possibility that I might not come in first or second in this event either. Quickly, that resignation stews into a bitter brew hardening an impulse hot in my forehead: *If they are going to win, I'll make them pay hard for it. I'll go out at a fast pace and see what happens.*

A fast start is not what you do best.

A fast start would surprise them.

Surprise doesn't matter diddlysquat at the front end of a race unless the surprise gets you across the finish line ahead of the others.

I should at least tail Dodd or Somerset early, ride them close.

What if they take you off your pace and you do worse?

Then I'll try it only if it feels right. I just want to ride one or the other; both of them if I can.

Don't wish for something you haven't thought through – you could get it, as Momma says. You should want to win, not ride them.

The half-mile is a shorter race, though. I can afford to ride them earlier.

Let's go through this again – what's the point here?

To try something different.

You don't just want to try something different. You're frustrated.

Dodd rode me on the last lap of the mile and beat me. I can get motivation and maybe a tactic out of this.

He rode you because you passed him, and he was trying to stay close enough to pass you back, which he did at the finish. You sped up earlier than you planned in the mile, and you ended up with muscles near paralyzed in that last push. Run your race.

I'll decide after the gun. I'll only ride them if it feels right.

Don't let them throw you off.

I'll figure it out.

"Third and final call for the 880."

In the lineup I'm placed between Dodd and Somerset. Red Bird is positioned behind the Oneida Baptist racer who made his move in the mile too early to keep it up. I breathe deep to pump oxygen into my blood until I feel light and seething on the trigger. The starter instructs us, orders us to get ready, to get set, and bangs us into a stampede that sorts itself out in fifty yards.

The leaders enter the first curve in a tight line:

1 – Oneida Baptist

2 – Red Bird

3 – Clay County off Red Bird's shoulder

4 – Somerset

5 – Bobby Dodd of Knox Central

6 – Me

7 – I don't know

You're in the middle of this pack tailing Dodd, and what does he care? You're using up your oxygen high, going faster than your pace. Now what?

I can't drop back.

Why not?

I'm up here on Dodd's back.

He won't miss you.

I'll miss him.

Out of the curve and onto the straight, the spitfire pace feels good so far, but *am I running my race or theirs?*

You said you would think about it.

I think I'm running theirs. I have no choice.

You always have a choice.

I'm not going to drop back unless my body makes me.

I hold on. Everyone ahead of me holds on. At the start of the second curve I see that our front group has pushed ahead of the second cluster. We have two races going.

Midway around the second bend, Dodd challenges Somerset. *Trying to take on the favorite on a curve in the first lap? This is new.* I wait to see what happens before deciding what to do. Dodd follows through and edges around Somerset and Clay County. *Big move.*

Out of the second curve we straighten out:

135

1 – Oneida Baptist

2 – Red Bird

3 – Dodd

4 – Clay County

5 – Somerset

6 – Me

I'm on the back of Somerset who is going to overtake Clay County and I have to go with him. As we drive between the spectators bulging on both sides of the starting post, Somerset strides past Clay County; I gear up with him.

Somerset moves on up the line and passes Dodd as I follow, running fierce and feeling it at the halfway mark. *What have I gotten myself into?*

Near the third curve Somerset sails around Red Bird, not my style of race but I follow along, churning blood and breath through me in high dudgeon – cells yelling in the lungs and arteries, "What's going on here?" – but they can't stop long enough to hear anything over the muscles firing work their way.

Out of the third curve:

1 – Oneida Baptist

2 – Somerset

3 – Me

Just behind: Red Bird, Clay County, Dodd, in that order last I saw them.

Dodd's not going to stay back there, and I don't know how Oneida Baptist is hanging onto the lead because this bunch is not coasting at all.

On my right a pair of legs chunk up to me with shorter steps than mine, like a toy gone mad – *Red Bird?* Yes, Red Bird spins a half step ahead of me, so I push up to keep him from getting a full step out. I don't see how anyone can whirl legs like that past a quarter-mile. *Dodd's the one to worry about because that boy can last and surely he is going to get up here close before this straightaway ends.* Red Bird can't switch to the inside lane in front of me because I am tailing Somerset close, with just enough space to keep safe from the slash of spikes. *Here comes Dodd, what did I tell ya,* wide on the third lane around Red Bird and me, angling in next to Somerset, leaving me behind Oneida Baptist and a two-man wall of Somerset and Dodd, with Red Bird at my side. *I'm trapped in here. When is Oneida going to overheat the way he did in the mile?*

Maybe this is Oneida Baptist's kind of race. You wanted a surprise.

I wanted to make the surprise. This is chaos.

You love it.

Three-fourths the way down the backstretch, *somebody's got to break.* Red Bird gives in to the grind and drifts back from my shoulder. Near the last curve Oneida Baptist maintains his lead, followed by Somerset who is blocked by Dodd to his right while I am stuck behind both of them unless I swing wide on the turn.

Halfway around the curve, Oneida Baptist speeds up enough to give Somerset space to angle into the second lane in front of Dodd. I shove myself into Somerset's old spot on the inside lane before Dodd can take it for himself. His field clear, Somerset unleashes and takes the lead, but Oneida Baptist blocks me in front and Dodd holds me in on the right. I want Oneida Baptist to give me clearance the way he moved up enough to give Somerset a corner in which to slip out, but this time Oneida Baptist does the opposite – he slows and forces me a step behind Dodd. *I'mrunningoutoftimehereCRAP!*

Out of the last curve:

1 – Somerset

2 and 3 – Oneida Baptist and Dodd, side by side

4 – Me

Fifty yards left – I can't stay behind the wall. I have to gamble, so I sling all the way out to the right of Dodd who has Oneida Baptist on his left, a three-man line. Somerset is gone, out front by himself, his girlfriend probably shrieking so high only a dog can hear her. This is a fight for second place.

Each second gets a life of its own as Oneida Baptist pulls a notch ahead of Dodd; *sudden death – this is it.* Dodd loses just enough ground to give me hope, so I unload what's left against Oneida Baptist. He unloads what he has left against me and edges ahead, slow motion in the center of a fast film. I am losing to him, *no no no,* but I will hold off Dodd this time, *push it, push it!*

      1 – Bradshaw Perkins, Somerset
      2 – Vernon Wallis Jr., Oneida Baptist
      3 – Jeremiah James, Harlan
      4 – Bobby Dodd, Knox Central

I'll be back.

25

Recognition

I WAS BACK ON THE RISE OF IVY STREET, ON THE LONG ROAD TO THE 1957 season the day after my losses in the regional meet. When Bradshaw Perkins of Somerset took the state championship in the mile and second place behind a Louisville runner in the half-mile, I was relaxed to be running on Ivy Hill once more, waving back at people in cars, stopping to talk to well-wishers in driveways and yards and sidewalks, sprinting only when I needed to release the charge that made my legs restless if I sat too much or moved too slow too long.

The week before the summer break, school took on the ease of spring despite the last exams, and I looked forward to the Friday evening assembly where student accomplishments would be mentioned, settling the glory into memories among friends. Marci drove in for the occasion and walked with Sarah, Mother and me to Harlan High for Recognition Night. Dad felt a little dizzy and stayed home. When I sat down with my family women, I realized that my seat was the same one I sat in as an eighth grader when we were herded into the auditorium for a mental health movie. In that movie I expected to see someone who, for example, thought he was President Eisenhower though he didn't even look like him.

Instead, on the screen I saw a boy about my age, in a regular family, with a little sister, even. The boy screamed because he was upset over not getting dessert. As if that weren't enough, he smacked and threw a toy that didn't work. The kid was spoiled and twitchy on his trigger, I could see that, but did he have a mental health problem? I never yelled for dessert – not with Dad in

139

the house – but as soon as I was big enough to cut the grass I found it relieving to kick the gas mower when it wouldn't start even after I pulled the cord so many times my shoulder hurt. Sometimes when I kicked the lawn mower it started after another pull or two, so I understood this kid in the movie. After seeing this film, though, I realized that when I wanted to kick the lawn mower, I had to keep enough control of myself to hit it in a place where nobody would see me.

On Recognition Night I anticipated the satisfaction of being mentioned as the district champion miler and half-miler before an audience of my schoolmates, mother, and sisters.

After the program opened with the Harlan High School fight song, three girls from the Awards Committee took the stage – senior Samantha Brock, a girl I didn't know well except as a cheerleader who could jump to the ground in a split; junior Gretchen Ames, who sold me those two kisses at the Halloween booth; and sophomore Lucy Giddon. After recognizing the valedictorian and salutatorian, they presented the Drama Award to curly-haired Jessica Dandamus who, when reading Shakespeare, fell into talking in his style. After Jessica returned to her seat, other schoolmates went to the stage for being the best this and best that. Applause, applause.

The second half of the program honored the athletes. The football team was called to the stage first. All-conference players like Horse listened politely to summaries of their accomplishments. I missed the seniors already.

Then the basketball team was brought to the stage. Same thing. Then the baseball team. A few all-around athletes, like Ricky Seals, didn't even bother to walk all the way back to their seats between recognitions.

Mother pressed my arm. The only sport left was track.

Samantha announced that was the end of the program and that

everyone should be given a round of applause. Mother looked at me, stunned. Sarah asked, "What?" Marci's eyes squinted under furrowed brows.

I looked across the way to see Scotty Lanier's reaction – a sour half-grin and shrug of his shoulders.

As the audience streamed out, Mother kept her seat a minute to cool off. I wondered what she would do to a cranky lawn mower if she had one at this moment – shove it off the hill, I bet.

When the people around us cleared, Mother fumed, "I am going to talk to Dr. Clark about this." Dr. Clark was the superintendent and a friend of my parents.

"No, Mom," I said. "Let it go. It's done."

"It's not done."

I patted her hand, "It's done." The day her father died in the VA hospital in Memphis in 1937, a World War I veteran in the next bed told Mother that when Granddad couldn't take his medicine, the nurse shook him so hard he had a coughing fit that took him into a coma. Hearing that, Mother – the gentlest of women – tromped to the nurses' station to find that nurse to kill her with her own hands – that's what she said. Grandmother and Aunt Betsy stopped her. I didn't want Mother going after someone in the school hallway. Besides, I didn't know who did what, though I figured Lucy Giddon didn't speak up for me.

Marci exclaimed, "I can't believe this."

I said, "Maybe they forgot."

"That is too big to forget. Something is very wrong here."

"It's done," I said, "let's go," and dealt with it as best I could. Late the next morning, in the heat of the day, I hauled the mower out of the basement to cut the grass around the house. The engine puttered to life on the first pull of the cord and kept running without so much as a cough even when I shoved and yanked it horizontally across the slope so steep that gas dripped out of the

141

air hole of the tank cap. This mower knew how to be a friend when it really counted; and it knew that, from this day forward, it could take as long as it wanted to start and I would not say a cross word to it ever again, nor let it die of anything except a peaceful, natural death.

Sarah's diary – June 1, 1956

JJ cut the grass on all the slopes in less than an hour. It usually takes him more than two. I was IMPRESSED!

26

Priscilla

THE WINDOWS ALLOWED ENOUGH AIR TO COOL DOWN DAD'S HIGH-ceilinged, second-floor office looking down on Main at the corner of Central where the bustle pulled us all the more outside, to the mine offices up the hollows of Martin's Fork and Clover Fork. Yet through the day, when my mind unlocked from my work, I thought of Jenny Lee and looked forward to talking with her in the evenings.

In the midst of all this, two weeks into the summer break, our family sat around the dining room table for a Sunday after-church dinner with Uncle Clyde and Aunt Clara. Halfway through the salad – a split banana topped with a streak of mayonnaise holding crushed peanuts, on a leaf of lettuce – Mother turned to me and said that Mrs. Handley next door mentioned that her nieces were coming for a visit on Wednesday.

"Oh?" I said, "Priscilla and Patricia?"

"Yes," she said, "from Dayton."

"That's nice," I concluded. Full force I remembered Priscilla coming to me in my seventh-grade desolation – the girl who, prettier than imagination, held my hand in the woods behind my house; who kissed me in the heat of the attic, and who drove away in the husky blue Hudson. The summer she left, whenever I walked down my steps to the sidewalk along the stone-block retaining wall, I remembered that sedan leaving with barely an engine sound, just brake lights to slow the descent, drifting around the corner to Second Street, where Priscilla waved goodbye one last time through the window.

After Uncle Clyde and Aunt Clara took their leave, I headed downtown, thinking about my seventh grade summer and how the only thing that stayed fairly still since then probably was the look of T.C. Hunter's store, where I paused to see if his display was the same as the week before and it was, including three women's hats, the kind I saw in old-time black and white movies where everyone talked fast. I wondered if Priscilla had changed as little as his display.

On Wednesday, Dad and I drove home for lunch after a meeting at the Brookside mine. As we finished the deviled eggs and baked beans Miss Becker cooked for us – she knew I liked those, and I thanked her heartily – I heard a car door slam, so I casually excused myself to go upstairs to Sarah's room to look through binoculars out the windows that faced the Handleys' house and yard. Two trim girls, along with sportily dressed parents, unloaded luggage from a car – a red and white 1956 Ford; *how times change*. There was Priscilla, still classically cut, even from a distance. I tracked them until they and the voices disappeared into the house. During the rest of my workday I wondered if they would call me. By bedtime I had my answer: No.

The following day, as my father and I leaned up the sidewalk on the way home in mid-day, Dad stopped to catch his breath and a "Hi, there!" spilled from a brick-walled landing off the front steps of the Handley house.

"Is that you, JJ?" A girl, in sunglasses and a swimsuit looked down.

"Patricia?"

"Long time, no see."

"It has been a while."

"Come on up."

I came on up as Dad continued home. Looking shiny with Johnson & Johnson Baby Oil mixed with iodine, Patricia came down a few steps to kiss me on the cheek, reminding me how nice baby oil smelled. Without rising from her aluminum lounging chair, Priscilla gestured with a polite but unexcited "Hi."

Patricia said, "You are looking good."

"Thanks. You, too." Whenever I could, I studied Priscilla to find the old picture in her and update it. I asked Priscilla, "How long will you be here?"

"Ten days."

"How have you been?"

"Fine, and you?"

"Fine."

Is this all? Even if the childhood passion passed long ago, isn't there some nostalgia about it, some curiosity about how it settled out?

Priscilla let her head fall back on the chair. She wanted her tan.

Sitting with me on the low wall, Patricia asked about Chief and Stoner, so I offered to organize a picnic with them Saturday. Agreed.

Without raising herself from the plastic webs that would crisscross-mark her skin if she didn't turn over often enough, Priscilla saluted her left hand above her brow to shield the sun as she looked at me with a "Bye."

What the heck, I thought, and invited Zorro and his whip to the picnic. I called Jenny and invited her. "Sure," she said, without asking her parents first.

On Saturday afternoon I led the other two cars up Black Mountain and onto the rocky road to the cabin in the clearing by the pond. As the group carted food, records and Sarah's hi-fi player from the cars, I ordered Zorro to let everyone know we were there.

Zorro slumped quietly to a clearing, unsnapped his bullwhip from the leather holder on his belt, and, as if transformed by a full moon, whirled the whip over his head until it made a propeller-like noise, and then cracked it front and behind, startling us with the sharp loudness of it. He lashed combinations of one crack, two cracks, three cracks, then leather-snapped a beat, finally aiming the tip at a pile of leaves he POWed loudly off the ground. After pausing to let the echo play out, he jerked the length of the whip to him in gathering circles he caught with his left hand, looking sharp.

When the firecracker dance faded out of our eardrums, Zorro, back to normal, smiled his thin lips and took a little bow to the applause that sounded spindly in that aftermath. Jenny and Patricia laughed. Priscilla looked bewildered. I wanted her to be bewildered.

Jenny walked up to Zorro, held out her hand and offered, "Here."

He opened his hand. "What is it?"

"Red dog," she said, as she handed the smooth pebble to him.

I explained, "It's made from burned slate. Natural combustion."

"Thank you," he acknowledged. "What do I do with it?"

Jenny answered, "Whatever you want."

We set out the food on the porch and started off on a hike to an overlook on a ridge. A late-afternoon breeze followed the yellow cast of the sun through the leaves, keeping us from sweating on an easy climb. By the time we scaled a hump of rocks on the spine of the mountain, the whole group was talking familiarly. Only the sweeping view of the lumpy-green valley southward quieted us. I stepped to the back of the boulders so I could study Priscilla and Jenny together. Trying to make sense of these two, whose images had streamed through me like two seas now brought together, I compared Priscilla's short brown hair to Jenny's, glistening dark; Priscilla's straight and slender nose to Jenny's nose upturned; Priscilla's perfect mouth, on a jaw line smooth and feminine, to Jenny's dimpled smile; Priscilla's sleekness to Jenny's shapeliness. *So, what is the difference, really?*

146

The difference was that Priscilla did not look back. Jenny turned to see where I was and, finding me, momentarily lifted her shoulders to her chin with an exaggerated, almost giggly, smile before returning to the view.

27

Life Savers

LATE IN THE AFTERNOON THE DAY AFTER OUR MASON POND OUTING I didn't even have Priscilla as a friend, but I had Stoner as a friend, sitting behind the wheel of his Plymouth ordering milkshakes and onion rings from the carhop at Denny Ray's and telling me that *he* liked Priscilla. I thought that if the world was going to spin us around, let's spin and see where we land; couldn't stop it anyway. I told Stoner I didn't blame him for liking her but asked what he was doing with me in the car. He said he was talking. I told him to go to the pay phone and call Priscilla. He said he didn't know if she would go out with him.

As he said that, Chief carefully wheeled his father's Lincoln next to us. All Chief's movements, outside of football, were methodical, even his laugh. Beside Chief sat Patricia. Chief's clothes had a clean bleach smell from ten yards away. Chief was usually clean, thanks to his mother's laundering, but this night there probably weren't more than three germs on him when he left his house. I told Stoner he should find out where Priscilla was. He said he might.

"What do you mean, 'might'?"

"Let me do this my way," Stoner said.

"By the time you do it your way," I told him, "she'll be sailing out of Harlan in that Ford, heading up to her boyfriends in Dayton, Ohio. They probably keep them in the National Guard Armory up there." I rolled down my window and shouted, "Where's Priscilla?" I had courage asking about girls when I wasn't asking for myself.

Patricia shouted back, "Hi, JJ. She's at the house."

"Thanks," I said. I looked at my watch and told Stoner, "Go to the pay phone and call her. The Handleys' number is 193."

Hulking into the restaurant, Stoner leaned into the pay phone and returned with sweat on his upper lip. "I'm taking you home."

"Good," I said. The carhop brought our food. We paid and told her to take the car-window tray, and I told Stoner we needed to take care of the Sunny Acres dog.

Stoner motored us through Sunny Acres, slowing down for the spike-haired little dog to bark close enough that I could douse him with the ice water. Dead-on. The dog yelped extra. "This is a good night. I get this dog and you get Priscilla. Where are you going to take her?"

"Denny Ray's," Stoner explained.

"Then give me your onion rings."

"I'm saving my onion rings for when I bring her out here."

"These are high-powered onion rings, not the sweet kind they usually fry. You don't want these onion rings if there is a chance you will kiss Priscilla or talk to her closer than two feet. You want Life Savers, peppermint; five at a time is better."

"I didn't say I was going to kiss Priscilla."

"You have a week. After that, you can kiss her goodbye."

Back on Ivy Street, Stoner pulled his car close to the small, grassy embankment that rose from the curb to the sidewalk, got out, inhaled, tucked in his shirt, and ascended to the Handleys' door. I walked halfway up my steps next door, sat, and leaned back to watch the twilight sky and listen to the sounds of Stoner and Priscilla getting in the car. I was happy for my friend. I had known one Priscilla and he knew another Priscilla. My Priscilla was better, but mine was gone, and Stoner's would be soon.

My porch screen door slammed. Sarah's footsteps approached. Her voice asked, "What are you doing here?"

149

"Looking at the sky. Where are you going?"

"Denny Ray's, with Bernie and some friends."

"Are you packed for camp tomorrow?"

"Done."

"Then have fun."

"What are you gonna do?"

"I'm gonna think about what to do. At Denny Ray's, make sure Bernie tries the onion rings. They're good."

"I know what you're up to," Sarah said.

"I ate some."

"That's why you're outside by yourself."

Sarah is growing up, I thought as she stood at my side, smelling of a light rose perfume, no match for Bernie's cologne. Recognizing that I had better take advantage of the evening before everyone disappeared and left me on the cement of the steps, I asked Sarah if she had any Life Savers. She did. Spearmint. Close enough. "Can I have some?"

"How many?"

"The pack."

She gave it to me, and I put five pieces in my mouth and went inside and phoned Jenny to ask what was going on. Jenny said she had just come back from Bessie Harper's, her parents were at the country club, Barbara was in Lexington for the weekend checking out the University of Kentucky campus where she was headed in the fall, and Miss Mira had given Jenny a rock from Stonehenge if I wanted to see it, which I did, so up the hill I went.

Taking my hand as I came through her door, Jenny led me to the display shelf and took from it a fist-sized stone, gray-blue, marbled with white.

"Miss Mira said her cousin picked it off the ground about a hundred yards from the megaliths. Look, it's bluestone," Jenny glistened at it. "Maybe some pieces got chipped off and scattered as people scavenged the monuments."

I examined the stone. "Heavy."

"Miss Mira said that in medieval times people around Stonehenge thought the bluestone had healing powers. Some would place it in their baths for cures."

"Then it would be a good thing to hold."

"It couldn't hurt."

After I turned the stone a few more times and handed it back, she held it in front of her, as if weighing it, and then asked, "Would you like something to drink? Seven-Up? Grape juice?"

"Seven-Up." I didn't want blue teeth just now. As Jenny clacked ice and piffed open the soft drink bottle in the kitchen, I sat on the sofa, slipped two Life Savers into my mouth, and observed the large wall photographs of her and Barbara as preschool children. The chubby-cheeked Jenny in the picture wore a large bow on the back of her head, and looked at the camera with the same alert eyes.

She asked, "Would you like some chips? Music?"

"Music sounds nice. Something light."

She stepped to the stack of long-playing records on the radio-record-player cabinet and offered, "Mozart's Number 27 Concerto for Piano and Orchestra is nice. Or there's Frank Sinatra."

"Let's do Frank. Would you like a Life Saver?"

She took one. I took the rest.

With the record in place, Sinatra started singing *One More for the Road*. I asked to see her family photo album on the table. She sat beside me as I leafed through the black and white Kodak prints of Jenny – sitting up as a baby, riding a tricycle, smiling in her mother's arms, holding her father's hand, graduating from kindergarten, and then looking straight at the camera for her school picture, so young. Now she was technically in high school.

Frank Sinatra finished his *One More for the Road* song to the bartender. Some violins started up a tune, sounding familiar. His voice drew us in to *Autumn Leaves.*

I said, "That's my song."

"Do you want me to skip to the next one or let it play?"

"We'll let it play."

With the orchestra floating behind Sinatra, the lyrics of the leaves fell lightly on me as Jenny pressed her head against my shoulder. At that, the wiring of my chest ran its overload enough for me to hear my pulse on the edge of the song as I bent forward and kissed her once and then again for a longer, gentle time in the center of my storm. As we sat back on the couch, we talked of parents and sisters; of Mr. Cobb fidgeting; of how colors made us feel; of Walt Whitman's words; of moonshine; and of the cheap movie sets in *Thunder Road,* the film that supposedly showed Harlan, with mountains not really ours. We guessed at the mysteries of Stonehenge, a time I couldn't see, but I could see ahead enough to know this summer would be mine, almost no matter what.

Sarah's diary – June 15, 1956

Bernie, Linda, Amanda, Willa Mae, Dinky, Bear and I packed in Pooch's Chevy and went to Denny Ray's. Willa Mae and Amanda's crinoline took up a lot of room. So did Bear. When I sat on Bernie's lap he put his hands on my waist. I think he enjoyed having me close, though his leg went to sleep, and he had to get out to walk around.

July 3, 1956

I was thrilled to get my second letter from Bernie with his little handwriting all scrunched up. The longer I am at camp the more I miss him and look forward to his letters. Writing each other is even better than being together sometimes.

At Rock Loop yesterday Jane and I met Bobby Joe and his friend Cotton, with blond hair and GREEN eyes. Cotton gave me a lanyard key chain he made.

July 12, 1956

We met Cotton and Bobby Joe at Rock Loop during free time after supper. Cotton asked if I wanted to see a secret cave he found, so I sneaked off with him. The cave was not more than six feet deep. Sitting close, I felt warm in it. We didn't hold hands or anything, but I got very happy and confused. What would I think if Bernie sat close to another girl? I would not like it – if I knew about it. Cotton lives in Knoxville, so we won't become girlfriend and boyfriend. We're just camp friends. I'm meeting him there again on Tuesday just for fun. (!!!!!)

28

To the moon

SUMMER WARMED UP ZORRO. HE ASKED IF HE COULD HELP OUR Scout troop load newspapers from Mrs. Hacker's house when I told him that Mr. Crane had bought a 1947 Ford pickup truck, which we would use for hauling. On the appointed day, the other Scouts milled around the corner of Cumberland Avenue while I met Mr. Crane as he pulled up to the white frame house in need of fresh paint, in contrast to the shiny red of the truck.

I told Mr. Crane that Zorro would be helping us because he wanted to see the restoration work on the pickup.

"Larry Baines, eh?" Mr. Crane pulled back his cloth fishing hat in order to scratch his thick, white-streaked hair. "His daddy would have liked it."

"I should have guessed that."

"Cat Baines knew how to drive and how to fix anything with wheels. He died in '49 coming down the south side of Cumberland Gap. He ran moonshine back before the war."

I couldn't have guessed that one. "Risky business."

"You'd think a riskier business would be driving a fuel truck for Patton's tanks as he fought through Europe, but Cat came clean through that. In '49 he slid off the road all by himself, on ice. Isn't that the irony? He lost control on those curves south of the gap whipping down to that little slice of Virginia. Going to Tazewell for machine parts. He fixed up coal trucks after the war, and did machining work on mining equipment for me."

As Zorro arrived and leaned into the pickup to smell the truckness of it, Mr. Crane punched his cousin's doorbell. Mrs.

Hacker, in a loose white cotton dress and fuzzy slippers, peeked through the curtain, opened the door and told him he could come in and "bring the boys." As we entered, Mrs. Hacker stood watch at the corner of her living room, probably wondering if I remembered she owed me $18. She kept her post as we grunted armloads of the *Enterprise*, the *Knoxville News-Sentinel* and *Courier-Journal* from the stacks that hid two walls of her back bedroom, barely leaving space for a window obscured by a yellowish pull-down blind. We filled the truck bed, tied a tarp over the load, and filled a second pickup truck Chief borrowed from his father.

Mr. Crane asked Zorro if he wanted to drive. Zorro was alert enough to say, "Yes, Sir," instead of his customary, "Yeah." The rest of us followed in Chief's truck to the paper-collection site at the incinerator east of town. After unloading, Mr. Crane dropped me off at Huff Park for my workout. Zorro said he wanted to come with me. At the field, Zorro took the same spot in the center of the bleachers where he sat the winter afternoon he told me he liked Sarah. He seemed satisfied to have Sarah as a friend these days.

In the middle of a five-lap run, I saw Lucy Giddon and her friend Verna emerge from the city pool entrance, their hair combed back damp. As the girls strolled to the sidelines of the field and neared the bleachers, Verna threw down her swimsuit bag and held Lucy. I cut short my lap, dashed across the field to them and asked what was wrong.

Verna exclaimed, "She's light in the head."

I helped Lucy sit on the lowest bleacher plank and told her to lean forward and put her head between her knees. I had learned that in Boy Scout First Aid but never used it before. My main First Aid interest was treating snakebite with a tourniquet, razor blade and suction bulb I carried around in my kit, but nobody ever got bit, so this fainting had to suffice.

As Zorro tromped down the stands, I asked him to bring my

windbreaker, which he draped across Lucy's shoulders. I asked Lucy how she was feeling. The back of her wavy brunette hair was messy from how she gripped it. Weakly she reported, "Better."

"Wait a while," I suggested.

"Yeah," Zorro added, "take it easy."

After a few minutes, Lucy raised her head slowly and asked to stand. With help, she steadied herself and reported she felt stronger. I asked where she lived and if she wanted me to get my folks' car to take her home.

"No, thank you," she replied. "I live on Rain Street, across the river, not too far. I'm taking the bridge by the school. I need to walk."

Zorro said, "Then let me go with you. Is that OK?"

Lucy nodded yes, removed my windbreaker and handed it back to me, saying, "It's pretty, the way you run."

A compliment? "Thank you."

Zorro gave her his arm and she took it, escort style, as the three of them walked along the field and up the steps to Clover Street. I resumed my workout but did not feel like pushing at full speed. This was a time to run steady and even, the way the summer was going, with Sarah active at Camp Sochee and I content to work for Dad.

From camp, Sarah wrote me that she had been thinking about what she wanted to do in high school, that she would not resume ballet lessons with Miss Mira in the fall, that regular dancing suited her. She also wrote that talk of Jenny Lee and me was getting around in Harlan. I didn't know whom Sarah was writing, but I had waited for months for the talk to surface around me, and now I heard it only from my little sister in the Smoky Mountains. So at Sunday school, while the teacher tried to explain the Psalm, "Be still and know that I am God," I fidgeted and asked Lois if she heard any talk about me. "Nothing new," she replied. "Aren't you still walking on Ivy Hill with Jenny?"

I was free. Even the smell of fresh-cut grass on a hot summer day greened the season in me. My runs were long and easy, and life in the house was cheerful, too, especially when Sarah returned from camp, slimmer and restless to see her friends and Bernie. Except to see my friends occasionally, I didn't drive to Denny Ray's, for I knew Jenny would not be there. On some evenings I brought Jenny to the porch to relax and listen to Gogi Grant sing *The Wayward Wind* and even listen to some of Sarah's music.

On an early Friday evening in August, as I picked up Jenny for an outing, I asked her what she would like to do. "I'll let you choose," she offered. "Where would you like to go?"

In a sorry attempt at cuteness, I answered, "The moon."

She thought about it for a moment – "Then I will take you there," and navigated me to Brookside, east of Harlan, then up the side of a hill used as a mine dump. Fascinated, I strolled with her to the edge of the slate leavings, black and gray. Here and there along the slope, smoke curled and flames lit out of what looked like shattered flat-stone armor from a long night war that left nothing standing. The destruction cascaded to the edge of the downhill forest bracing against its progress.

After a long while gazing, I took the hand of Jenny, whose cream-colored dress and summer skin glowed life against the barrenness. I turned us to each other, as in a one-step dance we knew, and told her that I loved her. Almost in a whisper, she replied.

29

The law of physics

THE MORNING LIGHT, SO WELCOMED IN THE KITCHEN WHERE I lugged three fresh bottles of Chappell's Dairy milk from the back door, gave no warning. As I scooted past Dad I caught a trace of his Old Spice aftershave lotion that Mother liked. He wore his pressed khaki work clothes because we had an appointment at Crummies Creek, eleven miles south of town near the Virginia border on highway 421. I always had an uneasy feeling about the Crummies commissary after Mother told me how, before I was born, mine operators brought out machine guns and union miners shot at coal trucks and beat up other miners – scabs – who crossed the picket lines – for me, too much meanness on either side. But despite strikes now and then, Harlan had moved past the organizing war days when National Guard troops rumbled in to keep the peace. These days mines and miners mostly seemed to be trying to hang on to what they could keep.

After putting away the milk, I slid into my seat at the kitchen table as Dad bowed his head to say the blessing.

"Father..." he began. After a few moments of silence, I opened my eyes.

Dad nervously pressed his fingers to his forehead and blinked his eyes as if to see more clearly.

Mother asked, "What's wrong, Steve?"

When Dad rose from his chair weakly, I jumped up and held him, saying, "Let's get to a place to lie down." As gently as I could, I gathered him. Dad mumbled unintelligible words, and ten minutes later we had him in the hospital emergency room, outside of which

158

I sat stone still on the bench in the waiting room, talking only to encourage Mother.

After half an hour, Dr. Benton came to us and said that Dad's stroke had paralyzed his left side again and attacked his speech. They were doing all they could, and he would need more physical therapy when he was released.

The family gathered in Dad's hospital room, a fair location for him because it fronted Mound Street on the third floor where he could see the rooftops and hear the life of the streets. We divided up duties, giving me the overnight watch to give Dad water or turn him when he asked, to talk to him and help him with his eliminations, and to rub his limbs. When he slept, I napped on the floor until five in the morning, when Uncle Clyde came.

Dad showed no frustration, so I grew more hopeful that he would walk and talk again. He enjoyed listening to me reading him Ernest Hemingway's latest work, *The Old Man and the Sea*, at once his favorite book; he loved to fish.

The third day after Dad's stroke, Jenny asked to visit, so I brought her to his room shortly after Uncle Clyde helped Dad take lunch. As Jenny entered beside me, Uncle Clyde stood, the gentleman. Uncle Clyde was deep blue-eyed like Dad and strikingly handsome with his white hair. Whereas Dad as a young man would have nothing to do with guns, Uncle Clyde had packed a revolver when he returned from battlefields of France. Dad and Uncle Clyde seemed fearless to me, but in different ways.

In one of the chairs at the side of the bed, Jenny talked with us about what families she knew vacationed where, about what the stores were selling, ordinary things, and after an hour of so touched my father's hand and told him she would see him later. Dad paid attention, mumbled some and looked pleased to have her company. When she was done I walked her down the pale green hall, down the steps and to the paned-glass entrance room where, years before, polio patients were wheeled in so they could feel sunshine on their faces as they laid encased in iron lungs. It was as appropriate a place as any to wave to her goodbye.

My vacation came in pieces. The week before school resumed, I met the Lees at Norris Lake where Jenny's father took us in his outboard boat to a shallow cove where I had camped with my Scout friends the year before. Trusting us to be safe alone, he idled his Johnson Sea Horse engine as Jenny and I slid off the side, then he sped off. I followed his daughter the few yards to the shore and fetched a smooth, bark-stripped log bobbing in the wavelets.

Pushing the trunk into deeper water, I crawled onto it and tried to hold it steady as Jenny threw herself across the middle and twisted in order to sit up. The twisting rolled us over. For the next try, she mounted first, and I worked my way onto the log until I sat facing her, about two yards away, sensitive to every motion.

I challenged her: "Can you get me off without getting yourself off?"

She countered, "If I roll the log to get you off, I go off, too. It's the law of physics."

"What law of physics?"

"That for every action there is an equal reaction."

"It's not the law of physics that you will fall off if you move yourself counter to the motion of the log the way logrollers do."

"It's the law of physics if I'm not a logroller and can't move myself counter to the motion of the log. But I'll try," she ventured, then shrieked into the lake, tumbling me with her.

Back on the water horse, watching her laugh nervously when the log turned or bounced, I thought of how she had become the transparency through which I saw the brighter part of summer. Even while tending to Dad, I looked forward to the day and her presence in it. Balancing on the bobbing tree, I thought of how, a year from now, I would go off to college while Jenny would have three years left in high school. I knew she loved me with a young girl's heart, but I also knew that she would change as she got older, and I didn't know what the result of that would be.

With one hand gripping the log, she used the other to pull her wet hair back from her face, smiled the contrast of her sheet-white teeth against her skin that tanned easily, shrieked briefly as the log trembled, and asked, "What are you thinking over there? What are you up to?"

I confessed, "I'm wondering what you will think four years from now."

Closely monitoring the tree for any shift, she replied, "I'll think: four years ago I was on a log in Norris Lake with Jeremiah James, and it is time for him to call."

With that, Jenny disappeared off the side, causing the twirl of the log to sink me. Swimming beneath the surface, I emerged beside her and declared, "I'm calling now."

Frantically, she asserted, "You're early!"

"I have to be."

Sarah's diary – August 28, 1956

I have to quit biting my fingernails. People who chew their nails look weak and nervous.

Daddy needs me. I can't walk around gnawing on myself. Mama tells me how unsanitary it is. Willa Mae lets her dog Butch lick her lips as a "kiss" – now THAT's unsanitary!! The worst thing is how a stubby fingernail looks – worse with nail polish on it.

30

Some kind of phase

AT FIRST I HARDLY NOTICED THE HEAVINESS OF MIND THAT BEGAN TO slow me down, like a headache that didn't hurt but kept the zest of the brain for itself, in a fist. It started shortly after school began, after I brought Dad home from the hospital and carried him up the steps to the lightweight wheelchair that had seen temporary use with his first stroke. Now Dad also wore a fitted, latex-rubber groin bag to catch the urine that collected in a drain pocket strapped to his calf.

When I asked if he was ready to work his way back to normal, he signaled yes with a shake of his round head, now sunk deeper into his neck, his torso seeming smaller as his suspenders loosened from the slouch. With his good right hand he shakily picked up his left wrist and placed it in a more comfortable position on his lap.

On school days I helped dress Dad and get him to breakfast. Mother re-hired Homer to assist him in the middle of the day and take Dad to physical therapy at the Miners' Hospital across from Sunny Acres. We closed the office over the Cumberland Hardware, though I determined not to think about that and to concentrate instead on the fact that he was with us and would improve. We brought home his files for Mother to manage. Except for the metal swivel chair, which I kept, we gave the office furniture to Harold and Uncle Clyde, and sold his maps and blueprint machine to a fellow civil engineer, T. Basil Howard.

Two weeks after my father's return home, I felt the drag draining me when I tried to run up Ivy Hill. So I stopped at the

162

hairpin curve to rest on the hip-high stone wall where, during Christmas holiday snows of younger years, firefighters built bonfires for us and opened a fire hydrant to freeze Ivy Street so we could sled down it. As I waited for a signal in my body that its battery had found some amperage, Birdseed clumped down Ivy Hill around the turn, and, *what the heck*, I shouted to him, "How strong are you today, Birdseed?"

"A little strong, but not too much." With downhill-heavy steps he galumphed over to me, grinning funny, his shirt sticking out of the back of his pants.

I said, "I hope you don't want me to race you up this hill."

He glanced back at it. "Too steep."

"That's what I'm thinking. What do you do to get fired up for a run up a hill like that?"

"I don't run up nothing that hard unless I have to. If something is after me, I get fired up automatic-like. Why do you have to run up it?"

"To stay in condition."

"Run on somethin' flat."

"I've been doing that. I need to go up something tough like this."

"Then do what I do."

"What's that?"

"Do it tomorrow."

"There's a saying that 'tomorrow never comes.'"

"Who says? Tomorrow always comes. Yesterday was Tuesday. This is Wednesday."

"Good point, Birdseed. Thank you."

"Glad to help," he walked on down the street. "Just run up this thang tomorrow."

The following day I did as he said, determined to push my thickness past Jenny's cliff, past the second curve, past the hilltop

163

houses. From there I walked on the eastern loop toward the second flat, going to no place in particular. I hadn't been to the little cemetery since my walk there with Jenny the previous year, so I meandered up to the grave of Jerusha Tess, high above the Clover Fork River. The grave still had its little dip, and suddenly everything seemed immensely sad.

What do you want to indulge in, the sadness or the pretty woods?

I think I'll try some of this sadness. I cried for fifteen seconds.

That's enough. It's kind of a nice day out here.

Maybe this is some kind of phase.

Throughout the week the early fall leaves of Ivy Hill shimmered an invitation, but I didn't have the strength to lift my heaviness into their changing color, so I walked down to Huff Park as a way to get my body moving around the easier field on the faith that I would break out of this hold.

Mother grew concerned because I went to bed on time, after getting Dad ready and reading him *The Upper Room* lesson, one of them being how Jesus went into the desert for forty days to fast and pray, with the question being how much effort we put into devotions.

"What do you say to that, Dad? Can you manage that, forty days?"

Dad nodded yes, causing me to laugh. I added, "That's a long time."

Everything took a long time. In the lunchroom I asked Stoner if he had ever felt closed in, without energy. He said he had, but it passed; he advised me to wait it out. I didn't want to mention this seeming weakness to Jenny, and though I thought of her as much as before, I didn't see her as often, it was taking me so long to get other things done.

I saw Dozer forty minutes a day, in study hall where he, not Lois, now sat beside me, so in early October, as he stared out the

164

north windows facing Ivy Hill, I asked him if he ever had days it was hard for him to move.

"Every morning."

"I mean in the daytime, when you want to play football but can't."

"I always want to play football. Are you dragging? Is that it, Jaybird?"

"I'm dragging."

"There's some meaning behind it."

In English class Miss Garn had us looking for meanings, symbols, metaphors, and parallel themes in poems and passages. I asked Dozer, "What would you figure that meaning to be?"

"In my case, not wanting to get up in the morning is symbolic of the fact that I stay up too late. Or is that a metaphor?"

"Either one, I guess."

"It symbolizes the fact that I'm tired of the way Bell County plays dirty inside the line. Get it? I'm 'tired' of it. The satisfaction I want is to punch a hole in that line so hard that the guy in front of me rises off the ground before falling on his butt. You coming to the game Friday?"

"I don't know."

"If you do I'll show you how that symbolism works out. You don't have the flu, do you?"

"No, this isn't a body-ache thing. It feels more like a low battery."

"Good. I don't want any virus before the Bell County game. Last fall half the team was sick with flu on that trip to the Big Sandy Bowl. Lordy, lordy, we were like a TB ward that had been put up against Ohio State." Dozer gazed out the window a short while. "What were we talking about?"

"Death."

"There's a metaphor for you."

165

Sarah's diary – October 5, 1956

JJ didn't want to go to the game against Bell County because he said he had homework to do. I never heard that one before. He should have gone. Harlan won 18-13. I went to see Bernie play, but he didn't get in the game. Ricky Seals scored near the last when Dozer and Stoner busted a way for him at the goal line, so exciting.

Jenny went with me to get popcorn. We talked about the majorettes. She looked disappointed that JJ didn't come, but she doesn't talk with me about those things because she is going with JJ. If she told me what he said to her when they were alone that would be AWKWARD, but it wouldn't be if JJ told me.

JJ isn't talking as much as he usually does. He needs me, but he doesn't say so.

I think I might try out for majorette next year.

October 9, 1956

Miss Mira came to the house for tea with Mama this afternoon and asked about my studies and what books I was reading. More and more I like Jane Austen and the way English people talked in her time. I wished we talked more they way they did, it's so much more intelligent. The conversation with my girlfriends is so immature. Half our sentences have "cute" in them, and the boys are all the time saying "Huh?"

31

Into the wind: the coach

TWO SCRUFFY DOGS JOINED ME AS I THUDDED DOWN THE STEPS TO Huff Park where an erratic wind played out of the east through the valley of the Clover Fork River, now and then catching the dogs' fur from behind. I hadn't looked forward to the workout, but now I looked forward to the dogs' company.

After a few stretches I lurched ahead but halted ten yards out and walked to the end of the field, summoning the will to run. The dogs had no lack of will. For seven laps they frolicked along my circuit with little discipline before abandoning me for a livelier attraction at the river.

Alone again, the wind proved my weakness when I faced it. After half an hour of pushing into a sweat, I plopped onto the Dragons' bench, my thoughts as dull as my body, prompting me to lean back and gaze in my blank way at the shedding trees on the slope behind the visitors' stands. For a while I sat there staring, figuring that if I couldn't do anything else, I would just wait.

Through my stupor I heard a car door chunk closed in the parking lot beyond the swimming pool. I paid no attention until I got the impression that someone was coming. Focusing out of my blur, I turned my head enough to see a trim woman in cream-colored slacks and sweater, with a thin, orange-tinted scarf that curled in the gusts, an unlikely fashionable sight on this empty field – even more unlikely to be crossing in my direction. As she came closer I recognized that she was Mira Crane, so I stood.

"Isn't it just beautiful, JJ?" she enthused, sweeping her arm. "What a lovely day. How are you?"

"What are you doing here, Miss Mira?" Responding to her gesture for me to sit back down, I did so with the grip of an old

167

man who had eaten too much meat.

"I parked there," she said with her North Carolina drawl – *Ah pahked theah.* "I came to shop at the A&P, but I saw someone here on the field and thought it might be you, so I came over. Surprise."

"Surprise," I spoke the refrain as she rested herself in her poised way on my right.

"How is school?"

"Going well."

"Your father Steve?"

"It's hard on him that he can't talk, but he has a determined attitude."

"And how's your training going?"

"Doing fine."

She didn't respond.

"Well, I've been slow lately. Why do you ask?"

"The question came to mind."

"It's been slow."

"How slow?"

"Like I'm dragging."

"Oh, goodness. For how long?"

"About a month."

"Well, that's no fun at all."

"It's a phase."

"Can I help you?"

Hearing that, I almost choked up but fought it off by thinking of the dogs sniffing around when I came to the field. "It's up to me to get going."

"Perhaps you would give me a try as a coach."

A coach? "Thank you, but I can't ask that. I run for hours every day except Sunday. I can't take up your time that way."

"I would be part-time, say, three afternoons a week, not every day. I'm sure Coach York would approve."

"You just walk on the field by chance and offer to do that? I don't understand, but that's awfully kind of you."

"I doubt you've given a second thought to what you've done for

168

me."

"No ma'am, I haven't given it a second thought because I haven't done anything for you."

"What about Halloween, when you stopped that prank fire on Sadie's porch?"

"You know about that?"

"She's Herman's cousin, you know, so her condition is a concern. To Sadie, what you did was a great favor, like saving a life. You would never guess it, would you? She told Herman about it after you and the boys picked up the newspapers at her place in August."

I thought, *plus, Mrs. Hacker never paid me my $18.*

"I'm here to repay you."

"I beg your pardon – what?"

"I'm here to repay you."

"For what?"

"For the debt."

"You mean for what I did?"

"Yes."

"You give me too much credit, Miss Mira. But if you want to give me a little coaching, I would be glad to have it. I'm not at my best this week."

"We'll get you to your best. I just ask one thing – that you follow my instructions."

I worked up enough humor in me to be cheeky. "What if you ask me to do splits?"

"I might ask you to do splits."

"Oh no, please," my humor ran out. "I'm not a hurdler. I'm a miler. You know I'm a miler, don't you?"

"I know that."

"What if I come apart, strain something?"

"You won't come apart."

"If I have a woman dancer coaching me and I hurt myself with a split – boy."

"You won't hurt yourself following my directions. Let's make a

169

deal. If you should not want my instruction, I would finish and we would still be good friends."

"That's very kind of you. Thank you." I thought about it. I didn't want to hurt her feelings. She was nice company and such an interesting woman, always listening respectfully to young people. "That's a deal."

"Good. Now I want to earn your confidence."

"Why? You're the teacher."

"Why should you trust a dancer to help you run?"

I thought about this briefly. "Maybe you could tell me how to stop dragging."

"That is a good test," she nodded approvingly. "Would you mind if I put my hand near your back?"

"No, I don't mind." I leaned forward from the bench. "What are you going to do?"

"I am going to sense your energy."

With the scarf draping from her arm, she placed her left hand between my shoulders without touching my jacket. Then she seemed to shift her hand to the center of the back for a minute, then to a spot a few inches lower for the same length of time, then to the base of the spine, then behind the neck, and next in front of my forehead. Then she placed her right hand above my right knee for a minute or so, making my leg twitch. When done, she folded her hands in her lap and sat a while, looking ahead contemplatively. Finally she took a deep breath and told me, "You will feel better. This is what you will do. You will not run until Thanksgiving Day."

"Thanksgiving?"

"We'll make sure we both have something to be thankful for. Can you come to my house tomorrow to talk about what you are doing?"

When I agreed, she proceeded to give me some breathing exercises to do while walking in fresh air. She told me to inhale from the abdomen and through the nose to whatever count was comfortable, then hold to half that count and exhale through the

170

mouth to the same half count, a dozen sets at a time, if possible. She said I could do any other exercises or calisthenics – sit-ups, push-ups, jumping jacks – as vigorously as I liked, but I could not run until Thanksgiving.

"That's hard, not running for so long."

"Lately it looks as though it has been hard for you to run at all."

"Why do you think that is? I was doing fine in the summer."

"Stress. Sometimes it catches up with us. Tomorrow I will have another question for you: In running, what do you want?"

"I can tell you now. I want to win."

"Is that all?"

"That's kind of basic, isn't it?"

"Kind of," Miss Mira bent her head forward and covered her mouth as she laughed. Straightening up, she suggested, "Think about it."

I said I would.

"The coach gets a hug," she asserted, giving me a brief, light clasp, and walked back across the field toward her car, the fringe of her scarf fluttering behind her.

At home I found the family at supper, with Dad wearing one of mother's aprons for a bib and feeding himself cooked spinach. After I took my chair and dished out a small serving, I told them, "Guess what. Miss Mira saw me at the field. She wants to coach me."

"Such fun!" Sarah exclaimed. "Maybe I can go watch. What will she have you do?"

"The first thing I have to do is not run until Thanksgiving."

Sitting at the head of the kitchen table, Mother held her gaze steady for a moment, the way she did when she computed bridge cards that had been played, and informed me, "Forty days."

Dad worked his mouth and throat hard to say a word that I understood on his third try. "Tutu." He laughed so hard at himself that he had to wipe his eyes with his napkin. It was a happy sight.

32

Intake interview

HALF-SETTLING INTO THE SOFT-BACKED CHAIR ACROSS FROM MISS Mira in her sunroom study, I felt as if I had awakened from a nap unsure of the day or time or where I was, though in this case I knew all those things; it was just that two days earlier I would never have thought I would end up here. On the wall behind Miss Mira were paintings of Paris and New Orleans, a richly colored backdrop for her lean, aristocratic face and whitish-blonde hair that looked even more striking in contrast to her dark pants and sweater top. Around her neck a gold strand held a large pearl against her chest.

"Nice pearl," I commented.

"Thank you. My mother gave it to me. Would you like something to drink? Mint tea?"

Yes, thank you. From a blue and white teapot on a tray atop her desk she served me a cup and took one for herself, with a little sip.

"How is Sarah doing?"

"She's dancing a lot. It helps get the tension out of her."

"She has nice movement. I love to watch her when she improvises. How is your dancing?"

"I don't step on girls' feet, thanks to you."

"That's important."

"I have a question."

"Please."

"When you hold your hand close to a person to feel the energy, how do you feel it?"

"You practice at it. First you learn to calm your thoughts to be receptive. Then you concentrate."

"On what?"

"The energy, or lack of it."

"What does it feel like?"

She asked me to imitate her as she rubbed the palms of her hands together, and then told me to stop and hold my hands in front of me. "Feel that?"

"Yes," a tingling sensation from the friction.

"That's what it usually feels like. If you sense it on another person, the energy might feel more like static, or heat, or pressure. A master could see the energy intuitively."

"Can you see it?"

"No."

"Where did you learn this stuff?"

"The way to concentrate and meditate I learned from a saintly man who was in Cincinnati on a lecture tour back in 1928, when I was a young woman. He taught a different technique, but this seems to suit you. He taught how to sense the energy, too. It's all very simple, really."

"How do you know when the energy is right?"

"Ahhh," she acknowledged, "that takes more practice, feeling the disturbed points on the body and harmonizing them with your energy. That's why people hug – to give and receive that energy, but they don't think of it as a technique. Consciousness and energy – whirling atoms – are what we're made of, you know. You will feel the finer energy."

"How?"

"By calming yourself and knowing what to concentrate on."

"How can I calm myself, running for my life out there?"

"By practice. Does it sound that strange?"

"It's not what I'm used to."

"What are you used to?"

"Just running."

"Do you think while you're running?"

"Sure. Like a madman sometimes. It's not dancing."

"But like dancing, racing has an art as well as a science to it."

"I think a race can be beautiful. One of the most impressive things I ever saw on TV was a film that showed a leopard chasing a gazelle – stunning, the speed and turns – I could hardly move, it was so dramatic, except the end was bad, when the cat killed the gazelle." I paused to finish my recollection of the pursuit. "Sometimes the stride feels fast and easy. That's when I think I'm really running."

"Tell me about that."

"I like the pure feel of running, when I'm not even pushing hard because the movement is carrying me almost. It's interesting to hear you talk about energy, because every once in a while I feel a certain strength. You may think this is strange, but I think of this energy as intelligent and friendly."

"How do you reach it?"

"I don't know. I run to a certain level and hope it comes through. It won't be bossed around, but when it's on, I'm telling you... What do you think it is, or do you think I'm going off the deep end a little bit here?"

"You're not going off the deep end. If this strength is a second wind, which you get when you push on and on with concentration, I would say that energy is glandular. But if you break into a different awareness without first making a great exertion, that is another matter, even if the glands facilitate it."

"If it's a psycho state, it's a humdinger, because what's behind it seems happy and unmatchable."

"Is that what you want?"

"Yes, ma'am. That's what I want."

"Thank you for telling me."

"You're welcome."

"Others would want that but don't realize it's in them. You're fortunate. Are you ready to start?"

My left leg jiggled. "Yes."

She tapped my moving knee and told me I was breathing shallow. "Let's get out of the nervousness. If you would, sit up straight so your spine doesn't touch the back of the chair. Make sure your posture is comfortably erect, not strained."

I did so.

"Put your hands upturned on your thigh so your shoulder blades are pushed a little back."

Check.

"Close your eyes. Look upward between the eyebrows as if you were gazing at a distant star. Don't strain the eyes."

"Why am I looking up there?"

"Because when one enters the superconscious state the eyes are pulled upward by the energy reversing from the body into the spine and brain. To get the state we want, we first imitate it."

Superconcious? Like Brahms? "OK."

"Before you start, visualize something or someone of spiritual importance to you and invoke that presence."

I did that and said, "Ready."

"Breathe in deeply and slowly through the nose, using the abdomen rather than the chest. Keep your eyes comfortably up-turned, as if looking into the screen of your forehead, and keep your attention on the breath. Breathe in a dozen times, holding your breath to the same count and exhale through the mouth to the same count. Let's do it together."

We inhaled, held and exhaled together, making me feel light.

"Now," she said in a voice turned quiet, "Keep your attention on the breath. Mentally say the word 'Amen' in two parts."

I interrupted in a soft voice, "Why not say it the regular way?"

"Because you want to go into the sound, not just say it. On the incoming breath, imagine the first syllable as 'Ahmmm.' With the outgoing breath imagine the sound 'MMnnnn' stretched out. You don't have to do anything but watch the breath and mentally make those sounds, the incoming breath being 'Ahmmm' and the outgoing breath being 'MMnnn.' Don't force it. When the breath slows down of its own accord, feel the calmness in the brain during the intervals of not breathing. Ready?" Yes. "Begin."

I concentrated on the breath until I remembered my dog Biscuit, and then Mr. Tundrell who poisoned him. *Lucky for Mrs. Tundrell she got the insurance money when her husband died.*

Miss Mira reminded me, "Gently bring your attention back to the breath."

The sounds of town traffic grew more remote until I felt as if my torso and arms were stretched long with no feeling in them. The distant sensations rested in my head.

"There," her voice drifted into me, causing me to breathe more and feel my body again. "We went for fifteen minutes."

"It felt like five."

"You concentrated well."

Resting back in my chair, I didn't want to get up, and my leg didn't jiggle.

"This is central to your training. Do this in the morning, and in the evening longer, or whenever you have a few minutes during your day."

"I never read anything about this in my track and field book."

"You want more than is in that book."

AFTER SUPPER I flopped down in Sarah's room to do homework with her. While penciling through algebraic equations, she played Elvis Presley's hit, *Love Me Tender*, and then my Johnny Cash song, *I Walk the Line*. It was easier for me to do homework in the room with Sarah these days because she didn't play the same some song ten times straight. Even so, after half an hour, I returned to my own room to study, preferring the quiet.

Sarah's diary – October 20, 1956

After church I called Willa Mae, Bessie, Linda and Samantha, but nobody was home. I can't call Bernie. He should call me. What would he be doing on a Sunday afternoon? Nothing. Sunday afternoons are boring. It would be worse if the grandfather clock in the hall were working. Then I would hear all that ticking.

33

Holidays

SHORTLY BEFORE SUNRISE IN LATE OCTOBER, THE RUNNER FLASHED across my sleep like an impressionist's brushstroke, a vague thrust of legs cutting around trees, the momentum of the sidesteps pressing across his body. Then it was done, leaving me at the edge of wakefulness. I thought, *so there you are,* and before the scene faded, closed my eyes to fall back into the body of the Cherokee or into the woods where I would find him. Failing that, I recalled the particulars as best I could before they vaporized into a general sensation.

Sarah knocked on my bedroom door to let me know I'd overslept, and it was time to help Dad to breakfast before I left for school. The only thing I really wanted to do was put on my sweats and run the roads. I didn't care whether I was running against anyone or with someone or alone: I just wanted to let the long gait out the door. Yet I could not: Thanksgiving was almost a month away.

A week later I visited Miss Mira. Seated in a director's chair across from her in her dance studio room, I told her that I had gotten back the running fever so maybe we didn't need to wait until Thanksgiving; we could get started now. She said no, that we needed to wait, but that she would check me over.

She inspected my feet, the wear of my shoes, and studied me as I walked up and down the floor. When she asked me to sprint one length of the room, I relished the release, like finally getting to bite into a sandwich after a day of eating raw carrots.

She asked me to raise each leg to the side, to the front and to the back, onto the bar, and then directed me to a mat for side stretches, lunge stretches, and from a sitting position a hurdler's

177

stretch with one knee bent to the side. I accomplished this with some ease and was relieved to hear her say that this was as close to a split as I would get.

The following day at lunch I found Zorro at Cornett's Store on the corner across from school, a shadowy, wood-floor haven with display counters along the front and scratched booths in the back where we ate hot dogs, RC Colas and chocolate-wafer Moon Pies because we thought they were better than cafeteria food, which included such items as milk, vegetables and fruit. Zorro wore a fresh blue-and-white striped shirt with the collar up. I had heard that he was spending time with Lucy Giddon, so after I slid into the bench across from him and told him I would resume training on Thanksgiving, I asked how he and Lucy were getting along.

He leaned over close, so others couldn't hear in the noisy place, and told me, "Cool. She's coming to eat with me."

"You're going together, it looks like."

He bit his lower lip and nodded long and slowly in a yes motion.

I continued, "She thinks of me as a friend, right?"

"Yeah."

"Good."

"You know what else?"

"What?"

He leaned in closer. "I don't understand girls."

"Sarah tells me girls don't understand boys."

"You know why they don't?"

"Why?"

"We're a mystery, that's why."

"We're a mystery to ourselves, Zorro."

"Yeah, buddy," he acknowledged as he sat back again, proudly. "A big mystery is what we are."

A bigger mystery to me was why Zorro and Lucy showed up in the bleachers at Huff Park field on Thanksgiving morning to watch my first practice with Miss Mira. After I talked with them in the stands, they looked on as Miss Mira asked me how I felt.

178

"Good."

"May I touch your forehead?"

"Yes, ma'am." *Zorro and Lucy can figure it out for themselves.*

She placed her warm right palm firm across the front of my head for ten seconds or so, brought the hand down and said, "After your warm-up, please run your sprints toward me."

After the first sprint she reminded me to breathe in my nose and out my mouth. I couldn't tell how she knew whether I was breathing in my nose or my mouth. She added, "To breathe in your nose, you don't have to close your lips. Instead, place your tongue on the roof of your mouth to block the breath from entering your throat. The more you do this, the more natural it will become. If you become desperate for air, inhale any way you wish."

At the end of my last sprint, Miss Mira declared, "Excellent. The stride is straight. Run as long as you feel light. Then wrap up with three 100-yard dashes using a high extension. Don't be concerned about the speed. Reach out without making a bounding leap. You want an even glide, not a bouncy one."

For half an hour she observed me from beneath the goalposts, then from midfield. After we finished and Miss Mira departed, Zorro and Lucy descended to the sidelines. Awkwardly, Lucy asked how long the actual races would be, the equivalent of how many times around the field. I pointed to the approximate place at which the mile would end in a fifth lap if I began at midfield on the south side. Lucy asked me to take her to it and asked Zorro to wait. When we reached the mile spot, she took a deep breath, rubbed her chin, tightened her lips and confessed she had been the one who had caused me to remain unmentioned on Recognition Night the year before "because I liked you." *Liked* me? "As soon as it happened, I was sorry," she confessed in a low voice without looking into my eyes. "When Zorro asked me why you were overlooked, I lied to him and told him it was an oversight. Today I told him the truth, and I'm telling you the truth."

"Thank you. I wondered what had happened."

"Too many mixed feelings can make you crazy."

179

"Yes, they can," I admitted. Two years earlier a classmate had told me that my friend Becky Deeds Smith was snootily indifferent about being elected class princess to the Football Queen's court. I passed on the accusation, and when my words got around to Becky, she leaned over from her desk beside me in algebra class and asked me why I said those things about her. Worst of all, her eyes were red. I said I was sorry, and I was sorrier than the sorry I told her, but it was too late. She remained nice to me, which pressed my conscience all the more. That's when I realized that folks like Mr. Tundrell weren't the only dangerous people loose on the streets, and that I could do damage myself. I didn't actually understand Mr. Tundrell, but I understood Lucy all too well, and I told her, "We're friends now. Let's just go on from here."

That's what we did. We went on from there. We returned to Zorro and together walked up to Clover Street and on our separate ways.

At home, Marci and Alexander brought the turkey and gravy. Harold and Judith brought sweet potatoes and a bean casserole cooked without fat so Dad could eat it, sitting in his usual place, at the end of the dining room table set with rose-patterned Spode china and red goblets reflecting Mother's gently civilized taste, pleasing even to the young.

Mother said the blessing, not nearly as long and detailed as Mr. Garrett's full-voiced prayers in church. Mr. Garrett didn't even have to turn around for people to hear him on the sidewalk if the doors were open. Mother's tone was just right, a Mississippi lady's voice, smooth as ice cream warm at the edges.

I had looked forward to this day, and it was better than I expected, with holidays to come.

MISS MIRA'S TRAINING began not with stopwatch times but with concentration on the angle of my lean, the lift of my legs, the extension from the knees, the looseness of my arms, and the straightness of the forward motion. She wanted beauty and a strong fluid motion. Increasingly I felt and enjoyed the more rounded movement of the legs and level thrust of the body, judging it by its smoothness.

She smoothed me in other ways as well. On one mid-December afternoon I strode onto the field and greeted her, trying to be pleasant while repressing the mood of the hour previous when I went to the basement to wash my running clothes and left Dad alone on his bed for a nap. Mother was away, shopping at Kroger's because she wanted to collect S&H Green Stamps to finish up a coupon book and redeem it. Unknown to me, Dad had awakened early and wanted to get up. Frustrated because I didn't hear him above the noise of the washer, Dad rolled onto the waxed oak floor and dragged himself to the hall where I finally heard his strained, wordless calls and hurried to him. Flushed with anger, he chastised me in sounds clear enough to make the point. I argued back, insisting that I would have gotten to him before too long, so why couldn't he just wait? That bothered him all the more. After I helped him to his easy chair, the backwash of his predicament flooded on him as he bent into the shrinking of his body and wept into his good right hand. I apologized and hugged him, wishing I had done better, finding no consolation in the fact that he was a prisoner alone, no matter what I did.

On the field I tried to move beyond the downdraft of all that as I circled through my first warm-up lap. When I neared Miss Mira at the bench, she arose in a straight way like a dancer, stepped onto the field and motioned me to stop.

"Let's walk a lap and do the breathing exercise," she ordered matter-of-factly. "And here is something else I want you to do, every moment your mind isn't on some other duty. Be aware of the point between your eyebrows, as if it represents the source of your life. Be grateful to God this life is coming into you." She pressed her forefinger briefly against the low center of my forehead. "Don't focus your eyes there in this instance, but be aware of that spot until it becomes a habit. Whenever you are not busy thinking of something else, whenever you have a spare moment, rest your attention there. Do this for the rest of your life." Just like that, she said, *do this for the rest of your life.*

Around the field I walked beside her, doing as she said. As we came back around to the Dragons' bench, she asked, "How is your father?"

"He had a frustrating afternoon."

"And now?"

"He's at physical therapy."

"Does he like the therapy?"

"Yes, ma'am."

"That's good to hear – at this moment he is doing something that he enjoys."

"Yes, ma'am."

"When you get home, give him my regards, will you?"

"I'd be glad to."

Slowly she turned to look at the backdrop of bare trees on the sides of the slopes, causing me to look around some myself. After absorbing this, she concluded, "You're ready to run."

Off I went down the field and, on Sunday, down the church aisle, rolling Dad into the handshakes and pats of parishioners in the stained-glass amber softness of the sanctuary where Marci played a cello medley of Advent hymns.

Rev. Boswell preached about the prophecy, in the Book of Malachi, that Elijah would return before the "coming of the Lord," and quoted from Luke and Matthew that Elijah had returned as John the Baptist. Feeling frisky, I nudged Mother, "I thought we didn't believe in reincarnation."

Not feeling frisky, Mother pressed my hand, to be quiet.

After church, the family proceeded to the Lewallen Hotel for dinner and sat at a table next to Olivette and Petro Blackburn, who talked with Dad about Harlan in the old days, before the streets were paved, when the site of our house was just a hillside garden. "Back then, before I was born," I asked Mother with my enduring peskiness, "who do you think I was?"

"A baby waiting," she answered with a scrunch of her right shoulder. "Not Elijah." Having dispensed with that, she told the

Blackburns we would like to have them over for a little social.

"That'd be mighty fine," Mr. Blackburn acknowledged. "We'd be much obliged." Turning to me, he added, "Be sure to get your daddy out into the mountains."

"Yes sir."

I had time to keep my word on that during the Christmas break when I drove Dad someplace every day after lunch, reciting family stories Dad had told me in relation to particular places. When I recalled something in error, Dad tried to inform me, but I couldn't catch all the words. Sometimes, after struggling to get the information across to me, he gave up, turned silent and gazed out the car window, seeing whatever he saw. His retreat from the sharing of his life came as a warning to me that there would come a day when the silence would be harder than this.

But not yet, not quite yet. We moved through Christmas warmly, singing carols and opening gifts. I gave Sarah pens, paper and more blank journals from Bissell's. From Mother I received a cushioning pair of adidas road-running shoes for practice, to replace the ones I had worn down to a hard slickness. From Marci I received soft-leather spiked shoes for the cinder track. Sarah gave me an Elvis Presley album with *Blue Moon of Kentucky* on it. Dad opened his gifts with Sarah's assistance, and we adjourned to Harold and Judith's house for dinner. I had made it to another Christmas with all my family.

On New Year's Eve my parents went to bed early, though Mother would lie awake or close to the surface until Sarah and I returned from our parties. I brought Jenny to the gathering at Chief's house down the street. Because Zorro joined the Explorer Scout troop the week before, quite unexpected, Chief included him in the party, and Zorro brought Lucy.

For the first time I noticed how well Jenny fast-danced – not as elaborately as Barbara did, but better than I. It was if I were seeing her develop, not so much in looks as in her expressive traits. Most often she seemed to be looking at life from an altitude of awareness, but when she danced fast, she seemed fully immersed.

183

And she seemed fully immersed when she danced the slow numbers with me on the brick-tile floors of Chief's sunroom. As we counted down the last minute to the New Year, I led Jenny to the hallway off to the side that I might kiss her across the years' divide without an audience. I asked, "Who are you, really?"

Without a pause she answered, "I'm the Kid."

Sarah's diary – New Year's Day, 1957

At Willa Mae's party, Bernie took me outside to kiss THREE times. We could have done five but it was cold, and we didn't have our coats on. I could take the wind better than he could. Imagine that, and he plays football.

34

Storm

THE MOST STRIKING THING I NOTICED ABOUT MISS MIRA AS SHE stood on the field in mid-January was that she hardly blinked her eyes beneath the brim of her hat as the snow whipped across us all of a sudden and stuck to our eyelashes.

"I feel a storm coming. This winter looks like it will be hard against us," she ventured. "Let's make the most of it."

I shifted from one leg to another to keep them warm. "When it's really bad like this, I can run in the gym before school."

"That would be handy. Let me know when you are coming to the field."

"I will. What do you want me to do?"

"Do the same thing you did last winter. Breathe the way I told you. Run whatever variations you think you need. In March, we will review. How does that sound?"

It sounded good enough, and true to the omen of the day, the winter drove me indoors much of January and February. With feet taped to avoid blisters from leaning around the tight circles of the gym, I traded the dark of evenings for the dark of mornings, clean and warm but confined, relieved by watching Friday night basketball games in this gym with Jenny and my friends, and by weekend walks with Jenny in any weather except rain.

By March I was back regularly on the field with Miss Mira, enjoying the expanse of sod and daylight when, halfway through a workout, Miss Mira arose from the bench and stopped me midfield.

"You're done," she said with considerate firmness. "Go home."

"But I'm not finished with the routine."

"It's OK, darling. Go on."

As I ambled toward the bench to put on my sweats, she added,

"Quickly."

"What is it?"

"I have a feeling you might be needed. If I'm wrong, forgive me."

She wasn't wrong, as I found out in my run up Second Street when I reached the hospital where the ambulance backed into the bay as Mother and Sarah frantically trotted down the sidewalk.

As soon as I saw the medics roll my father out of the ambulance I felt the tremors not unlike those from the boulder reappearing through the tree break down the hill. But we, the family, were readier than before, veterans of the hardship we had gone through, knowing our duties by now, half-numbed by the war on the brain but practiced at hope, if only Dad could hold on, as he seemed to be doing.

At the field the next day, between hospital stops, I asked Miss Mira, "How did you know something was wrong yesterday?"

"I felt troubled in the heart, and I thought of your father."

"You didn't see anything?"

"Only what the feeling made me think of – your family."

"That was all?"

"That was all."

"Do you ever ask to see more?"

"Oh, darling, no, I never ask to see more of a difficult thing, not something like that. I only ask for ways to make it easier."

"When did you first have these impressions?"

"As a child."

"When you knew something would happen?"

"Yes, hunches."

"What did you do?"

"I paid attention to what I felt when I was right and what I felt when I was wrong, so I could learn what to trust."

"Do you know what's going to happen to me next?"

"Yes," she smiled. "You're going to run."

For two hours I sped up and down that field in the curious reassurance of her company. I thought that, because she seemed to see beyond what I saw, everything would turn out all right

186

somehow, and that my father would enjoy more of the satisfaction of family and friends.

But the quaking of that boulder rolling, breaking one thing and clearing another, was not finished with me, quite unsuspecting when the Blackburns came to the house for tea in the living room. Taking note of my open windbreaker releasing the heat of my workout, Mr. Blackburn asked how far I ran.

"I'm not sure when I'm on the field. I don't add it up except in hours. On the road, maybe ten or twenty miles."

"Then you can run a good ways." With her wrinkles lined up with the smile of her round face, Mrs. Blackburn said agreeably, "You would have liked that Indian fellow."

"I would have liked to have met Jim Thorpe, you bet."

"No," she said, "the Indian man here when we were little 'uns."

"Who?"

Mr. Blackburn explained, "An Indian who ran special mail to Pineville before the railroads were brought in. Thirty-some miles."

"There was an Indian runner to Pineville?" I looked straight at him. "Where'd he live?"

"Somewhere on the east side of Ivy Hill, out toward where the Rosenwald school is. He wasn't from here."

Mrs. Blackburn informed me, "From North Carolina. One of them Cherokees."

"A Cherokee?" I asked Mother if she had ever heard of him. She hadn't.

Mr. Blackburn added. "He came up from the Smoky Mountains."

"You saw him? What did he look like?"

"About six feet, I would say. Black hair, not too long. No fat on him. If you run the river and the ridge, I guess fat don't get a chance to stick."

"How'd he dress?"

"Regular. Light clothes usually."

"What happened to him?"

Mrs. Blackburn chirped, "Why, you're inquisitive, aren't you?"

187

"Yes, ma'am. I like history, very interesting. That's a good story. Good story. Do you know what happened to him?"

"Never heard."

"Who was he?"

"Sounded like Solomon," Mr. Blackburn held his head back some as he spoke. "Salaman."

"That was it, almost like salamander." Mrs. Blackburn agreed. "Salaman something."

I commented, "That doesn't sound like a Cherokee name."

Mr. Blackburn agreed, "No, it don't. I don't know how they came about their names, if they took them from somewhere or their folks married white."

After the Blackburns left, I walked with Mother to the hospital where Dad's bed was cranked up enough to let him eat his supper off the tray, and I asked him if he knew of the Cherokee who ran the trail to Pineville. He nodded he knew, but he didn't know his name and didn't remember telling me about him.

I asked Mother, "You remember that dream you had of Granddad? How did you know it was real?"

Twitching her right shoulder, Mother relaxed her hands on her crossed legs and thought about it before answering, "There's something about a dream like that that's steady. Everything is clear and normal, and a feeling of certainty comes out of it. It's hard to explain but not hard to accept when it comes to you."

Dad put down his fork and mumbled that he was finished, so I pulled the tray away from the bed and sat in the vinyl-cushioned metal chair beside Mother's. "Mom, since I was small I've had dreams of a Cherokee running. Do you think someone told me about him and I don't remember that part?"

"I don't know, son."

"Have you ever heard sounds in dreams?"

"Songs sometimes, but not when my father came to me."

"Not deep sounds?"

"Regular music in some other dreams. Not often."

"Well, I heard beautiful sounds in my dreams of the Cherokee.

So maybe that's not realistic, huh? I mean, we don't usually have an orchestra around us, right? That's more like a movie."

"It sounds unusual."

"But," I remembered, "those dreams with the runner and the sound, they're precise, very clear, never crazy-like. I see different parts in different dreams, and sometimes one of the old parts is replayed."

"Then pay attention," Mother advised. "See what proves true."

On Saturday morning I walked down to the county courthouse to see if anyone heard of Salaman, first pausing in front by the bronze doughboy to hear the preacher tell us, "The time, huh, is near, huh, the TIME, huh, TO BE REVEALED, yes," but he didn't reveal it and the clerks at the deed office couldn't reveal anything either. They said they never heard of any Salaman, but if I could get more information they would be glad to help unless it involved a record before the Civil War when the old courthouse and all its contents were burned to the ground by a feuding hothead under cover of Confederate leanings – in this case not Grandpa Dannon but probably a friend of his.

On the field Tuesday with Miss Mira, I pushed through a workout in which she asked me only to run around the field a hundred times at medium speed – quite unusual not to have any sprints thrown in – and told me that was enough for the day.

I told Miss Mira I was concerned that I might not be getting fast enough. I was preoccupied by all that was happening, whereas Bobby Dodd might be running hard, working late, gunning for me. She said I would get some hard runs later, to go on home and be with the family.

At home Mother sat me on the sofa with her to talk – never a good sign – and told me that Dr. Benton recommended that Dad be placed in a nursing home with skilled care.

Dr. Benton had suggested that we inquire if there might be an opening at the Bluecrest Home in Lexington, more than three hours away, and if so, we might want to check it out. He had heard good things about the facility's medical care. Finally, full force, I was in a race to a finish line I couldn't see, and I didn't know how to win it.

Sarah's diary – March 8, 1957

Dad likes for me to rub his head. He hasn't much hair, and what he has is around the sides. I like his freckles on top. I wish I were Jesus, who could heal people. I can make Daddy comfortable, that's all. No matter how much you love people, it doesn't feel like enough sometimes. The person I love might think it's enough, but I don't.

35

Dog run at Bob's Creek

As my friends on the football team warmed up for spring practice, Miss Mira huddled with me on the sidelines and asked what I wanted to do.

"I want to run hard for an hour and go home. Marci is coming."

"Run hard on another day."

"I need to kick out."

"You can kick out Friday or Saturday when I'm not with you. Save your strength for now and concentrate on your extension."

"I get strength by running hard."

"You get strength by willing it through you."

"What's the difference?"

"You are thinking about how to get the energy out. I'm thinking about how to get it in."

"The only way I know how much energy I have is to test it. I don't know if I am faster than the guys I will come up against. In eight weeks we go to the district meet. I haven't been in a race since last May."

"Then let's get in a race."

I cocked my head. "How?"

"Ask for one."

"Ask who?"

"First ask, then think of who to ask."

"I'm asking. I want a race."

"Ask again."

I'll do what she says. "I want to race."

"Who can get you in one?"

"I'll ask Marci to ask the Union coach how I can get in one. Maybe he knows."

"Maybe he can let you run with Union, not as a team member, maybe as exhibition."

The prospect of racing sooner than May 11 gave me something new to think about as I alternated short and long runs through the hour. At home I went straight to Marci – she was in town because of Dad – and told her I needed a race and asked if she would request this favor of Mr. Sands. He seemed to like me and had offered to help. She agreed to ask.

On Friday evening, after Mother read the headlines to Dad, she told him how Dr. Benton suggested that Dad get good nursing home care and asked if he would consider the Lexington facility if it looked acceptable. He nodded yes.

I asked him if it would be hard to leave for a while. I wanted him to grit his teeth and say no, but he nodded yes again, almost helpless. His answer shredded through me, and the wreckage would not stay still. I asked mercy for him. Hearing no further answer through the night, the attempt at mercy fell to me. On Saturday morning, while Homer drove Dad to physical therapy, I found Mother, Marci and Sarah at the kitchen table going over business and insurance papers, and declared, "I don't want to take him to Lexington. That's too far away. He needs to be home."

Mother answered, "I don't want to send him away either, son, but we don't have any good choices in the matter. You see how touch-and-go it has been."

"We have the choice to keep him. He doesn't want to go."

Strained, Marci put the question to me: "What if he needs special care and can't get it here? What if he is further hurt or dies because he doesn't get good enough attention in an attack?"

"What if he dies alone there? What if it's the loneliness that kills him?"

Moist-eyed, Sarah looked at whoever talked. Mother kept her composure and stated, "It hurts me just as much. I can keep him comfortable, but we are at the limits of what we can do to keep him alive, and that matters."

I considered how much of a burden I was throwing on Mother

by making this more difficult for her. "Then what if we bring him home for the summer after I get out of school?"

"We will look at the situation when school is out."

"Good, thanks," I finished by embracing Mother. Upstairs in the bathroom I cried into a towel so no one would hear, washed my face, slipped into my shorts, T-shirt and shoes, and told the family I would be out a long time running. I couldn't hold it back any more.

Heading south of town on the narrow path hugging the curved road, I didn't care about the traffic or the heat coming on. Two miles out of town, cars honked near Denny Ray's. I waved back, but my mind didn't reach far outside my rage of measly powers. Hardly sane, all I could do was chase the invisible and try to crash headlong through whatever showed itself.

Four miles out, on the bend past Harold's house, the strain threatened to choke in on me. I bolted my attention to my forehead. Six miles out, the glassy river shoved further west of the road as the railroad track pulled closer and forked a spur to the mines of Lenarue and Mary Helen.

Across the spur I accelerated, expecting the push to get harder when, like a brother out of hiding, a second wind joined in, fueling a high pace, opening the door for more. Seven miles out, walkers by the highway stood aside to let me pass. I knew that more narrow and unwelcoming footpaths lay ahead near the place where the bullet had zinged through the hat of my great-uncle Steve and into the roadside cliff, so I swerved right to the nearby cement bridge and small café at Bob's Creek where a clutch of boys loitered. To avoid making a scene or seeming inconsiderate, I slowed and waved as I went by them, but one of the boys heckled me anyway: "What are you running away from? Scared of us?"

I didn't look back. Their badgering triggered the attention of other boys playing baseball in a field between the café and the railroad tracks: "Hey, chicken! Too yellow to say hello?" When I reached the crossing and cut onto the railroad, the baseball players swept toward the track to intercept me, stirring the group outside the café to join the chase belatedly.

As the spread-out gang at Bob's Creek swarmed toward the tracks, I watched them with trance-like disdain and throttled back up to my previous speed to keep from being caught. A strangely calm thought – not a wish but an acknowledgement – came out of me numb and straight: *I'm going to run these boys into the ground.*

When the mob neared the rail bed, I sprinted beyond the angle at which they could cut me off, causing them to make chicken sounds and shout louder about how I was running to mama. The left flank merged with the other pursuers behind me on the tracks – about eight in the front group with the rest struggling behind.

The posse slowed. *Aw, c'mon guys.* I braked to a light trot and looked back.

They started up again. I started up again.

They slowed; I slowed. Concerned that they would give up altogether if they thought they couldn't gain on me, I let them come within ten yards and hoped they wouldn't throw gravel. At this distance I could hear them panting through their talk and having a hard time thinking up anything new to say.

I let them get within five yards, close enough to glance back and see their faces crimson until they burst forward, and I burst forward. We repeated this three more times, including a fifty-yard stampede. About three-fourths of a mile from Bob's Creek they halted, not even yelling as loud as before. I turned to them and walked backwards, not easy to do on rail ties. As they came at me again – I couldn't understand why they didn't throw gravel – I pivoted ahead and saw six dogs hightailing out of the woods in the distance. In full bark, the pack headed onto the railroad and dead straight toward me.

When the pack got within forty yards, I slowed to a walk, turned to the posse and yelled, "You'd better not run while these dogs are around, and don't look them in the eye."

One of the boys shouted back, "You do what you want; we do what we want!"

As the dogs barked in closer, another boy yelled, "Walk! These dogs get worked up if you run!"

So everyone behind me clenched carefully into the crescendo of barks, with fur rising off the dogs' backs as they parted to approach us on either side. A burr-covered Doberman mix snarled and barked the loudest, nothing friendly about him, but he and the other dogs moved on past. When the animals scrambled off the tracks and across the field, I turned to the gang compressed between the rails and asked, "Do you want to chase me some more, or are we done with that?"

"We're not after you anymore," announced the boy in front. "You're not a chicken. That's all we need to know."

"Good," I said. "Let's go back."

At that, I set off at a good speed toward home, wondering who else would give me a race on the way. Nobody, as it turned out. I counted myself satisfied anyway, enough to get me through the day.

36

Departure

THE DAY AFTER THE RUN AT BOB'S CREEK, HAROLD DROVE MOTHER to Lexington to check out the Bluecrest Home. Ringing into the uncertainty and quiet of the house, Marci called with good news: Coach Sands said he would arrange it so I could run the mile in Union's April 21 meet against Cumberland College.

When Mother returned, Dad was happy to see her but not happy to be closer to being put in a nursing home. I told Dad that maybe we could bring him home for a summer break and that in the fall I would be in Lexington with him. That quieted him and me.

At practice two days later, Miss Mira asked what I thought I needed. More closing speed.

"Very well," she agreed. "Sit on my right." I did so. She asked me to go through my concentration exercise with her and then told me to visualize the race up to the part I needed to kick. She told me how to think of energy being drawn into the back of my head and how to perceive the motion. It felt good.

I asked her if she was hypnotizing me. No, she said; she was showing me how to control my mind, the opposite of giving control to someone else. She said I should never try hypnosis and never leave my mind blank. That injunction disappointed me. In ninth grade I watched a magician-hypnotist at school invite volunteers, including Harley, to the stage. The performer hypnotized them so they would shiver when he said they were cold and sweat when he told them they were hot. He told Harley that he was as strong and as stiff as a board, laid him between two chairs and sat on him. I thought that one of these days I would like to do that to somebody, and now I never could.

With the racing procedure practiced in my imagination, I ran a series of hard sprints of varying distances, alternating with a medium pace.

Friday in the doom of evening I helped pack my father's clothes and necessities, and tossed with a fractured sleep into the morning. Dad was in a better mood because we were meeting Marci at Sanders Café, a restaurant where she liked to have breakfast, on U.S. 25 north of Corbin. By 10 o'clock we pulled up to the white, Alpine-like building with three peaks and a yellow sign out front. I wheeled Dad into the busy, country-like dining room to meet Marci and Alexander. Mother put the white-and-red checked napkin on Dad's shirt and read the menu:

"Kentucky Country Ham – with Two Eggs, Red Gravy, Hot Biscuits. Not Worth It – But Mighty Good – $1.70."

Dad wanted that, but it didn't suit his diet. Marci suggested No. 4, a "Choice of Juice – Golden Brown Wheat Cakes, Coffee or Tea – 75 cents."

Dad agreed. I asked for the same. The others ordered the two eggs with grits, toast and jelly, for 60 cents.

As Mother poured the cream in her coffee, I watched the heavy white swirl into a light brown, just as I had watched the cream as a child when she let me stir her cup on the kitchen table. The waitress brought my orange juice in a thick glass, as ruby red as Mother's dining room goblets. The restaurant's maple tables and chairs reminded me of the maple furniture in Sarah's room. Home followed my father in pieces.

The goateed Mr. Sanders emerged out of a front corner office and from behind the cashier's counter to walk to each table, asking how we liked the food. We all said we liked the meals, and would have said so even if we didn't, but if Aunt Betsy were with us and didn't like something, she would have said so.

I told Dad that the next time we drove through Corbin we would eat here again. He liked the idea. But soon after, he didn't like the idea of leaving Marci. He wept harder than usual and made Marci cry. I held onto the thought that our time was not up and that I would bring him back home in the summer.

197

In Lexington, when we said it was time for us to leave after spending Saturday evening and Sunday morning with him, he cried again. What else could he do?

Bluecrest Home was clean, Dad's room was private, and the aides were cheerful and friendly. But nothing could quite mask the smell of oldness, its medicines and leavings, or the finality of the lives slumped in beds and wheelchairs, waiting. All the tenderness and mercy that this place might offer could not overcome the loss of what these people had done and been, the same as was lost in the silence of my father as we walked out the door with the history and bounty of his life, in a hurt that was mine as much as his, the depth of which I had never known before.

37

Lesson of the trees

THE FIRST THING MISS MIRA ASKED ME ON THE FIELD AT MY NEXT practice was when Dad would be having visitors, so I told her the schedule for family visits and that I hoped to bring him to Barbourville for the district meet in May. She expressed delight at that and suggested we increase the workouts to three hours a day and increase the length of my meditation exercise at night.

"I'm going to run out of time."

"That's our life story, darling. Do it and you'll have more time."

For my training schedule she laid out sprints of various lengths, from thirty yards to a hundred, interspersed with jogs and medium runs. She told me not to think of a competitor yet, but to put my attention in my body and visualize the energy. I did that as best I could, sweating my T-shirt so wet I had to wring it.

On Friday evening I took Sarah to the Musette's spring concert in which Jenny sang, but this time I didn't sit in that seat where I had watched the mental health movie; I already had enough to think about. After the program, Jenny took me to Katie Bingham's house on Marsee Drive for an after-show party where more people talked than danced, so I pulled Jenny to the yard bordered with colorful paper lanterns. Two cushioned lawn chairs stood close to the path of the boulder that had bounced across the yard on its way into the sheriff's cruiser, but not so close that I wanted to move the chairs out of the way, though I glanced up the hill. As she sat, Jenny pushed her hair back with her left hand, clearing the way for me to see her eyes where she blinked away the gold of lantern light and asked, "Can I be your teacher?"

"I don't know."

"Please, please. I'll make it short."

"What's the lesson?"

199

She shifted in order to face me. "Trees."

"OK."

She tapped my forearm. "What's your favorite kind?"

"The oak, like the one outside my window."

"Well," she emphasized, "this shows you appreciate the strength of nature and its durability over time. The oak is part of the beech family, and it is related to the chestnut. The chestnut was very common in the last century, but a fungus killed most of the chestnuts. You know how wide the branches go. You know what else? The tree's root system is as big as the crown. Isn't that interesting? That's a lot of roots."

"Lots of hidden roots."

Smiling satisfied at the life of trees, she concluded, "That's my lesson. How did you like it?"

"It was perfect."

"Thank you." She sank back in her chair and gazed ahead at the night edge of Ivy Hill. I leaned forward to tell her that I liked the way she saw things, she couldn't know entirely why.

With Dad out of the house, his bed unused, his chair empty, it was hard not to think of him, and I looked forward to giving him a break from Bluecrest Home where on Saturday afternoon we found him at the end of a hall, beyond a clump of men sleeping in front of a TV set. In a wheelchair parked in an alcove, Dad was reading a newspaper as best he could hold it with one hand. We were glad to see each other, and he seemed to enjoy looking out the car window as we toured west of Lexington through Woodford County, thoroughbred country where picture-perfect double fences bordered pastures, barns and mansions. Dad had always wanted me to drive slower than was my habit, and on these back roads through the swelling green sea of meadows, I had no trouble drifting at an amiable pace. Sarah from the back seat leaned forward to keep her hands loose around Dad's neck until we returned and left him at Bluecrest.

On the way back from Lexington we stopped at Marci's for supper. After the meal, I said I wanted to go to the track. Marci went with me, an unusual thing, because we did so few things together and she was leaving the company at her home. As we rounded the oval she asked what it felt like to run the mile. I described it the best way I could as I strolled on the lanes where in a month I would be moving and thinking in fast time.

"Promise me this," she asked before we stepped off the track. "Be at my concert the evening of May 17th, at the chapel. I'm playing with a group from the Louisville Orchestra."

I was touched not only that she wanted us there, but also that she asked me first, with a childlike earnestness. She was always admiring of others and unassuming about herself, yet when she put her bow to the strings she opened up a world with the kind of surprise that Zorro let loose when he put his whip to the wind. So of course I would come to hear her work, and Mother and Sara agreed. I only hoped that I would be qualified for the regional meet the weekend of Marci's concert. At least we shared a performance deadline.

With the track season in full swing, Coach Odell led his Rosenwald sprinters onto the field where I escorted Miss Mira to the runners and introduced her as my coach.

"You coachin' for Harlan? They ain't got no team, only Jaybird."

Making a little bow to them, Miss Mira explained, "I'm an unofficial coach."

Peanut asked, "What do you do?"

"I teach dance."

The runners whooped. "Can't no dancer except Loretta teach a man how to run."

Miss Mira countered, "Darling, don't tell your mama that."

They whooped more.

Coach Odell approached, tipped his cap, and said, "It's good to see you again, Mrs. Crane. Anytime you want to help me straighten out these boys, I would be indebted to you."

More shouts. As it turned out, Miss Mira, who had met Coach Odell when she conducted dance workshops at Rosenwald Elementary, was busy enough straightening out me. She suggested

I practice with Rosenwald, at Coach Odell's invitation. I couldn't catch Peanut and some of his friends in the dashes most of the time, but they made me laugh through the heavy burn of work up to the day I would test myself with no penalty for losing against the Union and Cumberland College runners, my first free ride and my last.

♋

Sarah's diary – April 11, 1957

Mama showed me Daddy's file where he saved the letters I wrote him from camp. Sweet Daddy! So I will write him three letters a week. Maybe he doesn't care much what I talk about as long as it is about the family. I don't think he wants to hear about what lipstick Linda is wearing. Maybe Jenny can tell me some things to tell him about the coal business. No, that isn't a good idea. So many mines are closing. The Forester and Spillman shop is going out of business. The jewelry store by the Cumberland Hardware is closing. The Margie Grand might close. Some days everything seems to be dying. That's not cheerful. I'll write him about other things.

38

Union

WHAT RELAXATION I BRING WITH ME AS OUR 1953 DODGE PUTTERS into Marci's driveway is overrun by the news. Alexander steps outside to tell us there's a problem about letting me run and that Marci has gone to the Union College field to deal with it. We quick-walk across the campus and find Marci at the side of the bleachers talking with Coach Sands.

Marci introduces Mother, Sarah and Miss Mira and explains to us that he's concerned I might interfere with the race and that the Cumberland College coach might object.

Miss Mira smiles ladylike beneath her white sunhat wrapped with a broad ribbon that drops its two tails off the back and with her soft-rolling Carolina accent says: "Why of course you would be concerned, Mr. Sands. You can't afford to have anything go wrong because of your generosity, which we appreciate *so* much. You must have our assurances clearly stated: JJ will start in the lane outside the other runners. He won't block anyone at any point in the race. He knows he has to be something of a loner today, but that won't bother him. He will only come to the inside lanes when he has extra room. I will go out to the field, and if JJ is in a position that might cause even the slightest problem, I will wave him off the track."

Mr. Sands says, "That's especially important at the finish."

Miss Mira assures him, "It certainly is, and you can be sure he will not break the ribbon. He will be off to the side, out of everybody's way."

I affirm, "I'm not going to try any close maneuvers. I just want to time myself and get some experience."

Coach Sands considers that and says, "Let me deal with it," a good sign. He confers with the Cumberland College coach, nods yes a few times, then laughs, another good sign, *thank you, Lord*, and returns to tell me, "You can run exhibition in the mile. We understand you will start outside and stay away from the other runners; and your coach here – you don't look like a coach."

Miss Mira acknowledges, "Life is so deceiving, isn't it?"

"It is. Your coach here will pull you off if you get in a pack; and you won't go through the ribbon."

I assure him, "That's correct."

"You're in."

Miss Mira says, "That's so considerate. I can see why he has spoken nicely about you. Thank you so much, Mr. Sands."

I thank him, too. With an hour before the start of the mile, we return to Marci's house for breakfast – milk and a slice of toast for me; no prunes. Looking fresh in her white blouse and slacks with an orange scarf-belt around her waist, Miss Mira strides back onto the campus with me and inquires, "Where is your attention?"

"On the track."

"Bring it back, darling. Let's find a place to sit."

We choose a bench beneath a sycamore on the front lawn. Beyond the buildings, the loudspeaker makes the first call for the mile.

She orders, "Concentrate. Let's settle out."

"Settle out? They just made the first call."

"You'll get there. Stay with me for now."

Over the past week I have not gotten too anxious about this race because I am a visitor, not a real contender, and I'm in high school, not in college, so nothing is expected of me by others; it's more like a dress practice on a track. Yet it's hard to rope in my mind after hearing that announcement. *This is a race, after all.* I fix my attention on the breath until it slows down like a wild mustang that can stand still while a person is looking at it from a distance as long as that person doesn't flinch, because once that happens, that horse is gone for no telling how long. After about five minutes I'm not close to a flinch, the mustang doesn't care what's around him any more, and Miss Mira's instruction

204

murmurs, "Now draw in the energy."

I follow her instructions.

"Think of the race now. Let's go."

As we near the track, the loudspeaker makes the second call for the mile, and I warm up, feeling ready but not tense. Afterward I think, *I'm probably not going to win against these college guys, but since it doesn't count, enjoy it.*

Miss Mira interjects, "Enjoy it, but run to win."

"Are you reading my mind?"

"I'm saying what comes to me, darling."

She crosses the track into the oval where she'll monitor me from the area close to where the 100-yard dash and hurdle events start. Behind the starting line, six milers limber up, three each from Union and Cumberland, a smaller group than I'm used to. I take my place alone on the outside lane, charging up.

The starter doesn't give instructions other than to line up, revving me up a half-minute sooner than I expect, so I inhale deeply from the abdomen to load oxygen. "On your marks!... Set!...POP!"

The clump bolts off the line and packages into the two inside lanes. *I'm back in business, back in business!* Careful to stay out of their way, I run in the free-range territory of the fourth lane – two notches from the outside – until we near the curve where I pull in behind the traffic at the last position; *no interference back here.* Through the curve I don't think of strategy but of how thankful I am to be in a race where I'm a guest and don't even look like I belong – a runner in green shorts and white T-shirt on the tail of Union's orange and black runners and Cumberland's maroon and white. Since I don't have any idea who's fastest, I don't try to distinguish who is who, but concentrate instead on the fact that I feel strong behind the pack led by a Cumberland racer fifteen yards ahead. The tempo is not blistering but quick and steady on the first backstretch. *We're moving, yes, we're moving,* I agree with myself as I trail at the rear down the corridor. Everyone else must agree because nobody changes positions, nobody feels the need to bolt to the front of the line because our spread isn't long and the Cumberland leader is doing our work for us, taking us along on the old burst of adrenaline that soon will be burned off and replaced by will and endurance and then the blood of the hunt. I'm thinking the leader must be a pacer, and if he is a kicker too, no telling what he can do to us, but I am not worried yet. We run as if in a choreographed ride to the battlefield, and those that get there in front get to fight – that's what it feels like. So far everyone is on the way together.

Cumberland leads us all out of the turn and in a beeline to the starting post. I am thankful to be in the flow and without pain, safe on the outside, enjoying the steadiness of the momentum, surprised to hear my time as it is called out because I don't feel I am running as fast as they're telling me.

My body still feels light and at ease through the third curve – where I suddenly gauge my resources and conclude I am too much at ease, no matter that what the stopwatch says – *I have to get out of here.* At the end of the bend I follow the empty third lane into the straightaway and accelerate up the line. Sensing the momentum as if watching a motion picture of myself, I hang wide like an escort behind the front pair and barrel around the fourth curve with them.

Heading into the third lap I expect to hurt, expect the frontrunners to pick up some, but I am not taking on pain as grippingly as I anticipated. They spin on at the same pace though a Union miler tails tight on the Cumberland pacer, positioning for a challenge. I wonder if they are saving up for a hard close, but I don't wonder too hard or too long; I feel the tug against the reins of my caution, nudging for freedom, not needing a flick of the rider's whip, just permission to be let loose, and for the moment I am a jockey on this playful force that wants to be in front, so I let up on the reins; I let the force loose and feel it shoving me forward. In an easy fashion I ride around the leaders until I have ample clearance to close in to the inner rim through the curve.

With no one in front to distract me on the backstretch, my

stride feels so automatic that the cadence comes up from my legs to my head, as if caught in the beat of a dance. Out of the fifth curve I spot Miss Mira standing near the edge. She neither signals nor calls as I pass, so I figure I am within the rules but glance back to be sure, expecting the other milers to be at least close, expecting I will need to move to the right to give them clearance, but I'm surprised to see that I have advanced beyond their easy reach and *it's not even hurting; it's not even as hard as practice.*

Past the lap line I shoot beyond the officials until I hear the final lap gun crack for a Union runner behind me. The track seems mine the way Ivy Hill is mine on a good day. Breathing deep, holding pain at the mind-edge of machine work and enjoyment, I fade out awareness of the other runners and reach inside the movement for the pulse of a music I cannot hear, subtle and harmonizing – imagination maybe, but as good as real or better.

Around the last curve I unwind with speed fixed high to the rhythm, straighten out from the tilt of the turn, alone in the fluid rush of the final stretch where I angle off to the outside lane, behind the helper holding the ribbon at the finish line, sorry to be stopping, sorry to be shutting down the thrust of the easy roll.

On the infield, Miss Mira comes to hug me, a risk considering the differences in our comeliness and sweat. "Beautiful!" she exclaims. "Just beautiful. How did it feel?"

Too interiorized yet to find words fine enough, I tell her it felt "good." As I thank the busy coaches, my family descends from the stands in high spirits to leave with Miss Mira and me. Still enjoying the undertone playing through me, I think of Bobby Dodd. He's surely on pace in his build-up to the district meet, but so am I.

39

The seat at the ledge

QUITE THE GRACIOUS LADY, MISS MIRA URGED ME TO REWARD myself on Monday with any workout I liked, so I drove to the Harlan Country Club. With the permission of the manager, a friend of the family, I ran barefoot on the rolling course at the base of Little Black Mountain where the fairway cushioned me past golfers and their caddies on the putting greens, a dimension away from the dark work inside the bordering mountain where miners crushed coal and shunted it to the tipple at Lenarue. Edging around the smooth grade of a hill, I wished that Jenny were with me, walking here, the landscape was so verdant and serene. Hardly a minute after that wish took shape, I lifted over a mound and descended near a foursome that included Mr. and Mrs. Lee. Pleased at their presence, I curved into their company to talk with them and ask if they had ever heard anything about Salaman. They had no information.

Neither did Jenny when I talked with her at her cliff the next evening. I didn't think she would have information, but I had learned not to underestimate what she could figure out. She said she liked the name Salaman, that it would have been a good one for me; too late for that. I asked her if she would go to the prom with me, and received her yes as appreciatively as if it were our first date. I also thought of asking her if she wanted to go to the district meet, but that seemed imposing. Although she talked with me about my running, she said nothing about wanting to see me race and, besides that, she would have to miss school and I couldn't drive her to Union because I had to pick up Dad in Lexington and bring him.

I told her the sparse history I knew of Salaman, though I didn't mention the coincidence of my dreams; that could smack of an overactive imagination, it seemed to me. For the same reason I hadn't mentioned Salaman and the dreams to Miss Mira. I needed to figure out more for myself, to put more of the pieces together. Little did I know how the next piece would appear.

At daybreak on Saturday, Chief, Stoner and I taxied in the mist around the neighborhoods of Harlan picking up Scout friends for a hike down the Cumberland River. Dressed in his new short-sleeve Explorer shirt and blue jeans, with a knapsack on his back and bullwhip strapped on his right side, Zorro clumped from his house to the truck for his first outing with us. With Jug, Two-Bit, Harley and Horse gathered, our caravan snaked into the lifting fog along Kentucky 119 to Bell County where we crossed a small bridge over the river and parked at a white frame church near a scattering of houses. From this point we planned to follow the railroad and paths on the south side of the river to a spot near Pineville, then return, looking for bypaths on either side of the Cumberland.

Feeling the spirit of a wagon master, Stoner sang Frankie Lane's *Mule Train* as we moved in a loose bunch in the middle of the tracks beside a damp face of rock layers exposed by the cut of the rail bed. In the cleanness of the morning air, the trees on the Pine Mountain ridge north of the river looked precise. Half an hour out, we maneuvered to the river and hiked along the edge except where mud and boulders blocked us.

An hour into the hike, Horse announced it was time to eat as we headed along a branch road toward a paint-peeled house where a pair of matted-fur dogs barked out of the yard toward us. I wondered what I was doing to attract these animals and thought maybe I shouldn't be throwing ice on that dog at Sunny Acres. Whatever the cause of these appearances, I recognized my calling and told my friends to line up two-by-two and not pay attention to them. The heaviest dog with the deepest bark, a German shepherd, feeling feral from his country living, crouched in front of us while the other dog barked at his side.

Jug shouted, "Now what?"

209

I said, "Don't look them in the eyes. They'll move on."

Stoner muttered, "Yeah, maybe they'll think we're just tourists."

As the lead dog advanced, all worked up, snapping close to my knees, a whip-end slashed "POW!" across his snout and sent him somersaulting backwards into high-pitched yelping. Zorro cracked after the other one "POW!" and then "POW," though only the cherry- bomb-like bursts could touch them as they dashed tail-tucked down the road.

With his whip curled on the ground at his feet, Zorro said with a shrug, "I'm sorry, I don't understand all the Scout stuff yet, but I'm hungry, man. I don't want to stand around watching dogs bite at me. I want to eat."

Ridiculing me and glorifying Zorro, the boys noisily traipsed their way down the gravel road that shrank into a path through a patch of woods where I stopped cold to figure out what was going on.

The trees and the lay of the land looked familiar. I wondered if my parents had brought me here as a child. I remembered Dad pulling the car off the road to let Sarah and me cross the river on a swinging bridge. I also remembered riding the train to Pineville for the fun of it, but the swinging bridge wasn't nearby, and the railroad didn't pass close to this stand of trees.

My friends walked into heavy undergrowth as Chief asked me, "Are you coming with us, or are you going to wait for more dogs so you can not look them in the eyes?"

Barely registering his words, I commanded, "Let's go this way," pointing into the trees where I thought a path would take us through.

Chief let me know, "We want to go by the river."

"This is a better way. I think the river bends and we can intersect it down here a little ways. It will have bigger rocks to sit on."

"Can you see it?"

"No, but I'm going this way."

I moved ahead while Harley and Two-Bit hacked at briar bushes around a fallen tree in an effort to get to the river quicker until Two-Bit yelled, "SNAKE!" and bolted with Harley out of the patch. Full-eyed and flushed, they clamped close to Stoner where Two-Bit talked loud about how you shouldn't suck the venom out of a snake bite because it might seep into a cavity in a tooth and make your head swell up double and the eyelids would be so fat you couldn't see out of them. I told Chief, "There might be a slope just beyond these trees, with a clearing around some small boulders."

Chief led us through the patch of woods onto a sloped clearing. The way around the small boulders seemed familiar enough but had more bushes than I expected.

I took the lead. "We'll curve around to the river after we get past that rock, and there we'll look for a boulder to sit on."

Past the rock we looped to a shed-sized boulder by the river. Chief commented in an elongated voice, "Preeettty gooood there, JJ."

On the boulder we pulled off our knapsacks and unpacked our lunches. Chief opened a can of chow mein, and I asked him for some because I knew he wouldn't give me any – he never shared his food. He cupped his hand around his Chinese noodles and protested in a higher pitch than usual, "Hey, you have your own." Feeling rewarded, I bit into my peanut-butter-and-jelly sandwich – and then a curiosity hit me. I told the boys, "Wait here. I'm going to go up that hollow a ways, past the tracks there. I'll be back." Off I jogged amid warnings to look out for dogs and snakes, not a worry to me at this point. I had the notion there was a path to a rock formation draining water from a crevice, and I found it. I looked for a natural bench about six feet wide along the wall of the hill along the hollow, and when I reached the path-like bench I stood on it. "Lord, Lord, Lord."

I scampered further up the path along the ledge until it leveled out and broadened into a view east to the river where my friends remained small on the boulder. I searched the wall until I found the thick roof slab and followed it to the water-scooped niche where I rubbed the dust off the glassy swirl of grayish blue in the web of white, not as blue as I remembered it in my dreams but otherwise the same. On what had to be Salaman's seat, I sat cross-legged, dazed with clarity, wondering at all this, so vibrant and real to the touch.

What now? Some questions I knew I had to ask, but some answers, like some of the questions themselves, came to me with a force that wasn't scary, that didn't feel as if it were out to get me, though I felt as though my brain had been blown into the air like sparkling confetti and I would be a while picking up the pieces and placing them back in my head, until which time I would have to act normal.

What should I tell my friends?

Nothing. I have enough of a reputation trying to save them from dogs.

Should I tell Jenny?

I think so. She likes these puzzles. .

Should I tell Miss Mira?

She's the one who tells me things. I'll wait and see.

AT MY NEXT workout, I dutifully did my stretches and jogged a few warm-up laps until Miss Mira called for me to stop as I neared her at the bench. She asked what I was concentrating on. I answered, "My body." Seeing that she was waiting for more, I added, "I've had some dreams and found out some odd things. I'm trying to get them out of my head so I can gear up."

Her expression stayed the same. After about five seconds, she inquired, "A dream of a runner?"

"Yes, ma'am."

"Do you know his name?"

"Yes, ma'am. I think so."

For a few moments Miss Mira gazed at me, then smiled contentedly. "Good."

I asked, "Do you know?"

"Yes, darling."

212

"Who?"

"Salaman. An unusual name for a Cherokee, one must admit."

"Salaman who?"

"I should leave it at that for now, you're doing so well."

"How'd you know about him?"

"It came to me."

"When?"

"When I met you here on the field last autumn."

"Why didn't you tell me before?"

"Because it is more convincing for one to realize such a thing than be told and wonder what to believe, don't you think?"

"Being told would have been easier for me. I'm still confused about this guy and what's going on here."

"Time is confusing, but you wanted to understand it."

"Yes."

"It's part of the illusion, darling."

"Time seems real enough to me." *Birdseed would agree. This is Monday. Tomorrow is Tuesday.*

"Don't you know it! I get so caught up in it myself."

"Can't you just tell me the rest and put me ahead of the game?"

"I would, but deep down you know. Deep down we all know. Just go inside, and work with what you find."

"Go inside? I have to run out here."

"Yes," she confirmed, "Let's get started. Today imagine the competition pressing hard against you. You can do that inside."

After the warm-ups she stood at the corner of the field and called the intervals, with the requirement that I never stop moving, even if it meant walking in small circles between sprints.

In an even voice she called out:

"Thirty laps. Each time walk to the mid-field, then dash to the goal line. Walk to the other side of the field and do the same. I'll count down the laps as you go by. Think of your next charge ahead, not how many laps you have to go."

And: "Start this five-lap run medium-fast, but each time you cross the fifty-yard line push all-out for fifty yards to pass the

213

leader. Breathe in through the mouth, out through the nose."

And: "Push but don't strain. Feel the difference. Feel the difference. On this five-lap run, press your competition at the start and at the end. On the first lap sprint all out. On the next three, hang in with a medium-fast pace, and on the last lap sprint all-out again."

Then: "I'll call out your lap times on this five-lap combination. Make the first one a medium pace. Make each subsequent lap at least a second faster."

And: "Do a middle burn, five times around. Start out medium fast. Run the next three at the top speed at which you think you can maintain the pace, imagining a gap between you and runners behind you. If you slow down, visualize the runners catching up; maintain against them. Close the last lap at the fastest rhythm you can hold steadily. Don't go deep into the pain. Stay on the tolerable side of it and push it away. Stay in the forehead and spine. Push the energy down the back of the head into the spine with a beat."

"What beat?"

"It'll come to you, darling. Medium-fast speed on this first lap."

As I passed by her on the second lap: "Take over the race and hold it steady!"

"Number three! Stretch your lead – same speed!"

"Number four: Drive them down, drive them down with the rhythm!"

Last go-round: "Take it back gradually and coast your lead! That's it!"

Finish: "That's it, darling. I could see the race. Do you have something left?"

"I have something left."

"Then you're done for the day."

My workouts reached a three-hour peak the Tuesday before the meet, and then eased off. On Thursday afternoon I drove to Lexington and found Dad in his room waiting in the wheelchair with his overnight case in his lap, ready to go. Happy as vacationers, we loaded up and headed down the road he had known all his adult life, through Richmond, Berea, Renfro Valley, London and then Corbin where we stopped at Sanders' Café for lunch. The waitress recommended chicken livers. Dad nodded yes; he confirmed that Bluecrest Home didn't serve him fried chicken livers. I asked the waitress if we could have the chicken livers without salt. She checked with Mr. Sanders, who had the cook prepare them special for us, and Dad ate his whole pile.

At Marci's house that evening, Alexander cooked a meat loaf dinner, but Dad couldn't eat as much as he normally did because of all those chicken livers in him. A dessert of peach cobbler and ice cream topped him off and sent him to bed early.

In the morning I helped Dad dress and walked him to breakfast at Marci's round table as Mother, Sarah and Miss Mira arrived. Miss Mira said her son Jack was on his way from Richmond to meet her at the track. Miss Mira told Mom about how hard Jack worked with his construction business and how he built the enclosed patio for her behind her house. Her sons resembled Herman Crane in build – a little stocky but not fat – though Jack had Miss Mira's straight nose and slender neck.

After the pleasant table talk, Miss Mira checked her gold wristwatch and said we should go. As we walked into the shade of the campus, up the sidewalk toward the classroom building with the tall bell tower, she asked, "How well did you concentrate last night?"

"It took me half an hour to get settled."

"What do you expect of the race?"

"A hard drive against Bobby Dodd, and I don't know what else. I hope to enjoy it."

"Good enough."

I walked on with her in the vibrant way I walked away from the ledge, this time not engaged with the mystery of why things happen the way they do, but with the work at hand, my race.

40

Counting down

IN THE WARM-UP JOG AROUND THE BACK CURVE, I SEE DAD'S HEAD IN the passenger seat of Marci's long Pontiac parked five yards from the track at the mid-point of the turn, sloping down a small grade. The dipping angle makes the view right for him because he sits short. Even in the car he wears his hat because he wants to wear his hat. I tell him that the mile race is one event away.

At that, I trot to Miss Mira who smiles unperturbed beside Jack, a quiet, no-nonsense guy. He and I look as though we live in Kentucky. Miss Mira looks as though she lives in Naples and it's cocktail time at the Beach Club Hotel. Beneath her ribbon-crested hat, her sunglasses hide her eyes in style; the necklaced pearl rests on the top of her freckled breastbone and a scarf of deep blue with gold trim wraps the waist of her white pants. "So much fun," Miss Mira remarks to Jack. Indeed it is, but my fun is packed beneath a radioactive layer of anticipation that turns on all the switches.

The final call from the loudspeaker prompts me to the gathering at the starting line as school names are drawn for lane positions. This is a loaded event, with challengers from Lynch, Hall, Evarts, Wallins, Loyall, Black Star and Cumberland as well as Knox County, Middlesboro, Pineville, Barbourville, Bell County and Williamsburg. Buford from Corbin, who challenged me in the backstretch a year earlier, has the inside position. Bobby Dodd, taller than the year before, gets a middle spot. I am placed next to the outside but at least I am in the front row. I don't care if there is a disadvantage to the far position at the start; I'm satisfied to face the white lines of the raceway, level and clear.

216

My clock of attention ticks tighter as details come together – the positions of the racers, the reminder to keep a pace, instructions of the officials, the make-or-break demand to finish first or second, deep breathing, my family and friends, limberness.

Counting down: The gun-hand rises.

Like a fusillade of buckshot we shoot out of the barrel, most runners spreading along the left side of the track while I hang wide on the right where I have room until the turn.

At the curve I fold into an open spot in the first lane, third from last. I don't know who is first or second or much of anything else except the shape and stretch of the clump ahead of me, a frenetic scintillation of legs and feet and backsides and colors of whatever school's miler is in my face, at this moment the orange, blue and white of Williamsburg, the whole lot of us in a tumult rumbling around the bend.

On the backstretch the momentum of the secondary herd starts to drag and threaten my pace, so I stream past one, two, three, four runners until I find an inside space behind the quick-moving front group.

By the second turn I lightly register the placements ahead: Wallins in front, Middlesboro second, Black Star third, Pineville fourth, Buford of Corbin fifth, Dodd – the one I care about – sixth, Barbourville seventh. I am about twelfth and steady, holding my attention in the beat. For a second I wish I could bring my family into my momentum, but at least they can see the movement and the ground I have to make up; that is enough to ride us together.

In the second lap the pace slows near the turn, pressing me to swing out on the bend and overtake a line of three. On the straightaway I stay in the second lane because my pace is pulling me up to a string of runners. Halfway down the track I pass the line of them and hit the curve behind Bobby Dodd until Dodd passes Buford. Beyond the turn I see with peripheral vision Marci beside Dad in the Pontiac and hear her car-muffled screaming. I think she is telling me to "Go," but I am not going to make a move against Buford on the curve because in my last race against him he

217

fired out his reserves in an attempt to keep me from passing, and he might have more reserves this time, so I resolve to overtake him on a straight.

Out of the curve heading toward the third lap, Bobby Dodd knocks Pineville out of fourth place. Wallins can't hold on in front; Middlesboro claims the lead but can't sustain it as he clenches into choppy steps and falls back along with Wallins; Dodd takes the forfeit of them both and sluices up to second place behind Black Star, who is new at the point.

It's time for me to move against Buford; I burst a sharp clip around him. *If you want a sprint like last time, come get me now.* He doesn't try, not yet, at least. I put some distance between us.

Dodd takes the lead away from Black Star. That's a final signal for me. I pass the others and pull up to a close second to Dodd. I'm going to tail him for now unless someone threatens us. A lap away from judgment, my chest pumps hard but isn't gripped by the load. My legs are yet light and efficient with the pace. Anticipation of the last lap starts to blend wild through my blood like moonshine as I hang close behind Dodd so he will hear me – *nothing personal, just a game - a serious game to me.* In our duet out front I follow Dodd around the sixth curve, through the incoherent yells of my professor sister. I wonder whether to wait until the middle of the last lap before bidding for the lead but decide to move early.

On the front straight I push up to near-full speed and pass Dodd. As I get the final-lap gun he is three yards back. Barreling around the turn and along the back straight, I stretch the spread between us until I feel safe out of the sound of his footsteps.

I want to drive the speed into the rhythm a millimeter from the strain and see how long I can hold it and what I can feel in it. Halfway down the backstretch I shift my attention deeper into the cadence of a straight-line roll. Mentally I try to latch myself into the heart of the pulsing flow, but I can't dissolve into it quite enough to stream free in the rapid, so I fire along with what I have, a wheeling reach and the pleasure of speed.

218

Angling into the last curve, with Dodd at least ten yards behind, I stay fixed in the fast gait, worry free, and from the last turn I sling into the stretch with enough reserves to speed up a notch, but I don't need to storm the finish line this time; I sail the wave of the high tide in.

In the noise I break the ribbon, surprised most of all that it was easy – work enough, but more in enjoyment of a smooth performance than in the wrenching of an unbridled burn as I coast to a stop, looking forward to the next race.

MISS MIRA CONGRATULATES me, and even Jack tells me I "did real good there." Refreshed, I jog down the center field and across the track to the Pontiac where Dad is laughing. I tell him and an energized-looking Marci that the half-mile race will be in two hours, so they back away to drive to her house for the break.

After watching the other events with Mom, Sarah and Alexander while Miss Mira talks with her son, I hear the second call for the half-mile and descend to the grass where Miss Mira sits with me on the slope in the shade of the bleachers. Standing so as to not intrude too much, Jack listens as his mother asks, "In the mile, you were in a rhythm, weren't you?"

"Yes, ma'am."

"What did you hear in it?"

"The stride."

"How is your energy?"

"Strong so far. In this race the matter might come down to sheer sprinting speed."

"How do you plan to run it?"

"Start in the middle and close in the second lap."

"Watch out for that runner from Black Star if he is in this race. He fell out of the third spot on the mile, but he has good speed if he doesn't cut his stride short."

"What do I do about him?"

"After the first lap don't let him get ahead of you."

"Why? Does he have a good kick?"

219

"It looks like it. In the mile he was near the front, fell back to the middle, but he moved back up and finished third. He almost beat that Knox Central boy. He can get emboldened by a few passes."

In the lineup for the 880 I take note of the curly-haired Black Star runner. The ritual of the starter winds down to the quiet pause, the gun, and we are unleashed.

Middlesboro on the inside moves in front; Buford of Corbin runs second; Wallins third; Dodd fourth; Black Star fifth; I'm sixth, in the middle.

Out of the first turn Barbourville advances to my side in a rumble of thick pounding while Black Star blocks me, allowing Barbourville to slip around and take the sixth spot in the closely packed front group.

Buford passes Middlesboro, so at the second turn it is Buford in the lead, Middlesboro on his shoulder, Dodd third, Wallins fourth and starting to fade, Black Star fifth, Barbourville sixth. I'm seventh, and I'm not going to stay here.

Midway down the front stretch I overtake Barbourville and Black Star and Wallins. My speed is there, *thank you, thank you, thank you very much.*

Crossing into the final lap, Buford holds onto the lead; Middlesboro struggles at second – I see his head come back with a chin-up strain; Dodd holds on with seeming ease at third; I am fourth, followed by Black Star. *Time to head up the road.* I cut outside and pass Dodd before he can get around Middlesboro, then I move around Middlesboro and slip inside to the rail going into the turn behind Buford.

Out of the curve I match Buford's stride, locking in on him, with Middlesboro behind me, followed by Dodd. I figure Dodd has to be up to something that could get me in trouble, so I swing wide to avoid being trapped inside, steal the lead from Buford and then hear footsteps clipping up from behind. Black Star edges into my peripheral view, what Miss Mira warned me about, so I pay attention as he comes up almost alongside me. Dodd emerges and

220

appears off Black Star's shoulder, just a little behind him, making us an angled, three-man wing. I try to mesh into the rhythm but it's hard to bring my concentration in because I'm so exhilarated by the threat of these two runners on my right trying to take me down. In the frantic crunch of cinders with half a lap to go, I want to keep the formation rolling, play a little, stay a little with the wing and risk and maybe energize their front-row hopes but not let them get so heady they overtake me, just keep the uncertainty for fifteen yards longer, maybe twenty, a fast-dance on a sword edge as we stampede in formation down the straight where Dodd pulls up some, edging ahead of Black Star and then up to me, the way a race should be, *Lord, I love it,* but now that we are closing in on the last turn where my father sits I have had enough of this, so I pull away from Black Star and Dodd and drive on the thrill in my chest.

Around the curve I try to immerse in the high cadence again. I catch a pulse through my mind's ear and want to keep as much of it as possible when I hit the last straight, but a warning-signal tightness starts to weigh through my middle to the point I can't pull my attention from my body and into my forehead, so I loosen just enough to keep my speed without gnashing. I don't hear anyone close, though I know Dodd will overtake Black Star. With a higher gear left unused, I'm sure I can hold off Dodd if he moves up to me.

He can't.

A reaching, rounding movement gives me a final taste of the rhythm and takes me through the ribbon where I coast down easy to a walk.

Breathing deep, strolling back to the other runners as my blood flushes into the sudden dam of me, floodgates closing for the day, I remember that I have to take my father back to Lexington tomorrow and leave him where he cannot walk, much less walk away. But today he is here, and my mother is here by the grace of God, and I am giving them what little I can from a playing field, for whatever it is worth: two races on a day I am still young.

221

Sarah's diary – May 12, 1957

I wonder why girls shriek more than boys do. Boys shout and yell, and when they are surprised they might scream some, like the time JJ and Scotty set off the firecracker near the bus station and made John Egred yelp and got arrested. But girls – Willa Mae screamed at Elvis on *The Ed Sullivan Show* last year, and she wasn't even in the audience. She was at her house with Becky and me. I don't scream at Elvis. Of course I only saw him on TV. But I screamed when the two boys pulled up to JJ near the end of the 880. That was the best part, but it wouldn't have been the best part if they had passed him or if I had had a heart attack. That would have ruined it all.

41

Music to my ears

ON SATURDAY, THE DAY AFTER THE MEET, I PAINTED THE WALLS AND ceiling of Miss Mira's dance studio room, as it was about time I found a way to pay her back a little for all the time she was giving me. During my work, Mr. Crane read his *Life* magazine in his living room easy chair, pleasant as ever. Miss Mira brought me limeade made fresh, sweetened just enough to take off the acid edge of the fruit, mixed with crushed ice, just right for the humid heat of the day, unseasonably warm. The heat held into the week when, on Tuesday, Miss Mira joined me at the field. I thought she might lighten the workout, but the first words out of her mouth were, "This is a day to be merciless," and she sprinted me for two hours straight with hardly a minute break between any of the runs, bam, bam, bam, bam through the meat-grinder.

Halfway through the Tuesday drills she fanned her face, bid me take a drink of water from my jug, and told me the Wednesday workout would be tough but short and that I might enjoy having some time with Jenny. I never mentioned Jenny to her but welcomed that suggestion because I wanted to take Jenny to the ledge in Bell County and see what she would make of it.

Jenny agreed to go with me if we returned by dark, her mother's requirement, so I picked her up promptly with my hair still damp from the after-practice shower. Listening to Big Bob Simpson on WHLN playing music and extolling Philco appliances from the Belk's store he managed on Central Street, we twisted along the old road to the turnoff closest to the ledge, crossed the bridge and parked the car in a clearing. An older couple on the porch of a frame house rocked slowly enough to watch us and advise us not to get too hot out there.

We hiked deliberately down the railroad tracks, then by the river and into the hollow, up the hill near the stream leaking out of the mountain, onto the narrow road-like rise of the ledge. Releasing her hand so we could walk freely around the cliff with the niche, I asked her, "OK, Kid, what do you feel about this place?"

"It's interesting. I'm imagining how it was made."

"What about this grayish blue in the rock? What kind of rock do you think it is?"

"It's sandstone, rubbed out by water. But that bluish part, hmm, it's so slick it looks like igneous rock." She touched it barely with the tips of her long fingers. "But any igneous rock around here would have to be way down, five thousand feet or more. I don't understand the white webbing unless it's some kind of limestone packed in there."

"It could be."

"This mountain doesn't look like it was upended the way that ridge across the river was shoved up. The seams are fairly level here. Maybe some other rocks or different colored sands washed into the formation." Her fingers traced the roof strata above the indention, then she lowered her hands and contemplated something – I asked what.

"I don't know," she reported. "It's a pretty place. And this blue in the cliff – it reminds me of the color in the rock Miss Mira gave me, from Stonehenge."

"That's what you're thinking about?"

"Yes," she said in a sober but withdrawn way. "And I feel like I miss you. Which doesn't make sense." She perked up a bit. "You're right here."

"That kind of feeling comes over me, too, sometimes, and I miss you out of nowhere."

"Do you?"

"Yes."

For half a minute or so I watched her study the niche until, with a long slow breath, she asked, "How did you find this place?"

"I came across it. I've seen it before."

"Oh."

"In my dreams – of the Cherokee. I've seen him sitting here."

She fixed her eyes on mine. "In dreams?"

"Sometimes I see him. Sometimes I see what he saw."

"What he saw?"

"Yes, through his eyes. Like I'm him."

"Oh, boy."

"Yeah."

"You saw it as it is now or as it was back then?"

"Back then."

"Well," she didn't look taken aback, "you said you wanted to see the past."

I had forgotten about that, because the past I told Jenny I wanted to see was the one of old Bible times and ancient Greece and Egypt and Mexico, the high civilizations with prophets and pyramids, not Harlan County in the 1800s when my grandfather ran around shooting people. Lucky for me I didn't have dreams of him getting killed in the barber chair.

Jenny said she didn't know what to think of all this, but I was gratified to have her to talk to, curious and open-minded with sparkle, not inclined to go around gossiping; I trusted her not to share this confidence, for who could tell how such a story could twist by the time it went from one end of the school to the other. The truth was peculiar enough as it was.

On the way from the ledge to the car I held Jenny's hand for comfort, and we didn't talk much. Once in the car, as I pulled out the keys to start the engine, she asked, "So you miss me sometimes?"

"Yes," I admitted, touched that she wanted to hear me say it again. I knew I needed to talk about feelings here. Sarah would be proud. "Out of nowhere."

"Is that when you call me?"

"Sometimes, but I'm not always at home when I miss you."

"Where are you?"

"Running distance."

225

"Are you going to invite me to the meet?" She was bold in her way – bolder than I expected, and I admired it, even as I admonished myself for not inviting her earlier without having to be cued.

So I asked her to the meet, she said yes, and I made arrangements for her to go to Barbourville with Miss Mira on Friday because I had to leave Thursday afternoon with Mother and Sarah to stay overnight at Marci's to hear her concert.

Miss Mira said she didn't mind driving Jenny. "I look forward to taking the Sister tomorrow," she bubbled at the close of the short Thursday workout. "We'll have a happy time. Jenny is so exceptional."

"She is," I agreed as I removed my sweats.

For the first time Miss Mira asked me a question about Jenny. "Do you miss her sometimes?"

I was caught off guard by her probe of my feelings, which could sound like the kind of young love dreaminess that amused me when I saw it in others, especially Sarah, though I enjoyed it immensely in myself. "Yes, ma'am, I enjoy being around her."

"I do too. She's such a dear. Well, are you prepared? It's all coming to a head these next ten days."

If I placed in the regional meet Friday I would advance to the state championship the following week. "I'm ready to put out whatever it takes."

"In your meditation last night, how did you do?"

"Not great."

"How much time did you give it?"

"Half an hour."

"Try for an hour."

"An hour? It's hard concentrating in there."

"It's harder out here, darling, if you lose your connection."

"That sounds like a warning."

"I'm just being a coach."

"I know. Thank you."

226

Mom, Sarah and I arrived at Marci's home in Barbourville two hours before the concert, not soon enough for Marci who had fretted that we would not get there on time. At her supper table Marci announced I was the guest of honor for having advanced to the regional meet. I raised my hand so my family would know I was the one, and Marci passed around the table a buttered and spice-speckled broiled salmon, *umm hmm*. After the meal we told stories about Dad until Marci declared it was time to walk to the chapel where the Louisville Orchestra had set up.

When the student usher offered programs, Marci declined for us and asked that we be surprised. After leading us to our seats, she kept me from sitting and beckoned me to circulate with her among the chaired musicians tuning up in a cacophony of scales. She introduced me to the drummer adjusting his timpani – a treat for me to meet him up close at the drums – and then pulled me to the flutist Marci said would also be featured in her composition. Walking among them, I relished the skills of the musicians and the anticipation that reminded me of the warm-up for a race, except more refined and without the fear, as the musicians were there to work together, not run each other into the dirt.

After I returned to my seat, the players settled down and the conductor led them through a Strauss medley and took a bow. Then he introduced Marci as the "solo violinist and composer of the next work. Her piece is titled 'The Final Race.'"

I blurted, "What?" – not too loud, I hoped – as Marci stood, raised her bow at the signal of the baton and freed a tune that streamed out softly, as if across a meadow on a light wind. I recognized the melody as the one she played for us two Christmases before, the unfinished composition that left me entranced in the love seat at the bottom of the stairs in our living room. I felt as though I were at the starting gun but couldn't run; the race was everywhere, and I was the ghost of it.

The flute joined her in a long and lilting rise, the deeper instruments filled out the sound and expectation, and then the timpani rolled in. With Celtic quickness, Marci's violin burst into

227

the sprints and paused for the orchestral movement of the field of runners and the churning stretches of endurance and positioning. The timpani and the smaller drums in their turns sped with her or answered her. I could hear the feet up close in riffs of glides and passes and sense the line of will through a deep chord. I could hear and all but ride the threats, the steadiness, the surges and the rhythm. When the piece was done, too soon for me, I wondered what came through my sister that she could run the mile in such a moving way, with music.

The orchestra played four other composers' pieces, the last a work of Brahms, but I was happy being left behind in the work of Marci's mind. Afterward I embraced her, and as we walked to her house, I asked how she composed it.

"I composed the opening for its lightness. It took months for the rest to come. Did you like it?'

"Of course I liked it. I loved it, especially that deep sound that came through."

"It's interesting you picked that out. I put that in to represent the holy sound."

"What holy sound?"

"The sound of the power some saints say upholds creation – Amen to us; Amin and Aum and Hum to other religions – different spelling and pronunciation, same thing they called the Word."

I thought, *so that's what's going on.* But I was too happy to make a serious comment. Instead, I responded, "The Word gets around, doesn't it?"

"It gets around."

"You did it beautifully."

"Thanks. You know how long it took. I was so relieved when it finally came through."

42

Company for the stone

THE COOL MORNING PROMISES GOOD RUNNING WEATHER FOR THE mile, and my arm on Mother's shoulder gives me added comfort beneath the shade trees of Union. In the upbeat company of Sarah, Marci and Alexander, we walk through the library archway toward the parking lot where, with perfect timing, the Cranes' car slips to a halt in a space in the direction ahead of us. The brake lights stay on for a while until Mr. Crane lugs himself from behind the steering wheel; driving or walking, he doesn't move as nimbly as his wife.

Miss Mira emerges from the front passenger seat, poised and purposeful. Jenny steps out from the back door, and I am glad to see her as she brushes back her shiny hair and lifts her purse strap to her shoulder. Greeting each other in the charged cheerfulness of game time, Mr. Crane jokes with me until his son Casey joins him, whereupon he repeats his jokes to Casey.

Walking beside Jenny, I reflect on the fact that I will race in the company of two women and two girls I care about deeply.

This would not be a good day to lose.

I don't take the race for granted, but I am confident I can contend unless some accident tears me down. My winning time for the mile in the district meet was fastest in the region, and I haven't slacked since then. Bradshaw Perkins of Somerset isn't here to whip me the way he did the year before; he's running for Eastern Kentucky University. Bobby Dodd is tough and out to get me.

I am within two seconds of the fastest district mile time in the state posted by Sam Davanni of St. Xavier in Louisville. I wonder what those Louisville runners eat that makes them so fast. They take turns dominating state meets, and because they do, I like the idea of going up against them alone – if I can succeed today.

Shortly before the first call for the mile, Sarah takes Jenny's hand, a confusingly touching sight to me, and leads her through the crowd to see people up close while I walk with Miss Mira to sign in and say hello to Coach Sands, then loosen up in the midst of the colorful action, and at the final call ask Miss Mira if she has any instructions.

"Remember your offering. Remember what runs in you," she tells me the same way she told me last year in a workout.

I take that to heart and report to the line where I am given the inside lane. I wonder for a moment what to do with that placement advantage since I don't seek the lead at the start of the mile. I will need this position more in the half-mile, but in this four-lap race I will use it only to save some steps and make the outside runners pass me in order to claim their inside slots before heading into the first turn.

I look around – at my people clustered in the bleachers, at Miss Mira on the sidelines, at my fellow runners, and at the Southeastern Kentucky Regional Track Meet sign that tells me I returned as I vowed the year before. I wish my father could be here, or at least not be alone, but he is alive and I expect to see him in Lexington next week and take him to the state meet – that's my task of the moment, getting there. For all these gifts and all these possibilities I give thanks until the gun hand lifts, signaling me into a crouch.

The mile is on. I take off more quickly than usual. Halfway down the straight I speed up to make it hard for runners to funnel into Lane 1 ahead of me. This isn't a good idea; I'm getting pulled out. I restrain myself so I don't get myself too caught up in this little game that has no strategy other than to give the early front-end runners a momentary problem. *But I do enjoy it.* Six runners crowd in front of me; the other five settle in behind. Dodd isn't ahead of me as he usually is.

On the curve two runners pass me – one from Lily High, another from Clay County. I think that passing at this juncture is unusual at this speed, with so far to go, but they are ambitious. On the back straight they charge all the way to the front and lead us around the oval.

Crossing into the second lap, Bobby Dodd steams past me and melds into the middle, leaving me third from the rear. He's ambitious, too. I'm feeling even and waiting for the buildup in me. On the back straight of the second lap Dodd goes to the front. That feels unsafe, so I quicken up gradually, pass three, and wedge into the middle of the line, a better shooting distance. Some runners ahead of me trade places with each other, but Dodd keeps the lead against Lily and Clay County who follow tight behind him. I'm feeling thrust and endurance, but as I go into the fourth curve I realize I am not locked into the rhythm; I'm focused on the positions of the others and wondering whether this lap is as fast as I think it is – too much outward thinking, all in all.

Going into the fourth turn I pull into my head an awareness of the pace, the cinder chops and leg movements until I blend myself into the beat and follow the leaders down the straight to the third lap and the call-out of my time which is faster than in my last meet, so I know I am rolling fast; these other guys just happen to be ahead of me.

I believe they don't have staying power. I need to drive them down, so I overtake two runners before getting to the turn where I slide to the inside and hold on. Rotating from east to west around the bend, with running sounds in my ears, I gear up for the showdown with the five in front.

Out of the curve I start picking off one runner at a time. I'm going to the front and I don't think anyone can stop me unless they burn themselves out early. I pass number five, number four, number three, number two, feeling steady in the surge. I catch up with Dodd three-quarters of the way down the back straight where I clip around him at the start of the turn, wondering if he will challenge me now or later, though I don't care which because I am in high gear and aim to stay in it.

I hear him behind me as I get the final-lap gun. Through the seventh turn I put distance between Dodd and me as behind him fade those who overheated early and are paying the price. Halfway around the last lap I sail alone in front with flashes of Marci's fiddle in the gait, low hills on three horizons, a crowd I perceive again as if out of a lifting fog as I wind out of the last turn with the pleasure of the movement coming on, down the stretch, toward the crowd and through the ribbon – so quickly done – and onto the list of regional winners who will compete for the state championship in the mile.

For a minute I walk in the echo of what I have done in order to absorb it, then celebrate with Miss Mira and head into the stands to be with my happy company. We all feel gratified, and I feel strong besides.

For a while I can enjoy the afterglow and keep the recollection warm for the wind-up of the half-mile race.

DURING OUR BREAK, Miss Mira chats with her family in the stands while Mother, Marci, Sarah, Jenny and I stroll to the college lake beyond the athletic field. At the narrow shoreline I pick up a few wafer-like stones and skip the first one on the water. Jenny orders, "Wait!" and pries open my left hand to see the other water-buffed rocks. "This one is pretty," she says of a white, glassy-smooth pebble she rubs with her forefinger. "Can I have it?"

I relinquish it to her, and she tucks it into her purse for the ride.

I ask Mother if she wants to skip a rock on the water, but she declines the offer, saying she can't throw well.

"You can cast a fishing line where you want it."

"That's different," she informs me. She doesn't make a big display of her emotions in public, other than to praise me to all her lady friends who politely act interested. She doesn't have to kiss and carry on for me to know what a mother she is. I know she

232

would give her life for me without a blink, and so far she has done that in every way but dying.

Back at the field we watch some sprints and low hurdles until it is time for me to prepare for the 880. My company seems settled until I get to the starting post and, in a last glance before the race, I spy Sarah and Jenny standing, with Jenny holding her hand over her mouth.

I'm lined up.

I'm ready.

"On your mark... Get set."

I start in a volley that lands me in the middle of the pack by the first curve. A runner I never saw before, a long-legged boy from Lynch, gallops in front of me like a deer, bounding two steps to three of mine. Miss Mira wouldn't allow that kind of bounce in me no matter how long my stride. His undulating thrust fascinates me so much that I don't want to pass him yet. I'm thinking of how he makes the rest of us look like little quick-stepping birds next to him.

By the end of the second curve, however, Lynch breathes hard and throws a heavier thud into his leaps, so on the straightaway I get around him and pass the group, push ahead of Bobby Dodd and edge up to the front-runner from Fleming-Neon High. Fleming-Neon doesn't want me to pass as we go side by side across the halfway mark. Approaching the turn, I don't have room to fold in behind him, where Dodd follows close, so I run at Fleming-Neon's shoulder and resolve it's time to let loose whatever I have stored up from all those drills called by Miss Mira.

I gun into the curve. Fleming-Neon shrinks back enough to give me space in front. I take it, round out the bend and wait for Dodd to exact his revenge.

Halfway down the backstretch, Dodd arrives. The race is on.

This guy is good, I give him that. This guy is good.

He tries to pass but can't. We're linked. Dodd's footfall matches mine. *One of us is going to break. All it takes is a thought.*

Don't think it. Stay inside the rhythm. Keep the lock on the mind.

233

Three-quarters of the way down the backstretch, Dodd relents. *Take him now.*

I ease ahead of him – two feet, three feet, *that's enough*. The track stripes swish beneath us. Dodd follows steadily, but I'm not menaced; a yard seems safe as I angle into the turn.

Down the final stretch, the notion of a makeshift glory all my own fades thin and blends into the fullness of being so alive, with friends for me and runners against me, and for a second I feel we are all the same, although I break the ribbon.

And it's all over so quickly.

As the loudspeaker calls my name, I steady myself in the achievement of the day and try to hold onto it.

My family, the Cranes and Jenny walk down to the grassy area after I collect my medals from the award table. I give both ribbon-hung coins to Jenny, who thanks me and rubs them a moment before placing them in her purse, company for the stone. With a shared sense of satisfaction we climb toward the parking lot behind the stands. At the top of the embankment I turn for a moment to scan the busy field, the place of two years' wanting, and it all passes before my very eyes: I know I will never race again on the Union track.

43

T.C. Hunter Special

THE DAY AFTER THE MEET – THE SATURDAY OF THE PROM – I MET Jenny at Lee Drug for a chocolate malt and some shopping, including birthday toys for her nephew, Scotty Lanier's little brother. I expected nothing but an afternoon of uncomplicated pleasure because of the dance and because I knew where to find toys that boys would like, from experience in my counter-high days buying cap pistols, trucks and soldiers at Newberry's and at Scott's five-and-dime stores, wonderlands for little people and bazaars for bigger people who didn't want to spend a lot on, say, prescription glasses when a pair of magnifying spectacles would do for $1.25. I didn't know where to find clothes for Monday's Senior Day, an occasion for members of the graduating class to dress freely. I had planned to dress the way I knew Stoner would, in a regular shirt and jeans, until Jenny said I should try a different, old-time look. From Powers and Horton to the big Belk store downtown we browsed, finding nothing old-fashioned. When I declared the mission futile, Jenny said no, wait, hey, we should go to T.C. Hunter's store. Why didn't we think of that before?

Along Central Street I marched with her to T.C. Hunter's, ignoring the aroma from the bakery on the way, easier to do with a stomach full of chocolate milk and malt and ice cream, though in my heftier paperboy days I would have worked in something extra anyway, maybe a few day-old doughnuts plus a cream puff to aid my digestion. As Mr. Hunter craned himself up from his rocking chair behind his counter to wait on us, I said hello and told him, "I would like some old – ", at which point Jenny's elbow against my arm stopped my sentence. So I rephrased my statement: "I would like some nice summer pants."

He asked what color and size. "Thirty-inch waist," I said.

235

Jenny added, "A light color."

Mr. Hunter adjusted his glasses, braced his legs in a crouch to pull some boxes from beneath the counter, and opened them in the light of the bulb overhead. I fingered the fabric of the pants in the first box. Too thick. I suggested something lighter.

Jenny picked up some light-cream-colored pants from the third box. "This one," she alerted me. "Try on this pair." In a crusty dressing room in the back, I slipped into the slacks, buttoned the fly, and presented myself.

Jenny pinched my pants at the side of the knee and flipped the fabric the way my mother did. "It feels nice and light. I like that very much."

I agreed.

Jenny asked, "For a shirt, do you have something with full, gathered sleeves?"

From a counter drawer Mr. Hunter lifted a stack of folded, paper-taped shirts. As I sorted through them, Jenny asked, "Do you have any earlier styles? The early ones are so classic."

Mr. Hunter followed me to the back of the store and brought another stack from which Jenny opened a white V-neck shirt with a large collar and ample sleeves. "This one," she concluded. "Try this one on."

I obliged. It felt comfortable, easy to move in.

"Oh yes," Jenny confirmed.

Mr. Hunter took me to a mirror in the back while Jenny looked over the goods near the front. I commented to myself out loud, "I wonder if Salaman wore something like this."

Mr. Hunter answered, "Yes."

"Sir?"

"You asked if the Indian man wore something like this. He paid a dollar a shirt."

A shot of voltage pricked me between the shoulders and tickled through to my ribs. "He bought from you?"

"From my old man, while I was a boy."

"What was he like?"

"The Indian? Quiet. Eyes deep set like yours. Ran the mail. For those who didn't write, he wrote for a dime."

"Was he married?"

"Yes, to that teacher woman."

"What teacher woman?"

"A Miss Jerusha."

"Jerusha who?"

"Jerusha Tess, I'm recollecting."

Hold on here. "His name was Salaman Tess?"

"That's what I said."

The Universe is fooling with me bad. "Was she a good-looking woman?" *I'm asking how good-looking she was, this woman whose corpse I almost dug up.*

"I'd say so. Bright eyes. She was about ten years older than he was, and there was talk about that, but more talk about how she was a mulatto. She taught the colored. She had as good a head as anybody here, knew what a mountain was made of, what was on it or in it."

"I saw her grave."

"Is that so? I never seen it."

"I think she died in the fall."

"He came back from a Pineville run and found her lost to typhoid fever, best I recall."

"That would have been hard on him."

"I heard it said he sat cross-legged near her grave for a week; didn't move day or night. Some wondered if he was dead himself because he didn't even brush the leaves off him. Spooky, if you ask me. You can't even sit up straight that long by drinking yourself stone cold."

"It would have been hard for him to keep from falling over if he'd been liquored up."

"Spooky, if you ask me. He came to town after that week looking fit enough, though, and in the winter he went on."

"Where'd he go?"

"I heard tell he said he was going to Oklahoma, to find his kin."

237

I thanked him very much and asked him to keep the change.

"No need for that. Business is good."

On the way to Francis Flowers to pick up the corsage, Jenny asked why I was so quiet, and with an apology I told her I was thinking about the clothes, that's all. I wanted the evening to be about the dance, not about the 3-D movie playing behind my life.

In the evening I drove to Jenny's house and pinned the flower on her lavender evening gown. In the Lewallen Hotel ballroom we danced amid talk and *The Pastels'* music as mixed as the happenings of the day. Zorro, Lucy, Stoner, Jug, Horse, Chief, Harley, Two-Bit and Lois wove through the crowd, and I was exuberant with them, paying attention to Jenny when she told me something or talked with her friends or looked around. At midnight we slow-danced the last number and drove to Chief's house for an after-prom party with snacks and more music. Afterward, outside Jenny's house, as we stood beneath the trees at the edge of her yard, she asked if I wanted to go walking on Sunday afternoon and if I would wear the T.C. Hunter clothes.

So on Sunday afternoon I dressed up in the full-sleeved shirt and pants and my adidas running shoes and met her at the door. In a light, long, puffy-sleeved dress – a little old-fashioned, though not too much – she strolled with me to the road toward the second flat. As we walked around the hill, near the juncture of the short road curving up to Tess's grave, she pulled my hand to a stop, pointed to the dip and rise of the road, and asked if I would run for her about a hundred yards and back.

"Sure. Why?"

"I want to see what you look like as you run toward me."

"Wait here." I broke into an easy jaunt out and a quicker run back on the pebbled clay road, enjoying the wind against the fabric of my clothes. When I reached her, she took my arm, smiling wide, and we strolled back to her house like two costumed actors in an outdoor play.

44

Passing through

ON MONDAY MORNING I CHECKED MYSELF IN THE MIRROR TO SEE how the new old clothes looked for Senior Day. Not bad; better than knickers of the fourth grade. At the breakfast table Sarah agreed I looked good, a little pioneer-like. Mother warned me not to get my sleeves in my food, which I was close to doing.

As I buttered my toast, Mother answered the phone in the hall. "Oh," she said bluntly.

I stopped making scraping sounds on the bread.

"Oh no. Thank you for telling me... Yes... I understand... Yes, thank you. We will be on our way."

I put down my toast and Sarah held her fork still. Mother came to the kitchen door and reported, "Steve had another stroke. He has lost consciousness. The doctor says it is serious and that we should come right away."

Sarah leaned her head in her hands. I jumped from my chair, patted my sister and said we should get ready to leave.

We abandoned breakfast, scrambled, packed and left the clean-up for Miss Becker who worked with the look of fear. As I grabbed our suitcases in the living room, the phone rang again. Mother answered, talked methodically in yeses and thank-yous, then laid the receiver on its cradle and told us Dad had died.

At that, she leaned onto the phone table and cried fully, the first time I heard her cry that way. I went to her and put my hands on her soft back as the first wave of hurt drained through her and swelled into Sarah.

I didn't cry this time. The thought that he died alone was a wave too large for me to take on while I had to pick up the part of the man of the family gone.

I called some relatives; Mother called others and some friends. I phoned the Anderson and Laws Funeral Home to pick up Dad's body. Harold and I met with the funeral director to make the arrangements, and I handed over the burial suit Dad wore on his last trip to church. We set the funeral date for 11 a.m. Thursday and I wrote obituary information for the *Enterprise.*

With Mother and Sarah holding up well by outward appearances, I sought physical relief. At three o'clock, in a mechanical state of mind, I walked down to Huff Park where, on the Dragons' bench, Miss Mira sat ramrod straight, with a white scarf draped down her shoulder. When I handed her a wildflower, she stood, removed her hat and held me. "I heard about your father," she said. "I am so sorry."

"The worst is over for him, I guess," I uncoupled from her, "but I wanted to bring him home for the summer. I didn't want him to die alone. That's the worst part. I failed him in that."

"You didn't fail him. Some things can't be avoided. We all pass through them."

"He couldn't walk out of there. I could. The less he could move, the faster I was able to. That's the irony."

"He's fine now," she said. "Have a seat, darling." She gestured me to the place next to her. I knew from experience that I could settle down easier in her presence than alone, but I didn't think that she could settle me this time.

"Just go inside," she requested and for a long time led me with her voice until my breath slowed. Like a broadcast signal losing its reach to the radio of the car leaving town, the loss distanced itself. As my breathing paused on its own accord, my gaze became locked in the peace of the stillness. The weight of my body dissolved. I lost track of time until, after a while, I heard Miss Mira: "I am going to touch you between the eyebrows."

A cloudy light filled the impression left by her warm finger. In the center of that cloudiness formed a round spot, like a bright violet-blue sun, as pretty a blue as I had ever seen. Then the spot

240

started coming loose and diving, cloud-like, into a white vortex in its center.

She left me in that pulsation until it faded. Her voice told me, "Open your eyes."

I didn't particularly want to, but I obeyed.

"You intended to run the tension out of you. Where is it now?"

"In a box."

"You wanted to run hard and long today."

"Yes."

"Help yourself, but keep your awareness there," she pointed to the lower center of her forehead.

"I'll stretch and warm up."

"You don't need to stretch and warm up. Just start gradually."

"How long do I run?"

"Until you want to finish."

From a fast walk I slid into a jog a few laps, then a trot for a few rounds. Passing by Miss Mira, I noted that she was sitting straight with her eyes closed, the same as when I sat beside her. Occasionally at first, and vaguely, I remembered Dad in the mines and on the Martin's Fork road waiting for me. I remembered him carrying me as a child; his good cheer in the hospital; his crawling on the floor in the hallway; and the times I had to leave him at Bluecrest Home. After about a quarter of an hour, those memories weakened like mirror images on a pond giving way to the water itself until the floodwall broke, and a happy energy of sureness cascaded through me as I accelerated into a full run, around the field again and again. I wondered for a moment where the pain and tiredness were. Loop after loop I gave myself to the speed building up, until there it was in full: the electric lightness, all through me, at last. On and on I streamed, enjoying the strain when I wanted, forgetting the strain when I wanted.

Zorro and Lucy strolled down the hillside steps and over to the bleachers. I acknowledged them with a single wave on a pass, but I didn't want to do anything to slip outside this power. I circled almost full-bore around and around for an hour until Zorro

241

and Lucy left and the shadow of the goalpost stretched to the east. Thus reminded of the onset of dusk, I turned off the fount, walked to the bench and stood in front of Miss Mira.

She opened her eyes. "That's it," she declared.

I acknowledged, "That's it."

We didn't need to say anything else. Words felt too harsh against my state of mind, and I realized her instruction was almost down to silence.

৽৽

Sarah's diary – May 24, 1957

Aunt Betsy drove up from Vicksburg for Daddy's service. She says she likes tradition, but she also does what she wants. She married a sailor in California right before the war and divorced him within a year. She drinks Coca-Cola by the case, reads all night and sleeps all morning. In Vicksburg, her customers wake her up by ringing the doorbell of her antique shop, which is in her big house. She knows a lot and likes to talk, and sometimes doesn't notice when the people she is talking to have left the room. Even after we leave and return she is still on the same subject. She repeats her conversations, so if you miss a point the first time you can pick it up later. She's not refined like Mama, except they have the same way of talking.

With Aunt Betsy around, it's harder to feel sad. Yesterday she took *Gone With the Wind* to the toilet in the afternoon and didn't get off the commode until this morning when she'd finished the book. We could hardly wake her up for the funeral. I'm glad she's here.

45

Resthaven

ON TUESDAY SARAH STAYED HOME WITH MOTHER AND AUNT BETSY because she wanted to, but Mother told me to go on, to be with my friends though my studies were for all practical purposes finished. I would attend for half a day. On the wide front walk to the school, Jenny waited, watching me approach, and when I reached her she gave her condolences with a brevity I appreciated. I just wanted to go through the motions with my friends around me and leave at lunch. When we poured into the lobby crowd, a cheer went up, and I realized the students were looking at me.

Standing on a step by one of the sports trophy cases, Coach York, conspicuous in his natty red blazer, motioned me to the front and announced he and the school were sorry to hear about my father and that I had their sympathy. Then he congratulated me for winning the regional races, wished me luck in the state championship, and said I had done the school proud.

I thanked them and pledged to do my best. Though I knew I had the regret of death sealed in me, I felt lifted by the words and cheers of friends and even schoolmates who didn't know anything about the meets but whistled and clapped anyway. I would take whatever I could get and believe on it.

On the way to my homeroom I told Jenny I would like for her to go to the state meet, at least for the mile run on Saturday. She said that, in case I invited her, she had made arrangements to room with Barbara in her dorm and that Scotty would drive her to Lexington.

At lunch another good thing happened to me. I wouldn't have imagined it. Zorro and Lucy asked if they could walk me home. I accepted, and we talked about small things. I wanted to talk about small things. Sometimes the mercy of the earth is small things. I

243

thanked them for their company and invited them to come to the race in Lexington on Saturday if they wished, and we could all eat together before returning to Harlan.

Three hours later I walked to the field where Miss Mira stood at the sidelines waiting for me. When I asked what drills she wanted, she answered, "You decide." When I told her the order, she nodded approval, took her seat, closed her eyes for an hour or so of my practice, then watched me for another hour as I ran in the lightness, barely in this world.

The following day I ran two more hours in that manner. Feeling cleansed and calmed, I left the field to get ready for the visitation at the funeral home. The Lees' flowers stood at the foot of the casket. Dad's face looked surprisingly young. I told him goodbye. The friendship of the people who knew Dad draped warmly on us. After the visitation, the family gathered in our living room to share each other's company. We did not lack for food in the abundance brought to the door by friends and the ladies of the church, dish after dish.

On Thursday I did not run but tended to my sister and Mother and the thought of my father gone. Washed and dressed by eleven, I waited in the living room with Mother, Sarah, and Aunt Betsy. Mr. Biggs from the funeral home kindly came to lead us down Second Street and Mound to the Methodist Church. The escort made the walk easier.

Behind the casket at the altar, the minister talked nicely about Dad and consolingly about the promises of Christ. Outside we followed the hearse. Every car and truck along our way stopped out of respect until we passed.

At Resthaven Cemetery our caravan curled the narrow drive to the granite monument marked "James." Flat headstones marked the graves of Ma and Dannon and their infants who never made it past childhood. On many a Memorial Day, Dad had brought Mom, Sarah and me to this plot so he could pay his respects and leave flowers. This day we would leave him.

Miss Mira and Mr. Crane sat with my family on the front row of folding chairs beneath the green canopy. Sarah held Mother's hands and wiped her eyes with her handkerchief as the preacher talked of rest and of dust to dust, and I wondered where Dad was and if he knew I didn't want him to die alone.

That's how my father was buried.

46

Doctor Sally

ON THE WAY BACK FROM THE CEMETERY, MOTHER DROPPED ME OFF to buy some fruit juice for our visitors and a pack of Coca-Cola for Aunt Betsy. With groceries in hand and a brain feeling as if it had too much pain-killer holding it, I stopped at T.C. Hunter's store in case he might tell me something else. First, though, I asked for a shirt like the one I bought earlier in the week. He pulled out the remaining two and I bought them both for $8. He said I already had gotten the last pair of those summer britches.

He punched the cash register to put away the ten dollar bill and give me two dollars change. I told him I would take two dollars worth of the candy with the 1930 date on the carton. I wanted to help Mr. Hunter out and was curious to find out if the candy had turned to stone. As he wrapped the candy boxes in brown paper cut off a roll on the counter, he said he was sorry to see Dad go because Dad was a fair-minded man. I told him I was sorry to see him go, too.

I thanked him again for telling me about Salaman and asked, "Do you remember hearing where Jerusha came from?"

"Louisiana, I'm reckoning. That's where the sister was from."

"What sister?" I guess I should have asked before, but then again, T.C. Hunter didn't say anything until he was ready to.

"Jerusha's. Sally Bell."

"Oh. Pretty name."

"Doctor Sally, they called her. It was Jerusha and her sister that the Indian fellow pulled from the river."

"What do you mean, pulled from the river?"

"On the Cumberland, nearer to Pineville than to Harlan. That Jerusha lady and her sister and their driver were in the wagon trying to cross at the bend when the mud and current caught

246

them. That Salaman fellow pulled them out. That's how he came to know them. Good a way as any, I reckon."

"Was Sally really a doctor?"

"She was a nurse woman, and she could talk tongues."

"What tongues?"

"French. They talked that down in Louisiana. She knew ways to cure, and the Indian fellow taught her some. The colored went to her because she was a mix and did well for 'em. Even whites went to her when regular doctoring wouldn't fix 'em. She dressed like a lady – gloves on a summer day, scarves. She bought the best. In the summertime she used a parasol."

"Did she buy the parasol here?"

"My best brand."

"Do you still carry it?"

"It's on sale now."

I looked around for a sale sign but couldn't find any except the "HOT DEAL" card against the mannequin sporting a lacey blouse and velvet hat with netting. "Could I see one?"

Mr. Hunter opened some cabinet doors beneath the counter along the wall, shuffled merchandise around, and with some grunting pulled out an ivory-colored parasol, though the cover said the original color was white. "I have one left."

I spread it open and asked the sale price. Mr. Hunter answered, "Two dollars and seventy-five cents."

"I'll take it."

Mr. Hunter confirmed, "It's a good price. You bought at the right time."

"I appreciate your telling me about the sale. Do you happen to know what became of Doctor Sally?"

He scratched his head. "I think she married and left."

"Did you ever hear mention where she went?"

"No, sonny. Some people, you never know where they end up."

I thanked him for the information and the goods.

Outside my home I punched a few holes around the yard and buried all but one piece of the candy in them, on the chance they

247

might be found by archaeologists some day, something for them to think about, these people who like to dig around and figure out the past.

47

Hard candy

AT THE BOTTOM OF THE ENTRANCE ROAD TO THE UNIVERSITY OF Kentucky track, Miss Mira waits for us near the back of the towering grandstands. With southern ease Mother and Miss Mira inquire about each other's overnight stays. Mother radiates appreciation to Miss Mira for what she has done for me and has told it around town more than a hundred times. No friend of Mother's will speak anything untoward about Miss Mira, not within Mother's hearing.

My breakfast pancakes are well digested, a follow-up to three big helpings of spoon bread the day before at Boone Tavern in Berea where I wore a blazer and tie to look respectable enough to gain admittance to the colonial-like dining room with Mother, Aunt Betsy and Sarah. Aunt Betsy had been upbeat for Mother, who was trying hard to make the time pleasant for Sarah and me in that time-pressed aftermath of the funeral. At the table we found some release in remembering amusing things Dad did: how he told me to grit my teeth but never told Sarah to grit hers; how he teased Mother by saying she was "good peasant stock" because he knew that would ruffle her.

Mother had commented that in the Old South a widow was expected to mourn her husband by wearing black for a year. She didn't think she would help herself or us by wearing black.

So today Mother wears a blue dress as we converge at the entrance to the UK track. I give Miss Mira a gag gift, the remaining piece of candy from the batch I bought at T.C. Hunter's store. Dramatically she exclaims, "How interesting! A ceramic of the candy I remember when I was little. It looks so real."

"It is real. But don't try to bite into it."

"Is it petrified?"

"Something like that."

Mother and Sarah climb to high seats as Miss Mira accompanies me to the officials' table and pins my number – 421, same as the highway through Harlan – to the front and back of my shirt. Heats for the mile relay draw my attention to the precisely lined, rubberized-asphalt track, eight lanes wide compared to the six lanes at Union. Watching the sprinters pass the batons to their teammates, I prepare to take my turn in the half-mile heats. For days I have run easily in the lightness, so I don't think to make special mental preparations. I figure the energy and strength are there for me as they have been all week. I figure I have everything I need; I can run this heat by rote and concentrate tomorrow, before the finals.

During the 100-yard dash preliminaries I walk with Miss Mira to an open area and review the schedule and lineup.

"You are in the second heat," Miss Mira confirms with her finger on my name in the program. "We have four heats, eight runners each. Eight go to the finals on Saturday."

I add, "And twenty-four don't."

"What is your approach?"

"Start in the middle and move up after half a lap. Who's in my heat?" I review the list. "The tough one is Nicholas Finn, Lexington boy, Lafayette High. In the regionals he ran the half-mile four seconds faster than I did, and his time is only a second off Davanni of St. Xavier, who's our top dog for the finals. Davanni is in the fourth heat; Bobby Dodd is up against him today. That should be fun for Bobby. Seven other guys in the 880 have times faster than mine. Wow. We have a lot of hotshots here. I'm going to have to sweat to make this cut."

"Where is your concentration?"

"It's out there on the track. It just went out there."

I notice she doesn't say "Good" or "OK," but "The first heat is organizing. It's time to get ready."

I pull off my warm-up suit, hand it to Miss Mira, stretch, and prepare with a light mix of runs and sprints. Walking along the fence I watch a first-heat win by a Bowling Green runner who clocks as fast as Davanni did in the regionals. That jars me. *These guys are awfully quick.*

The announcer calls for the gathering of the second heat. We're reminded that we will remain in our staggered lanes until we round the turn and cross the breakout line. I take my assigned spot in Lane 3. As I shake my legs and arms, waiting for the other runners to settle in their places, I feel the adrenaline charging me for a fight and I wonder what is missing, what is different from my practice runs all week. Too late, I know: my thoughts are scattered, without an offering among them.

"On your mark."

Do your best anyway.

"Set!"

The pistol pop unleashes me on my lane alone, asking myself whether to hold back or charge ahead early. I'm used to working from inside a pack in a single race, but in this run I have to win against unknown runners in other heats. I want to bring myself into the body rhythm, but I'm busy, busy, busy accelerating and sustaining the speed faster than usual through the turn. I see myself gaining on the outside runners, but halfway into the curve Nicholas Finn in a white uniform with red and blue trim catches up with me in his second lane, which means he's leading because he has fewer steps left to take around the turn.

The strength pumping out of me is primal, not light, firing more from blood than spine. At the break-field line Finn slots into the first lane and I follow him over, hanging on his right in the raw satisfaction of all-out racing, half a madness. Tall, tan and handsome, this Finn guy is, the dream of girls most probably, and a beautiful runner to me, fast and even with a long stride matching mine; I edge past him in the backstretch until I have enough space to cut to the inside lane. With a quark-flash of relief but no assurance, I lead him through the second curve onto the straightaway where he comes up to my right as I had done to him.

Before the turn he overtakes me fluid-like, makes it look easy, and keeps a yard between us in the tilt around the bend. On the backstretch, in an overdrive of will against the threat of burnout, I challenge him again, but he won't let me pass. As he speeds up, I accelerate by the small degrees I have left, splitting my attention between my desperate need and the calcifying strain I have not felt in a race for a year outside the pressure-cooker workouts – no lightness here, no trace of grace on fire. All I have to work with is a battle instinct that grabs my reserves – tumultuous remains – and pulls enough out of the sinews to pass him and swerve into the last turn with his footsteps staccato in my ears.

My advantage ends too soon as he edges ahead of me on the final straight toward the finish line. I demand more speed but my legs and gut are hardening into Hunter's candy and all I can do is keep my drive as Finn stretches ahead of me into the ribbon where I let go the breath-choked momentum. My time is as good as my regional time, but at a burning price, and a second and a half behind Finn's.

With my expectations collapsed against me, I walk off the track through the opening of the low fence where Miss Mira greets me as happily as ever.

"Excellent," she declares.

"It didn't feel excellent." I wipe my face on my sleeve.

"It's all right, darling. We all learn some things the hard way. You did your best."

"It didn't feel like my best. I have tasted the best."

"Someday," she says, "the connection will be natural, and you won't have to run to get it. Today you ran your hardest in the state of mind you were in and made a race of it, a real race of it. That experience is as valuable as any. There are other races."

Bobby Dodd jogs past and shouts, "Great race."

Great race? "Thanks," I acknowledge but don't believe it. "Good luck to you."

As it turns out, Bobby Dodd's luck doesn't hold either. He doesn't make the finals in the 880-yard run, despite my cheers. He has the tenth fastest time, his own personal best, and I end up with the ninth fastest time by a quarter-second in the heats, so I'm eliminated along with him.

Dodd looks dejected at not hearing his name announced as one of the finalists, and I know how he feels. Bracing against my own disappointment, I walk by him and tell him, "Tomorrow it's our turn." Caught off guard, he grins slightly and nods yes.

I don't want to stick around the track. Walking off the field with Miss Mira and my family, I skip my customary moods because I don't have time for them. I have work to do, and I have to do it alone. Quietly, I eat supper with my family in the dining room of the Lafayette Hotel where we are staying. Afterward, they say they want to take a walk and visit one of Mother's acquaintances. They want to keep occupied among friends, beyond the confinement of a quiet room. I want the room. Just let me rest, that's what I tell them.

After showering with cool water, I sit on the side of the bed and bring my mind into the breath. It's not easy because of the funeral procession and half-mile race playing through my head. For half an hour I tug my mind back patiently, hoping Aunt Betsy keeps Mom and Sarah occupied. After an hour and a half, my mind finally floats free from the senses. A calm settles into the intervals between breaths, pauses that lengthen and rest as a crystal clearness in the brain. By degrees I am stilled into a statue and for a moment imagine what it might be like to be mute and paralyzed on a slab in the morgue, like a character in a Tales of the Crypt comic, except I can talk if I want to, which I don't.

Into the stillness plays a faint harp note that enlarges into the resonance of a deep gong, the sound I remember from my dreams of the Cherokee. I hear a knocking sound, and then a great sea humming, immersing me. Mesmerized by an embracing peace, I'm not concerned about the race to come, so far away. I'll think of the race tomorrow. I'll stay here as long as I can.

Sarah's diary – May 25, 1957

JJ lost the 880 today. When he does that, he thinks a lot and doesn't pay attention to what I am saying. Sometimes when he is disappointed in a race, I am surprised because I thought he was so exciting. Maybe I don't see what he sees. He doesn't see what I see, either. I guess we're even.

48

The finals

"WELL, WHAT ON EARTH? THAT LOOKS SO NICE," MISS MIRA REmarks as Sarah, Mother, Aunt Betsy and I approach her and Mr. Crane and their three sons – including Michael, the architect – in the parking lot near the entrance gate.

I explain, "It's my warm-up outfit – pants and shirt courtesy of T.C. Hunter. And I have a gift for you." I hand her the parasol. She opens it and, with a slight twirl, places it on her left shoulder.

"Just what I needed! My mother used one during summer days in Charlotte, and I have always had it in the back of my mind to get one." She kisses me the way foreign people kiss from side to side, with a faint sound but no lips on the cheek.

I welcome Marci, who with Alexander joins us, and I wonder what other music Marci will hear in what she sees, and if she will just keep it to herself or bring it through.

"JJ!" Zorro's voice calls from the cab of a Chevy pickup parked nearby. He steps out of the truck with Lucy, explaining, "Graduation present."

"Big present."

"1949. I'm going to fix it up."

Scotty Lanier slaps my back. I turn to see his smile that's deeper on the right side of his mouth than on his left. Beside him glisten the smiling eyes of Jenny. I am glad to have her here, more than I let on. I tell her I wore my outfit for her.

"Thank you," she acknowledges, a bit shyly because other people are around.

"How's the Sister?" Miss Mira greets Jenny, who answers with a "Fine, thank you," and a lift of her hand.

At the gate we hand over our passes and tickets and stroll in a bunch down to the field where we huddle to talk. Grinning nervously, Scotty asks, "What's the situation?"

"I'm not in the 880. I didn't make the cut Friday."

The information shakes Zorro. "What happened?"

"I lost."

"Oh."

"It wasn't a pretty sight."

Sarah objects, "Yes it was. He went back and forth all the way with this good-looking boy from Lexington."

"That good-looking boy, Nicholas Finn, will run against me in the mile. So will this Sam Davanni guy from St. Xavier, who made it to the 880 finals, plus six other guys from the 880 who came in ahead of me. There were no elimination heats for the mile, so thirty-two of us will come out at the start. It's going to be fun. I hope you enjoy it."

Lucy asks, "Is this your warm-up suit?"

Miss Mira answers against the backdrop of her parasol. "Harlan High is in style today."

I tell them, "I'm glad you came such a long way to be with me. It means a lot. I'll do my best for you. The mile starts in – " I glance at my Timex – "forty-five minutes. I'll get with you when it's over." I embrace each one, even Zorro, a little stiff, and as best I can take their good wishes into me.

Staying with me briefly as the group strolls on and Miss Mira waits a short distance away, Mother tells me consolingly, "I know you would like for your father to be here. Maybe he's watching."

"Or maybe he has other things to do and can't see through to where we are," I tell her. "It doesn't matter. What's important to me now, Mom, is that you're here."

I hug and pat her briefly. I don't want to hug her a long time without patting because that would be a different hug, one that could take us back to the death. All I want today is life.

Mother moves on and Miss Mira waits for me to come to her and asks what I want to do next. I tell her I want to go sit for a while on the slope behind the grassy waiting area.

Without words we stroll to the chain-link fence and sit with our backs near it. After she leans her parasol on her shoulder and relaxes her hands in her lap, we close our eyes, and I ease down. I don't hear any inner sounds, but for a while I recollect the comfort and closeness of them. After enjoying a potent stillness, the prayer of the gathering of war, I rise in assurance and stroll with Miss Mira quietly amid the clatter of teams camped around. We proceed to the less crowded field beyond the grandstands, dressing rooms and track.

For this warm-up I keep on my long-sleeved shirt and light pants that fold with the wind against my body, and I feel at home.

At the final call for the mile I remove my outer clothes and hand them with a slight bow to Miss Mira. She receives them with as slight a curtsey.

On the way to the starting area I step alongside Dodd. "Hey, Bobby." He's surprised I am talking to him before a race. Usually we runners don't even look each other in the eyes at the starting line, we are so absorbed in ourselves. He says, "Yeah?" with a two-syllable mountain twang.

"Let's give the big boys a run for their money."

A slightly perplexed look doesn't leave his face entirely as he acknowledges this with an "OK."

At the starting-line mass, *sure a lot of runners here,* I'm placed in the front of the fourth lane because I had the fourth best time in the regionals. Davanni is in the first lane, Finn's in the third, on my left. Dodd's on the outer rail.

I make my remembrance and offering, and then bring my attention into my head that engages like a transformer, pushing into the body expectancy and heartbeat, sheathed in the evenness of the night before. I am ready.

Gun hand up. Countdown. Start!

The front line breaks away with outside runners sprinting to take the inside position. Davanni doesn't try to hold them off but stays near the front. Finn dashes to claim space in the second lane among runners ahead of me – I can't see him. My pace is quick enough and easy enough, so I concentrate on the rhythm as closely as I can through the first turn. I hope Bobby Dodd isn't cramped in too far back. I can't calculate where he might be, even from the view of the curve, because I am about tenth from the lead with two-dozen guys pattering like a hailstorm behind.

On the backstretch I enjoy the fast glide and full-bodied beat in the midst of the moving bunch. Three boys pass me; two of them are runners who made the 880 finals. I'm not going to get pulled out by them yet. I'm satisfied with what I have and where I am; come the final lap, soon enough, I'll pursue whoever is left in front of me. I'm withdrawn to the eye of the storm, scanning inside myself for the lightness or whatever is closest to it as we take the second turn – one third of the group still in front of me, two thirds lost.

Across the start of the second lap some of the runners directly in front of me make their move to get closer to the head of the line. By the third turn half this front group is wearing down and slowing back to me. One, two, three, four milers can't hold on by the time the turn straightens out along the back where someone moves up to me from the outside and makes a pass.

It's Bobby Dodd. "You're rollin'," I tell him.

He slants to the inside lane in front of me. Another batch of frontrunners grinds down, causing Dodd and me to string into Lane 2 for clear passage. I'm anchorman to the front pack of five, wondering where those other 880 powerhouses are, because we still haven't finished half a mile.

In the rhythm of the steady thrust I imagine fragments of Marci's music – strings and drums and flutes above the fast-train weight of the orchestra. I wish Dodd had some of this. Or maybe not – he's burning along faster than I reckoned in this wildfire.

As we swing around the fourth curve, I glance over to confirm that this race is still among five, including two who beat state record times in the half-mile the day before. Our line rushes between the judges and the stands. Davanni takes the lead. He is getting what he wants, but I am getting what I want, now more than I expected, a surge of lightness as I begin to feel the Cherokee in me, the wind in his clothes and mine. In flashes I am on the path of the Cumberland, then breaking out of the patch of tall trees into the clear. I don't hear the sound, but I know it's there, somewhere deep, somewhere in the stillness, moving, all-pervading. Its power streams down my head into my chest and spine, joyous and certain. With a choice between losing the race and feeling this, I would choose to lose, but I'm not here to lose; I'm here to win, to offer the best I have, and what I have, *O Lord o' mercy*, what I have is beyond me.

Fueled above pain, I follow Dodd and the lead group around the third circuit where we tighten our ranks for the breakaway: Davanni triggers the shot of the final lap; Finn powers up to him and runs at his side while the third-place runner from Paducah holds on behind them. *This is it*, time to move, so I pull alongside Dodd and tell him in a quick breath, "Let's go."

As I take the third position away from Paducah and lean through the seventh turn, Finn pushes into first place; Davanni spins on at second. We're down to an order of four – Finn, Davanni, me and Dodd. The curve looks more precise than I ever saw it before, a perfect arc rising as if off a giant blueprint, brought to life by that which swings me hard around it.

The string of us unwinds on the line of the backstretch where I come alongside Davanni and pull him out an inch at a time until he reaches the tightness of his limits. Dodd follows in tow as I pass Davanni and start reeling up to Finn a third of the way down the far straight. Finn throttles out with a tensing jaw to keep his lead, and he is magnificent, *but this isn't the 880 any more – this is the mile, this is distance, this is my race.* I move past him and increase my lead by the time I hit the last turn and swing around to an angle where I glimpse Dodd edging up to second place, and I glimpse Finn battling Dodd to reclaim the position from him.

From there on out I don't think of what is happening behind as a vibrant calm inside the roll of the fierce momentum plays a streak of memory through me, a blur of trees down a fast ridge drop along Pine Mountain, thrill in the stomach, a deep lean rounding out of a high-banked turn against a clay embankment beneath a wall of stone and – down the white-lined track of level black before me, smooth and clear except for the ribbon I spin toward, closer, closer, broken, done and gone.

I glide down. Finn follows, with Dodd only a footstep behind. Dodd and I clasp each other in the honor of two mountain boys, first and third against the best, the pageant as our witness.

This time I hold Miss Mira a long while, and she holds me. I sense between us more awareness than I can separate enough to bring to words just now. "Wonderful," she says as I loosen my embrace, knowing her work with me is finished. I thank her for coming to me that windy afternoon on the field, and for the distance she brought me, to the finish line that marks the start, with everything between.

Here at long last, in the shimmering of our lives, I look to my family, friends and Jenny in the stands. With gratitude and outstretched arm, I raise in lightness all I have; I raise my right hand to them.

49

Afterword

I ADJUSTED TO THE WONDER OF THE RACE, AND THE SUMMER PASSED brightly in the company of Jenny. She came often to the country club where Barbara worked as a lifeguard in alternating shifts with me, and Jenny and I walked the hills in the honeysuckle wind, played badminton in her yard, listened to music and relaxed in the freshness of evenings on my porch.

In late October 1957, I strolled with her to the cemetery on the hill in the canopy of color so I would remember autumn, this place, and her this way, alive with me, and young.

For the next few years I looked forward to seeing her on weekends and in summer, every meeting anticipated as much as when I first walked with her. Though I knew she would change through the years, I hoped to marry her.

By the time she went to Princeton I was an officer in the Navy, based in Virginia, with long tours on the sea. Her replies to my letters became less frequent. Though we did see each other when I returned, I realized she had another life before her. It took many years for my heart to reconcile with this.

After military service I opened my civil and mining engineering firm in Harlan, for work that would take me into the mountains. I married a sparkling Pikeville girl named Rebecca, whom I met at a business accounting seminar she led. An analyst by nature and a mother by instinct, she gave me her youthful spirit, a bright heart, sweet peculiarities, her life, and two daughters who at their births unfolded the father in me.

My younger daughter ran hurdles for Harlan High, bringing a generation full circle. Her coach was Wally Odell, the coach at Rosenwald who was given the same position at Harlan High when Rosenwald was closed with integration. She trained on Harlan's modern track by the highway 421 that bypasses the old downtown. At her state meet I cheered for her and her classmates, as did Sarah – an English teacher at Harlan High – and Sarah's husband Carl who came seven boyfriends after Bernie Cole. Sarah and Carl have two sons, now grown, and we eat dinner together every other Sunday after church.

On Jenny's birthday in 2000 I made a call to her in the snows of Montana where she, having earned her doctorate at Ohio State, was a professor of geology, and where her husband, whom she had met as a fellow graduate student, taught organic chemistry. That was the first time I had spoken to her in thirty-five years, and the brightness of her laugh had not diminished. It was as if not a month had passed since I last heard her voice.

On Jenny's cliff, saplings and trees have grown out of the crevices, giving new life to the rock race on which we once moved so freely and gazed with such an unobstructed view.

I can imagine her walking the mountains where she is, and I am satisfied that she is well. She shared her life in the blossoming, and as I found what ran through me, I came to know what loved through Jenny Lee. I appreciate her still for the heart she brought and the heart she led me to, as have the others dear to me and comfortably familiar, out of all the strangers on this earth.

IN THE FOUR decades since my last race, I have walked through the valley of the shadow of more than death, and I have had more blessings than I can count.

In my first year out of the service I lived with Mother on Ivy Street, then built my own house on Ivy Hill. Mother died of cancer in 1967, but she fought with courage and lived a year longer than the time she was given. She lived so she could see her first grandchild, my daughter. That decline and fall were hard on me, too, but at least she died at home where I was with her. The house went to Sarah.

I was also at the hospital with Miss Mira two weeks before her eighty-seventh birthday. I had visited her at home regularly and

262

helped her as I could. Many times she talked about Salaman and Jerusha and Dr. Sally as the impressions came to her, but on this afternoon visit we laughed at stories of living Harlan characters. Her hospital bed was cranked up to enthrone her in a sitting position, clad in a blue silk robe with white trim, wearing her bangle, earrings, and the gold-strand necklace with the single pearl. She alluded to abdominal discomfort, but except for being in bed she did not appear or sound ill, and mentioned she did not know how long she would have to stay there. I was later told that her son Michael visited with her into the evening until she motioned him to her, kissed him, and told him it was time to go. Around three in the morning the night nurse came to her room and saw that Miss Mira had passed on.

Barbara Lee took over Miss Mira's dance studio business in Harlan. Her husband and son bought out Mr. Lanier's asphalt company.

Marci shared with me her knowledge of sounds and ancient words when I became more curious about them. A mother to countless students, she retired as a professor of music at Union but still plays in the college ensemble, performs as a guest soloist with orchestras, and has sold recordings of her compositions. One recording includes "The Final Race," which my daughters also enjoy, though they remark that I play it loud yet ask them to turn down the volume of their music.

Stoner retired as a school superintendent in central Kentucky.

Chief, a building contractor, supervises children at Camp Blanton, the Boy Scout retreat west of Harlan, on weekends.

Scotty Lanier, handsome as ever, owns a stock brokerage firm in Louisville and a summerhouse in Maine.

In 1972, before she died, Mrs. Handley showed me photographs of Priscilla's wedding. She worked as a model and married a veterinarian in Chicago. Five years later Priscilla divorced and moved with her son to Seattle where she disappeared from my life altogether, into another husband's name.

263

Lamar Galion of Rosenwald High did not teach math, as he thought he would, after graduating from Kentucky State. Instead, the *Enterprise* reported, he became a career officer with the U.S. Air Force Logistics Command at Wright-Patterson Air Force Base.

Rustbucket died of throat cancer in 1998.

Lois married Jeff Ketchum to begin a life of children, grandchildren and teaching. We get together at class reunions.

Two-Bit and Harley own an outdoor-equipment business in Mayfield, Ky. Jug manages a mine in Idaho.

Dozer retired as foreman of a manufacturing plant in Indianapolis and coaches Pee Wee Football there.

Zorro married Lucy two years out of high school. He bought a garage-sized coal truck and made a living with it for a while until the coal business went down in a bust cycle, prompting him to form his Red Dog Trucking Company in Corbin. I stop by to see them at least twice a year. Their children look normal.

I ran with Bobby Dodd and Nicholas Finn at the University of Kentucky for four years, all of us on track scholarships. The teamwork made workouts and travel sociable, and the coaching was supportive, though Miss Mira's instruction was never surpassed, nor did it need to be. We won our share of races. Dodd specialized in the half mile, and I specialized in the mile.

Bobby was my roommate on road trips. After graduation he followed his ROTC officer rank into the Army and to Vietnam where he piloted a medical-rescue helicopter. That was a worrisome time for me until he returned to fly civilian cargo planes out of Nashville, where he retired.

THOUGH STRONG ENOUGH, my pace is slower now. More often I jog and walk the roads of Ivy Hill. But when I run beside a slope of flowering dogwood trees in spring, or in the gold of the maple leaves of autumn, I feel the silvery glide, the ease of movement, grateful to have it with me still, like a friend who stays long after the need to race is over, after the cheering crowd has disappeared.

When I think of all who have scattered, all who have gone – my mother, father, so many friends, the bustling downtown crowds – I sometimes lean into the life that I have loved. Then I struggle to remember, and take hold. I sit again with back erect. I close my eyes and pray and lift my gaze. Into the stillness I sink as best I can.

For many years I asked to understand the hand of Time, and in my forty-ninth year I saw the Cherokee again, this time not in a dream, but in my inner gaze, awake. I had hiked with my family to the ledge in Bell County and sat in the spot where Salaman sat. Rebecca and my daughters remained on the riverbank, preparing a picnic spread. When I closed my eyes upward, my breath paused and the Amen came on by degrees, catching me by surprise, it emerged so easily, filling my forehead with whiteness. As the light faded, I saw through Salaman's eyes the face of the hollow without the railroad laid across it, and a deeper bend of the river than is there now. As his eyes lifted, I saw a runner streaming around a winding path along sandstone walls, flickering the white of his clothes through the gaps of trees. On the hump of a small cliff the runner stopped, as did the sound. The quietness of the breeze gave way to the whistle and rumble of a long train pulling coal along the mountain edge of Harlan, and I saw that it was not the Cherokee who stood there, but I, Jeremiah James, as a boy of seventeen.

So I sit in the quiet of many evening hours to see what else lies behind this dream that I am in. On my better days, when my mind is tamed enough to let the restless body go, the past and future wash like a joyous wave into the moment, and Time loosens its hold. There I would say to you, if only I could, the words I almost hear: Just go inside. Beside me, go inside, and run with me.

When man becomes a little enlightened he compares his experiences relating to the material creation, gathered in the wakeful state, with his experiences in dream, and understanding the latter to be merely ideas, begins to entertain doubts as to the substantial existence of the former. His heart then becomes propelled to learn the real nature of the universe and, struggling to clear his doubts, seeks for evidence to determine what is truth. In this state man is called *Kshatriya*, or one of the military class; and to struggle in the manner aforesaid becomes his natural duty, by whose performance he may get an insight into the nature of creation and attain the real knowledge of it.

-- Swami Sri Yukteswar
The Holy Science
(Los Angeles: Self-Realization Fellowship, 1990)

The author, 1960

HAP CAWOOD taught English and coached track in his hometown of Harlan, Kentucky in 1962 after graduating from Union College. He also taught and coached as a Peace Corps Volunteer in Sierra Leone. During his career as an editorial writer and editorial page editor for the *Dayton Daily News*, he received for his editorials the SDX Distinguished Service Award from the Society of Professional Journalists, and the Walker Stone Award from the Scripps Howard Foundation. He lives in Yellow Springs, Ohio.

Printed in the United States
34113LVS00004B/61-84

9 780965 907514